ONE NIGHT IN MALIBU

Mac Reilly is a private investigator with a penchant for lost causes. One night in Malibu, he comes to the aid of a distraught woman in a black negligee waving a gun in the doorway of a fabulous beach house. When the woman then disappears and the gun shows up in his car, Mac is pulled into a web of deception and lies that entangle his whole life.

Elizabeth Adler titles available from
Severn House Large Print

Meet Me in Venice

ONE NIGHT IN MALIBU

Elizabeth Adler

Severn House Large Print
London & New York

This first large print edition published 2009
in Great Britain and the USA by
SEVERN HOUSE PUBLISHERS LTD of
9-15 High Street, Sutton, Surrey, SM1 1DF.
First world regular print edition published 2008 by
Severn House Publishers Ltd., London and New York.

British Library Cataloguing in Publication Data

Adler, Elizabeth (Elizabeth A.)
  One night in Malibu
  1. Private investigators--Fiction. 2. Romantic suspense
  novels. 3. Large type books.
  I. Title
  823.9'14-dc22

  ISBN-13: 978-0-7278-7782-6

Printed and bound in Great Britain by
MPG Books Ltd, Bodmin, Cornwall.

For lovely Aunt Bebe Sell,
still reading and still enjoying
at the age of ninety-two

One

It was not the kind of night, nor the kind of place, where you'd expect to hear a woman scream. It was just one of those Malibu nights, dark as a velvet shroud, creamy waves crashing onto the shore, breeze soft as a kitten's breath.

Mac Reilly, Private Investigator, was walking the beach alone but for his dog. His lover, Sunny Alvarez, had taken off for Rome after a slight "disagreement" concerning their future. But that was an ongoing story.

Mac lived in the famous Malibu Colony, habitat of movie stars and showbiz moguls and megabucks persons of every sort, each one richer than the next, give or take a couple of million, or in some cases billion. Their fancy beachside mansions didn't look so fancy from Mac's angle, but then the beach was also not an angle from which most people ever got to see them. In fact the public rarely got to see them. The Colony was gated and guarded, one gate in or out, and though the beach had free access it was only along the water's edge with no loitering. Any unknown caught prowling along it at midnight would be in for some tough questioning.

The Colony's mansions were mostly the simple second or even third homes of rich people, understated in their beach chic and with the narrowest bits of oceanfront deck known to man, at a cost per square foot that boggled the accounting.

Mac's own place was a more modest dwelling, a forties bungalow he had bought cheap years ago in the big real estate slump and which had once been owned, or so he'd heard, by the old-time movie star Norma Shearer. Or was it Norma Jean? Norma or Marilyn, it made no difference. A shack was a shack whichever way you looked at it.

The house's saving grace, apart from its ritzy location and the view, was a small wooden deck with steps that led directly to the beach. It wasn't unknown in a winter storm for the ocean to come thudding at the wooden pilings under that deck, slapping over the rails until Mac felt as though he were on a boat, but he liked the excitement and even the possible danger. He was happy in Malibu, he wouldn't live anywhere else if you paid him. Except maybe Rome for a week or two, in the company of Sunny.

Mac kind of looked the PI role, six foot two, longish dark hair still thick on the head, thank God, even though he was forty. Dark blue eyes, kinda crinkled from too many days on the beach and too many nights spent propping up bars in his youth. No facial hair—Sunny didn't like it. A lean athletic build, which since he was a lazy guy gym-wise, was mostly earned from jogging along the beach with his rescued three-legged, one-eyed mutt of a dog, Pirate, who was pretty fast when he had the wind behind him.

Pirate was Mac's best buddy, and you've never seen a more perky little tyke. With his long spindly legs and ragged gray-brown fur, plus a severe underbite that left his bottom teeth exposed in a perpetual grin, he'd win Malibu's ugliest dog contest easy.

Of course Sunny adored Pirate, even though she wouldn't let him near her Chihuahua, Tesoro. Strong on the claws, quick with a bite and weighing all of three pounds, Tesoro outsmarted Pirate at every turn.

Sunny believed it was the animosity between their dogs that was preventing their marriage, but Mac was not quite certain on that score. Why spoil a good thing? Sunny and he were *good* together just the way they were, i.e., unmarried.

Sometimes Mac thought maybe it was his alter ego that appeared on your TV screens Thursday nights, in real-life documentary style reinvestigating old Hollywood crimes, of which there were more than you might imagine. His show was titled *Mac Reilly's Malibu Mysteries,* with yours-truly looking extra-cool in the Dolce & Gabbana black leather jacket Sunny had bought him.

When she'd told him it was a Dolce, Mac had had no idea what she meant. It sounded like Italian ice cream to him. Later, he'd discovered it was an Italian designer and the jacket was without doubt the coolest garment he owned. Soft and pliable as wet putty it had become part of his on-screen image, though God knows he was more usually to be found in sweats slouching up Malibu Road to Ralphs supermarket in

9

search of beer and dog food, or breakfasting in Coogies coffee shop in a T-shirt and shorts rather than decked out in black leather.

Anyhow, the show, which took old murders and reckoned to solve them, had given him some kind of fame. It was all relative of course, because as everybody knew in Hollywood, once your show went off the air you were as forgotten as last week's dinner. And now it looked as though Mac's time had come and gone and the show was likely not to return for another season. Too bad, because the income had come in handy and he'd gotten to keep his day job, investigating for all those nice rich folk. And surprisingly many of them were genuinely nice. Plus they had the same troubles as everybody else. Sex and money. In that order.

He gave Pirate the low whistle that meant get the heck back over here, and the dog came running from whatever exciting secrets he'd found on Malibu's most expensive bit of shore. Together, they turned and headed for home. They were strolling along, minding their own business, listening to the crash of the waves, breathing in the salty ocean air and keeping an eye out for shooting stars, all that romantic stuff. And then they heard the scream.

High pitched. Quivering. Terrified.

It didn't take a PI to figure out that the screamer was female. And that she was in trouble.

Two

Mac quickly scanned the houses. All were in darkness save for a glimmer of light on a deck a couple of houses back. He stumbled through the soft sand toward it, followed by Pirate.

He paused at the foot of the wooden steps leading to the house, listening, but there were no more screams. What he did think he heard though was a sob. Muffled, but nevertheless a definite sob.

Telling Pirate to stay put, he inched his way up the steps onto the deck, which was only about ten feet deep, a usual size for the acreage-tight Colony. The house loomed in front of him, a glass-and-limestone cliff that was more modern than the millennium and more stark than the architecture of Richard Meier, famous for the design of the L.A. Getty museum among other things. It was also as dark as the night outside.

Suddenly a lamp was turned on. Through the window he glimpsed a woman. A redhead wearing a sheer black negligee and, if he was not mistaken and even though it was at fifty paces, very little else. Now contrary to the popular belief, this was not your normal bedtime attire in Malibu and nor was midnight a usual hour to retire. Most everyone in the movie biz had an early call and were in their flannel PJs, curled up in a bed, learning the next day's lines by nine.

Mac knocked on the window but the woman didn't seem to hear. She just stared down at her feet as though there was something fascinating there. Like maybe a body, Mac thought.

She was young, maybe twenty-three, and beautiful, with everything in the right place as revealed by the sheer bit of black chiffon and lace she wore. Plus she had the face of a naughty angel. Mac felt glad to be of help. He checked, saw that the glass doors were unlocked, and in his knight-in-shining-armor role he slid it open.

Her head shot up and he flung her a reassuring smile. "Hi," he said, "I'm Mac Reilly, your neighbor. I thought I heard a scream. Are you in some kind of trouble?"

The woman tossed her long red curling hair out of her tearful green eyes, lifted herself to her full statuesque height and pointed a gun at him.

"Get out," she said in a throaty whisper.

Mac eyed the gun. It was a Smith & Wesson Sigma .40, and definitely not to be messed with. He paused long enough to wonder why she was not pressing the button to summon Security from the gate instead of threatening him. And then the gun went off.

The bullet ricocheted from the polished concrete floor near his foot, shattered a crystal vase then buried itself in the back of a nearby sofa.

Mac didn't wait around for a second shot. He took off down the steps, sprinting back along the beach a couple of paces behind the cowardly dog.

"Oops, sorry, my mistake," she called after him, her voice floating eerily on the breeze.

Three

Sunny Alvarez was lying on the bed in her room in the Hotel d'Inghilterra in Rome, dialing L.A. every ten minutes and wondering where on God's earth Mac Reilly was. It was nine a.m. in Rome, which meant it was midnight in Malibu. Could Mac be out on the town the minute her back was turned? When the truth was she'd only come here to stir him up a little. She'd figured a little jealousy wouldn't hurt. They'd always said absence made the heart grow fonder. Now she wasn't so sure.

Restless, she got up and began to pace, running her hands distractedly through her long hair that swung around her shoulders like liquid black satin, with just enough wave in it to give it bounce. Sunny's eyes were amber brown and fringed by lashes so thick they were like miniature shades on the windows of the soul. Her skin was golden, her legs long and her skirts usually short. She was, as Mac often told her, in between kisses, a knockout.

"Even though you're ditzy enough to drive any man mad," he'd once said to her, causing her to swat him with a handy cushion, which in turn sent Pirate into a barking frenzy because nobody—not even Sunny, who he loved—was going to harm his "father."

The only positive news Sunny had were the postcards Mac sent her daily. At least she believed they were from him but since there was no signature she couldn't be absolutely sure. Except she knew nobody else who would be FedExing pictures of Surfrider Beach, and Zuma, and Paradise Cove with the anonymous message "From Malibu, with Love." Sunny was saving those postcards. She planned to stick them in her Memories book to look at when she was old and gray. And also, unless she could get Mac to the altar soon, still single.

Her room looked as though a typhoon had hit it. Her method of unpacking was to take everything out of the suitcase and toss it over chairs and the bed, then sort out whatever she needed from the various piles. Her apartment was kept mostly in the same state of chaos. It was a leftover habit from her college days when it had seemed the easiest—and quickest—method of getting dressed, and it drove Mac crazy. To compensate she would point out her kitchen to him, immaculate as an operating room, and where she would cook him delicious meals—plus she always did the dishes afterward. Food was her first passion. The second was clothes, as evidenced by the shopping bags from Rome's boutiques scattered around the room. The third was her Harley chopper, but that unfortunately was back in L.A. Rome was a city full of Vespas,

14

and they were definitely not the same thing.

She picked up the phone, got Mac's voice mail one more time, slammed it back down again and lay back on the bed contemplating her coral-pink toenails and her life.

Of course her name was not really Sunny. That's just what Mac called her. Her real name was Sonora Sky Coto de Alvarez. Quite a mouthful, as she was only too painfully aware. In fact she was truly grateful to be designated as Sunny. At least it let her off the hook of constantly explaining those names, which were the direct result of having a hippie-style mother who'd communed with nature as well as with the spirits, in the desert around their adobe-style ranch outside of Santa Fe, New Mexico.

Sunny's mom was still dreamy and offbeat beautiful and still prone to wearing floating shapeless garments with long strands of crystal beads, and often flowers in her smooth blond hair. Yet, oddly enough she'd always been a terrific mom, even if her daughters did have to spend nights with her out in the desert, communing with nature while keeping a nervous eye out for rattlers. Mom didn't even think about things like snakes. Her mind was on a higher plane, one that sadly Sunny and her sister never reached.

Their feet were more firmly planted on this earth. As kids they loved riding horses, chasing boys and raising hell. Later, they'd graduated to riding motorcycles, chasing boys and raising hell. That is until their father took them in hand, straightened them out and packed them off to college, where he hoped real life would not deal them a killer blow between the eyes after the gentle ministrations of their otherworldly mother.

Sunny's papa was something else again. Handsome? You don't know what that word means if you haven't seen her dad. He's Mexican, with that polished-tan skin, thick silver-gray hair, soft brown eyes and a trim mustache. Kind of like Howard Keel used to look in *Dallas*. Astride his black thoroughbred he was the epitome of the Mexican ranchero.

He'd thought Brown was the perfect college to tame a Harley-riding, boy-mad eighteen-year-old, and true, it had opened up Sunny's world to a kind of life she had never seen. But she'd missed her family, and she'd cried thinking of her beloved *abuelita,* her Mexican grandmother, and of the tamales, cooked the way only Abuelita knew how to cook them. The tamales were a Christmas Eve staple at the ranch and everyone from the workers and the cowboys and the local families gathered to enjoy them, along with a large amount of tequila and Corona beer and Mexican music and dancing.

Of course Mom also cooked the traditional turkey, albeit in her usual haphazard way. Sometimes it wasn't quite done and had to go back in the oven for an hour or two; and sometimes it was too well done and Papa said you needed horse teeth to get through it. Either way it was fun.

At college it hadn't take long for the golden-limbed raven-haired Latina in black biker

16

leathers zooming around on her Harley to get noticed. Soon, she was cooking tamales and handing out the Corona at her own parties. By the time she graduated, magna cum laude, with her proud parents and her sister beaming in the audience, Sunny felt almost ready to tackle the world. But before that came the Wharton School and a master's in business.

Later, she'd found herself a job in Paris, working for a fragrance house. After a year there she moved on to Bologna and a job with the Fiat corporation. Then back home and on to California, where she'd opened her PR business, which was doing very nicely, thank you.

She'd met Mac at a press party for his TV show. He told her he'd noticed her across the room. "How could I miss you, in that outfit," was what he'd actually said.

It was winter and she had on a tiny white miniskirt, her tough-girl motorcycle boots because she'd driven there on her Harley, and a black turtleneck. She was all long golden legs, sexy curves and tumbling black hair. She was always careful about drinking and driving and was sipping lemonade when he'd come up behind her and tapped her on the shoulder. Swinging round, she found herself looking at this rugged guy in jeans and a T-shirt, whose deep blue eyes were taking her in like she was the best thing he'd seen all night.

It's him, she'd thought, thrilled. *The man I've been waiting for all my life.* Of course she was smart enough not to tell him that and it was true, they were total opposites: Mac, dragged up by

17

his bootstraps from the streets of Boston and the Miami crime scene to the PI and TV personality he was now. And she, the wild child brought up on the ranch, beautiful and brainy and ditzy, but with the determination to be her own woman.

In fact life seemed set fair, romance-wise, until she'd invited him for dinner at her smart high-rise apartment in Marina del Rey, a few miles from his home in Malibu. Even her home-cooked tamales were no match for that first disastrous encounter between Tesoro and Pirate.

Let's face it, Sunny thought, sighing, Pirate was willing to be friends. Tesoro was not. And rather than have his dog harassed, Mac had departed, leaving the tamales uneaten. "Next time I won't bring the dog," he'd said, shielding Pirate from the marauding Chihuahua.

And that was how things now stood. She went to his Malibu house without Tesoro. He came to her Marina apartment without Pirate. "And never the twain shall meet" was Mac's motto. Which of course left them in their current uncertain limbo.

Sunny checked the time. It was after midnight in Malibu and Mac still wasn't home. She should get off this bed right now. Get out there in the vibrant bustling streets of Rome, pick up a charming handsome Italian and let him sweep her off her stilettos.

Heaving a sigh that this time came from her gut, she decided that she would call Mac no more. The hell with the diet. She could practically smell sugar and cinnamon as she ran her hands hastily through her long dark hair, pushed

18

her feet into black patent sandals and headed for the door.

The phone rang. She swung round, staring at it.

It rang again. Of course it wouldn't be *him.* How could it? Hadn't she been calling him for the past hour, damn it?

She picked up the phone. *"Pronto?"* she said sulkily.

Four

"Sunny?" Mac said.

"This is Sonora Sky Coto de Alvarez."

Mac felt a sudden frost in Malibu. She was giving him the full-name treatment. He was in real trouble. Only thing was, he didn't know why.

"You sound so Italian," he said. "Maybe I should be calling you Signorina."

"How would you know I'm not already a Signora now? Neglected as I am by you."

He grinned. "Okay, *Signora,* who popped the question?"

"Certainly not you. Where were you, Romeo? I've been calling for the past hour."

"Would you believe the beach? Just me and Pirate. Gazing at the stars and wondering whether you were looking at the same stars, all those miles away in Rome."

"Huh. Some story. Anyhow, it's breakfast time

here. There are no stars, except the ones out at Cinecittà Studios, where I expect to be spending the day surrounded by the cream of Roman manhood."

Mac's grin widened. "Don't let it go to your head, honey. Hang out with me and I'll introduce you to the cream of Malibu manhood."

"Like yourself, you mean? Thanks, but I can do without it."

"Listen, Sunny, something odd just happened..."

"Don't even bother to tell me." She sank back onto the bed, legs crossed, dangling one black patent sandal on the end of her toe, contemplating it as though it were the only thing of interest in her life.

Her indifference permeated the telephone miles, registering like the knell of doom in Mac's brain. "Aw, come on, Sunny, honey..."

"And don't call me by that ridiculous rhyming name."

It was Mac's turn to heave a sigh. "Okay, so you don't even want to know that somebody took a shot at me."

Unbelieving, she swung the sandal back onto her foot, uncrossed her legs and stood up. She was heading out that door right this minute. Espresso and sugar buns awaited.

"I'll bet it was a woman," she said.

Mac was genuinely astonished. "How did you know that?"

"Just call it feminine intuition. And I have no doubt you deserved it."

"Well thanks a lot for that vote of confidence.

Really, Sunny, I expected more from you. Y'know, like a little concern for my well-being, a touch of compassion, or at least an inquiry as to whether I might be bleeding to death from my wounds."

"She *wounded* you?" Sunny's knees were suddenly shaky. She sank back onto the bed. "Oh, Mac, darling, are you all right?"

Mac was laughing as he said, "Well, actually, no, she didn't get me. But she had a darned good try, I can tell you. And it was a Sigma .40 hand-gun I was facing."

Sunny gritted her teeth. "You rat," she said shakily. "Setting me up like that."

"How else was I to get your attention? Look, Sunny, it's the truth." He told her quickly what had taken place just fifteen minutes earlier, taking care to eliminate the red hair, the sexy black negligee, the spectacular body and the face like a naughty angel.

"What I don't get," he said finally, "is why she didn't summon help. I mean, why was she shooting at me? Her would-be savior?"

"Perhaps she's the murderer."

"What murder? I didn't see a body. But I'll bet she was the one who screamed. Plus she was sobbing. I saw the tears on her face. Look, babe, I'm in a dilemma here. I already called the guard at the gate. He called the house, got word from the owner, Ron Perrin—as in Ronald Perrin, billionaire investment mogul—that nothing was wrong. Said it was probably just that the TV was too loud. Now that's b.s. I *know* what I saw. So do I call the cops? Or do I let her get on with

21

whatever it is she's up to and keep my nose out of their business, because it's probably only the usual domestic quarrel and she was just making her point?"

"With a Sigma .40? Some point! If I were you, Reilly, I'd keep my nose clean and stay away where you're not wanted. Unless of course she wants to hire you for some fabulous fee that you can't refuse, especially now the TV show might be canceled. I mean, why work for free?"

Mac thought worriedly about it. "What if she's really in trouble?"

"It seems to me she knew exactly how to take care of herself. And so, I guess, did Mr. Perrin. Do me a favor, Mac, you're talking Malibu Colony. Nothing bad ever happens there, everything is sweetness and light. Just don't be the one to make waves."

Sunny was sitting on the bed again. The phone was clamped between her shoulder and her ear and she was wishing she had a cup of coffee and that Mac would talk about something other than business. Like them for instance.

As if in answer to her wish, he said, "I miss you like crazy. I couldn't take it tonight, just me, mooching along the beach with Pirate. And you not beside me, not there waiting for me, not in my bed ... in my heart."

Sunny's own heart shifted pace to an incredulous little jiggle. "What did you say?"

"I miss you, Sunny. How about I catch the next flight to Rome?"

"Oh, Mackenzie Reilly," she said, tremulously, "that would be heaven. I know this café with the best espresso..."

"Forget espresso. Make a reservation at your favorite restaurant. I'm taking you out on the town tomorrow night. It's nothing but the best for my woman."

Sunny sighed happily. All was right in their world again. And for her, the billionaire Ron Perrin and the woman with the Sigma .40 were temporarily forgotten.

Five

Early the next morning Mac strolled up the street to Ron Perrin's house. Of course he knew all about Perrin. Who didn't? He was a big shot who'd made his first money by successfully investing for the insurance business, and had then parlayed his investment firm into one of the Wall Street majors. And though he now seemed all power and success, the man had a past. He'd divorced his first wife amid a great scandal because of his relationship with another woman, who happened also to be married to a prominent man. Plus he had once been accused of mis-handling funds, though he had emerged, at least on the court records, as clean as a whistle.

Now Perrin was CEO of a string of high-profile companies, and even more powerful. And much, much richer. He was also married to a famous movie star, the blond, petite and beautiful Allie Ray.

As well as the Malibu house, Perrin owned a mansion in Bel Air and a desert compound in Palm Springs, a couple of hours' drive from L.A. It was nothing but the best for Ron Perrin. He lived like the king some folks claimed he believed he was.

From the street angle, Perrin's house in the Colony was a simple blank sheet of windowless limestone. The door was a lofty slab of unpolished steel that looked like a pewter coffin lid and without a knob or a handle of any sort. A discreet button set into the wall invited the visitor to Press.

Mac did so but heard no distant electronic chime. Even the doorbell was silent.

Over the top of the steel slab of the gate he could see the ruffled fronds of a couple of tall palms and some branches of bamboo. Like most of the houses in the Colony he guessed the gate led into an entrance courtyard, beyond which would be the front door proper.

He pressed the bell again and glanced round, waiting. No cars were parked on the yellow lines in front of the house that marked the owner's parking spaces, and the blank steel door to the garage was shut. He wondered what kind of car Ron Perrin drove. A silver Porsche? A Bentley? A red Ferrari, perhaps? It was sure to be expensive and flashy because that's the way the man was.

At last a male voice answered. "Who is it?" He sounded out of breath.

"Mac Reilly," he said into the speaker. "Your neighbor."

A pause, then, "Come in," the voice said.

The steel slab slid to one side and disappeared into a recess in the limestone wall. No crazy paving for RP, only a straight dark blue concrete walkway leading past a midnight blue reflecting pool, through a tropical courtyard where the jungle foliage reached out to grab Mac as he walked by.

Perrin was waiting at the glass entry. He was a short man with the wide shoulders and hard stare of an aggressive primate. He also had the slight forward stoop of a man who lifts weights, as though permanently about to bend and pick up a two-hundred-pound barbell.

Perrin's brow was wide, his hair was dark with a slight wave; his eyes were a light molten brown and his thick eyebrows were what a writer like Dickens might have termed "beetling." That is to say, they joined over his nose in a distinguished frown. His nose had a sharp look to it but his mouth was full-lipped and sensual. He was in good shape and even now, in a sweat-stained tee and gym shorts, Mac could tell he was definitely a man who knew his Dolce from his Italian ice cream. He was also attractive in an offbeat way and Mac could see why beautiful Allie Ray would have been drawn to him. Power combined with money made a formidable combination.

Perrin said, "I know you. I've seen you on TV. Come in."

Mac stepped inside and took a quick look around. The entry soared thirty feet to a beveled glass dome. The house itself was open plan and sleek. An all-steel kitchen to the rear; a jutting staircase of free-floating steps with no visible means of support to the left; and in front a wall of glass through which Mac could see, though not hear, the crashing ocean waves. All the windows were closed and the air-conditioning was blasting, as was a recording of Roxy Music's *Avalon.*

Perrin's expensive Malibu walls held a collection of even more expensive art, whose value was apparent even to a non-connoisseur like Mac. And the furnishings were unbeachy, with serious antiques, soft leather chairs and fine silk rugs on the dark, lacquered-concrete floors.

An odd feature was the model railroad that ran around all four walls, vaulting over the glass doors, undulating through the open-slab stairs, sneaking along the baseboards and climbing the limestone in layers of splendid, and pricey, miniature rolling stock. It was a child's, or in this case a grown man's, dream. Mac was immediately intrigued. But Mr. Perrin had matters other than model railroads on his mind.

"Take a seat, Mr. Reilly," he said.

Mac perched on the edge of a slippery green leather chair. He glanced at the place where he'd been standing when the redhead took a shot at him. There was a large chip in the polished concrete floor. The remains of the crystal vase had been removed but he guessed the ricocheting bullet was still buried in the back of the bronze velvet sofa where Perrin now slumped opposite him. He looked distinctly pale as well as haggard and not at all like the rich, successful party animal everyone was used to seeing in the glossies.

Mac noticed a shredder, the cheap kind you see in drugstores, standing next to its up-tipped cardboard container. Perrin had obviously bought it recently and Mac had interrupted him in the process of shredding documents, a pile of which still waited on the floor.

"I wonder if you know why I'm here," Mac said.

Perrin slumped forward, hands clenched between his spread knees. He nodded, still staring somberly at Mac. Then he said, "Mr. Reilly, you are looking at a frightened man."

Now of all things this was not what Mac had expected Perrin to say. He'd thought he would bluster it out about the girl, tell him he had been mistaken, that he had been seeing things. He'd thought Perrin would offer him a drink, slap him on the back, invite him to a party and advise him to forget about it. For once he was lost for words.

Perrin was staring at him with that intense molten brown gaze. It occurred to Mac that perhaps Perrin didn't want it broadcast around, especially to his wife, that there had been a beautiful half-naked woman in his house last night, let alone one toting a gun.

"Mr. Reilly," Perrin said finally, "someone is trying to kill me. He's been following me for the last few weeks. He's on my tail wherever I go."

Again he surprised Mac. "How d'you know he wants to kill you?"

Beads of sweat trickled slowly down Perrin's

neck and Mac wondered whether it was from a workout he might have interrupted or from genuine fear.

"I just know it," Perrin said.

"So why haven't you reported it to the police?" Mac knew this would have been the move of an innocent man. Or at least a man with nothing to hide.

Perrin lifted his shoulders in a bewildered shrug, spreading his arms wide. "You've no doubt heard my wife is divorcing me? What if it's her? Maybe she wants me killed? How can I tell that to the cops? Her attorneys would have me locked up in a second. They'd say I was trying to screw her out of the money they claim is rightfully hers."

"I hear it's half your fortune." Mac kept his tone light but he was still wondering what Perrin was hiding.

"Mr. Reilly, do you know my wife?"

"I've seen her movies."

"Hah. Of course you have. The famous Allie Ray. One of the world's most beautiful women. But behind that elegant blond façade she has turned into the most grasping avaricious soul on this earth. And maybe on a couple of other planets too."

Mac stared at him, surprised. This was not the image Allie Ray, America's girl next door, projected.

Perrin fell silent, obviously still smoldering. Then he added bitterly, "She married me for my money and I was dumb enough to fall for it. She'd married two other rich guys before she got

28

to me. Sure, I wanted the trophy wife, the one everybody else wanted." He glared at Mac. "I scratched my way up from the gutter, Reilly, y'know that?"

He got up and began to pace, twisting his hands together, as though he were hurting inside. "I thought she loved me," he said, sounding almost piteous, if a man that powerful was capable of such a thing.

Mac sat silently, waiting for him to spill the truth, which he knew was what usually happened when you acted like a fly on the wall and just let them get on with it. Perrin was a sad man, no doubt about it, but he still hadn't mentioned the Naughty Angel with the gun.

Perrin was pacing again, actually wringing his hands now, agonized, Mac guessed, at the thought either of parting with his wife or his money.

Perrin glanced up. "Y'know how much I've offered her, Reilly? Eighty million bucks. *Eighty mil,* buddy. Plus the Bel Air house that I shelled out twenty-five mil for and on which she lavished another fuckin' fortune. But is that enough for Mary Allison Raycheck? The girl from Texas with a no-good alcoholic father who beat her with his belt every Saturday night when he got back from the bar? And the hard-drinking depressed mother who neglected her?"

Perrin shook his head vehemently. "For the media's sake I helped invent and perpetuate the story that she was raised a lady, all sugar and spice. And of course now she is that lady. She heads up a couple of worthy charities, though I'd bet she doesn't part with a cent unless it's tax deductible."

He slumped onto the sofa again and put his head in his hands. "She wants it all, Reilly. And to get it, I believe she wants me dead. And that's why you have to find out if she's after me."

Mac thought about the blond movie star he had seen in magazine photographs, though there were none of her here in the beach house. Always smiling, often pictured holding the hands of sick children in hospital beds, or hosting parties at her Bel Air mansion in aid of the latest political candidate, and patronizing the smartest restaurants in town while arranging for them to donate their leftover food to homeless shelters. And always with a photographer handy. That was one way of looking at Allie Ray.

The other way was of a girl from a poor and abusive background who knew as a child what it was to have no money for doctors, never to have enough food and no pretty clothes. And no love. Maybe Allie was only giving back some of what she had been fortunate enough to acquire. Maybe Allie really cared and Perrin was maligning her so he could hang on to his fortune.

One of them had to be a liar. Mac thought he would certainly like to hear Allie's side of the story.

Meanwhile, RP had not called on Mac. Mac had called on him. So why was the guy suddenly spilling his guts to a perfect stranger? Plus there was still the matter of the Naughty Angel to be explained.

"I would like to hire you to find out who is

following me," Perrin said, fixing Mac with that sad-puppy gaze again. He went to the desk, took a business card and handed it to Mac. "I don't want to end up dead. And I don't want my wife to be known as a killer."

He sat there, waiting for Mac to speak and maybe pass judgment.

He twisted those hands anxiously again. "I'll pay double whatever your usual fee is. Triple, even." His eyes clouded as he thought about what he'd just said. "Make that double," he amended hastily. RP was a businessman first and foremost.

Mac got up. He walked over to the upturned boxes of files. "You trying to hide financial records from your wife?" he asked. "Is that what this is?"

Perrin hurried after him. "Yup, yes, that's all it is," he said quickly.

Looking down at him, Mac realized that Perrin was considerably shorter than he was. "Mr. Perrin," he said finally. "Who was the tall red-haired woman who was here last night? The one with a Sigma .40 handgun."

Perrin's face was suddenly suffused with color, a vein throbbed in his neck, then he got himself under control and said, "I was out until one o'clock last night, Reilly. There was no one in my house. There was no redhead with a gun. I already told that to the guard at the gate."

Perrin turned his eyes away. He knew that Mac knew he was lying. He walked back to the sofa and slumped down again.

"Would you care for a drink?" he asked with

a sigh.

Mac shook his head. "I don't drink in the mornings." He thought quickly about the job offer. With the TV show likely not to be picked up he could surely use the money, but there was something he didn't like about this scene. Perrin was lying to him about the redhead, and probably also about his wife, though Mac would bet, under all his bluster, he was still in love with her.

"Thanks for offering me the job," he said, "but I can't do it. I'm off to Rome in a couple of hours." He walked to the door. "I'll be away for about a week."

Perrin hurried anxiously behind him, sneakers squeaking on the expensive modernist lacquered floor.

"You're going to *Rome?*" His voice was as squeaky as his sneakers. "But you *can't.*" He was shouting now. "I've offered you the job. I need you to find out what the hell's going on."

"Thanks a lot for the offer, Mr. Perrin." Mac turned and they looked at each other. Mac handed him his own business card. "Call me when I get back and we'll talk about it some more. Meanwhile my advice to you is to go to the police, tell them you suspect you're being followed. They'll take care of things for you. They'll come up with the truth."

"Don't they always," Perrin said bitterly. Then added, positively, "No police."

Mac felt Perrin's eyes following him as he strode down the deep blue cement path. The steel gate remained shut and he waited, without looking back, for Perrin to open it for him. Soundlessly, it slid back.

He stepped out into the fresh clean air and the sunshine. The gate slid shut behind him, locking in a frightened man.

Six

Allie Ray Perrin was on her way to Malibu. The morning was gray with the kind of fog that left droplets on your hair and was known euphemistically in California as a "marine layer." Driving slowly over Malibu Canyon, Allie knew from experience that it was unlikely to shift before three p.m. even though behind her in the San Fernando Valley the sun was shining just as always. It was one of the penalties—or delights, take your choice—of living at the beach.

Still, she drove with the top down on her Mercedes 600 convertible, snuggling into her cashmere hoodie, uncaring about the mist. The large dark glasses were L.A. de rigueur, sun or no sun, though she doubted anyone would recognize the unmade-up woman they glimpsed quickly in passing as the glamorous movie star they knew from the screen. Except for the paparazzi, of course, who hounded her like bats out of hell. But today she had escaped them, taking the back route out of her Bel Air home, cutting across Mulholland to the Valley, then over the canyon to Malibu.

It wasn't her husband she was going to see though. She had been watching Mac Reilly's program Thursday nights and she thought he seemed a man of integrity. A man you could trust. And if anyone needed that sort of man right now, it was Allie Ray.

Turning left onto Pacific Coast Highway, commonly known as PCH, she idled through the fog, denser now she was at the shore. The guard at the Colony gate recognized her car immediately and the bar swung up. She waved to him as she drove in and he waved back. There were no grand iron gates here, no high stone walls. Low-key was the watchword at the Colony. Everyone liked it that way. Life at the beach, Allie thought wistfully, was nice.

At the T junction leading to the Colony's only street, she made a right rather than the left she normally took to her own place, heading instead for Mac Reilly's house. Checking the number, she found it at the very end, stuck like a worn green barnacle to the Colony's glossy façade. A shiny red Prius was parked outside. She parked behind it, glancing doubtfully at the exterior of the house. It appeared to have been painted recently, yet somehow it looked shabby.

Still, Mac Reilly's housekeeping was not what she was here for, and she tugged on the bellpull, which was in the form of a cracked brass captain's bell, long since oxidized to an almost matching green. She waited. And waited some more. She jangled the bell again, anxious now. He *had* to be here.

Stepping from the shower, Mac heard it ring.

He glanced at the clock. Because of Perrin he was running late. As it was he would just about make the flight. He knew it couldn't be his assistant, who was due to arrive any minute to drive him to the airport, because Roddy had his own key.

Cursing, he wrapped a towel around his loins then ran to open the door. And found himself looking into the eyes of one of the most famous and most beautiful women in the world.

She was wearing a gray cashmere hoodie, matching pants and Reeboks that were so pristinely white, Mac figured she must have bought them specially for the occasion. He corrected himself quickly. A woman like Allie Ray probably had a dozen pairs, all new, sitting in her closet, and she probably never wore them twice.

Allie stared back at him, waiting for him to take it in that it was really *her* standing on his doorstep. Then she gave him the smile that had charmed moviegoers for over a decade.

"I'm so sorry," she said, "I must have caught you in the shower."

Brought back to reality, Mac hitched up the towel. He apologized for his appearance and invited her into the tiny square that constituted his front hall.

Allie stared at the dog as it bounded lopsidedly toward her. Pirate gave her the usual investigative sniff, then sat back on his haunch, allowing her a full view of his one eye and goofy smile.

Catching her shocked look, Mac said quickly, "His name is Pirate. After Long John Silver. In *Treasure Island.* Y'know: the wooden leg, the eye patch." She frowned and he added, "Hey listen, it was better than the alternative. He was almost dead when I found him."

Allie bent to pat Pirate's head. Sliding the cashmere hood from her pale blond hair, which was pinned in a loose ponytail, she walked into the living room.

With her hair like that, Mac thought she looked like the college version of Barbie. Except for those eyes of course, which when she fixed them on him, had a haunting quality, like diving into a turquoise tropical sea where troubling undercurrents tugged at you.

Excusing himself, he hurried to put on shorts and a T-shirt.

When he came back he found her looking round his comfortable, if shabby, domain. At the squashy old sofas covered in a variety of plaid rugs, most of which Pirate called home, when he wasn't sleeping on Mac's bed that is. At the beat-up black leather La-Z-Boy with a cup holder where Mac stashed his beer and pretzels, with the flap on the side for the remote, and that little leg-lifting device that, if the Lakers game wasn't so hot, relaxed a guy so much it could put him right to sleep.

Allie's gaze moved to the old surfboard that in a fit of artistic triumph Mac had painted gold and converted into a coffee table. Then on to the mélange of wicker chairs surrounding the squat, solid-looking oak table, bought by Sunny at a flea market and which she swore was a valuable antique. Mac had told her he was hanging on to it so when that rainy day came he could make his fortune.

Allie had moved on to his eclectic art collection, if so proper a term could be used for the colorful canvases on Mac's walls, most of which he'd picked up on visits to new young artists in their Venice Beach studios, at prices that had left him worried, and wondering if he'd left them starving in their garrets.

Allie took in the sea grass rugs on the wooden floors, the shutters flapping at the window, the faux-zebra rug in front of the fifties white-brick fireplace, the unmatched lamps, and the collection of candles and votives, courtesy of Sunny.

She gave Mac that haunted turquoise look again. "I envy you," she said, surprising him. "You have exactly what you want. You're a lucky man."

"There's no need for envy, particularly coming from a woman like you."

She perched on the edge of the dog-hairy sofa, looking up at him. "Tell me, Mr. Reilly, what exactly do you know about women like me?"

She had put him on the spot. Did he tell her the truth about what he'd heard she was? Or did he go for the comfort factor? Tactfully, he took the middle path.

"I know you came from a poor background, that you married well. Several times. I know that you're a famous actress."

Allie ran a hand through her pale blond hair, lifting her ponytail and shaking it free from the folds of the cashmere hood. "Do you know what despair is, Mr. Reilly?" she asked quietly. "Do you know what it is to arrive at the realization that there is only one way you are going to get out of the stifling small town you lived in, away from the alcoholic father, and from the worn-out, depressed mother you dread becoming?"

A shudder shook her slender frame and she frowned. "Away from the brutality and the grinding poverty, and the stifling grayness of a life with no prospect of a silver lining. Away from the small-town high school football heroes who lied about their conquests with the shy pretty blond teenager simply to add to their own macho luster. And away from the preacher who from the pulpit kept on spelling out a life of damnation for the fallen, and then afterward would try to grope you?"

She stopped and gave Mac that haunted look again. "Do you know what it feels like, Mr. Reilly, to wake up to the fact that in order to get out of there, there is only one thing you can sell. And that is your beauty. Because that's all you have."

Her sigh dredged up like an ill wind from her past. "At least," she said, looking squarely at him, "if I had to do it, I decided it would be to the highest bidder. There was just one rule. He had to marry me."

"And you stuck to your plan?"

"I married rich men. And I kept my part of the bargain. I was a good wife for a while. But eventually they got bored with looking at me, I guess. Anyway, I had always wanted to be an actress—a movie actress. And now I have all the money in the world—and possibly even more when Ron Perrin comes through with the divorce settlement. Not that I need it. I'm successful in my own right, more successful than some men. And y'know what, Mr. Reilly? I'm still not a happy woman."

Her eyes met his. "You're judging me, because I told you the truth." She lifted a shoulder in a delicate shrug. "Obviously you don't know what it is to have no choice."

Mac said nothing because it was true. Yet he understood.

She got to her feet and went and stood close to him. "Look into my face," she said. "What do you see written here?"

Actually, Mac could see nothing. Although she must have been coming up to forty, there were no time wrinkles, no laughter lines, no marks of sorrow. Just a very beautiful face that photographed really well.

"Discontent, Mr. Reilly," she said quietly. "That's what you see. I'm the archetypical woman who has everything. Oh, believe me, there are dozens of us in this town, maybe even hundreds. And we all have the same expression. As though life passed us by. Real life, that is."

She walked away, staring through the picture window at the ocean throwing itself lustily onto the shore in a flurry of spray. "But one day," she said softly, "one day I'm going to find that 'real' life, y'know that?" She swung round. "I'll be me again. Mary Allison Raycheck."

Mac said, "Back to that."

"I see you know everything about me, even my

39

real name. I guess I should have expected that from a private investigator."

"Actually, your husband told me."

She gave a short bark of a laugh. "Of course. But then, he would, wouldn't he?"

She slumped onto the La-Z-Boy and flipped the lever, stretching out as it lifted into position under her long, slender limbs.

"God, I always loved these things," she said, half to herself. "Once, I thought the epitome of being rich was to have a leather La-Z-Boy and a coffee table from Sears with a glass top and gold legs. My, my, how times have changed."

A tear trickled down her lovely face and dropped with a splash off the cliff of her cheekbone onto the gray cashmere. "Now I have all this furniture an expensive decorator chose for me because it's in perfect taste. I wear designer clothes because that's what I'm supposed to wear. I eat the right diet at the right restaurants, attend the right parties." She glanced despairingly Mac's way. "You see, Mr. Reilly, what my trouble is, don't you? I just don't know who I am anymore. It's still the way it's always been. What you see is *all* you get."

And then Allie Ray, movie star supreme, curled up in Mac's tattered black leather La-Z-Boy and, to his horror, burst into floods of tears. She pounded the chair with her fists, howling and sobbing.

Pirate hauled himself to his feet and ran to her. That dog hated a scene, he'd probably had had too much of it in his previous life, before Mac became his father. He sniffed Allie anxiously, whining and pawing at her. And to Mac's astonishment the movie star leaned over and scooped him onto her knee. "Sweet doggie," she whispered as Pirate began to lick away her tears.

"So now you see why I envy you, Mr. Reilly," she said between hiccups. "I don't even have a Pirate. I just have the *right* dog, the one we're all supposed to have this year."

"Not a Chihuahua!"

She shook her head, scattering tears all over Pirate, who shook his head too, to get rid of them. "A miniature Maltese. By the name of Fussy. And believe me, she is."

Mac offered her a box of Kleenex. He thought regretfully that he would miss his flight to Rome, but knew he had no choice. Allie Ray needed his help.

"Tell you what," he said, "why don't we go for that walk along the beach? Now I know you better you can tell me why you need me. And why you are so desperate."

Seven

Pirate loped along the shoreline while Mac and Allie followed at a more leisurely pace. After all, they were not there for the exercise.

Allie took off her sneakers and brushed the drops of mist from her hair. Digging her toes into the wet sand she said, "I'm sorry. I didn't come here to cry on your shoulder. I came to ask for your professional help. I'm a rich woman, Mr. Reilly. I'm willing to pay lavishly for your exclusive time."

Mac raised his brows, surprised by the offer. It was surely coming at a handy moment, when his TV income might be suddenly cut off.

"Anything I can do," he said.

She stopped, then turned to face him. "For the past week, I've been followed. It's a black Sebring convertible with dark windows so I can't see the driver. There's no license plate at the front, and since he's always in the back of me I never get to see it. But lately it's always there, on my tail. I don't know whether it's my husband having me watched to see if he can get any dirt on me. Or if it's the same crazy stalker who's been after me for the last few months. He sends me letters—love letters he calls them, though it's all just filth. Of course I don't look at them anymore, I just burn them without opening them. Anyhow, it's scary."

Mac didn't like the sound of those letters, nor the black Sebring. He thought it strange that both Perrin and his wife believed they were being followed. He wondered if they were tailing each other, but when he asked her Allie denied it.

"Then why not go to the police?"

"Because I'm Allie Ray," she said simply. "You can only imagine what would happen. I'm terrified though. I feel eyes on me, as though I'm being watched wherever I go. I don't know what to do."

Mac made a quick decision. It wasn't only the offer of good money that attracted him. Allie Ray was vulnerable, and she was hurting, and it was more than just a scary stalker and a husband who no longer appreciated her. He got the feeling Allie was a desperately lonely woman who needed not only his help but also his support.

"So why don't I find out who it is, and if it's your husband or not?"

She threw him a grateful smile then turning away she walked along the edge of the shore where the waves hit the sand, uncaring that she was getting wet. Picking up a stick, she threw it for Pirate who galloped joyfully after it. Wagging his butt, he dropped it at her feet making her laugh and she picked it up and threw it again.

"That's the first time I've heard you laugh," Mac said.

She shot him a mischievous glance. "Except in the movies, you mean. Then I laugh all the time."

"Unless you're kissing someone."

She laughed again. "You're right, I am always kissing someone. It used to drive Ron mad. 'You're my woman,' he'd say, whenever we had a fight, 'and all I see is you in bed, half-naked with some poncey actor.'"

Mac could just imagine Ron Perrin making that remark. Ego had no boundaries even when it came to the fact that acting was his wife's job.

"I didn't tell you everything," she said. "It's not only that I'm afraid of the crazy stalker. You see, Mr. Reilly, my husband is having an affair. And this time I think it's serious."

"It's not the first time, I assume?"

She shook her head, sending the ponytail and the drops of water flying. "It's not. But the truth is I still care about Ron. He's the only man who ever bothered to look behind the façade. The only man who wanted to know the real me. Without him, I don't know who I am." She sighed as she tossed the stick again, then turned to meet Mac's eyes. "Look at me," she said sadly. "What you see is all you get. I'm a public success. And a private failure."

Remembering the redhead with the gun, Mac thought Allie had a right to be worried. "Let me see what I can do," he said. "I'm off to Rome for a week, but I'll get my assistant right onto it.

"Anything else on your mind?" he asked as they made their way back to his house.

"Plenty," she said, smiling ruefully. "Unfortunately, it's nothing you can do anything about. My new movie is to premiere in Cannes in a couple of weeks and I know it's a mess." She

44

shrugged sadly. "Of course, they'll say it's all my fault, that I'm difficult, that I made changes, that I'm getting older."

She stopped at the top of the steps, watching as Pirate hobbled back up. "So now you understand why I envy you, Mr. Reilly."

"I think it's time you called me Mac."

She smiled. "The simple life has so much more to offer, don't you think, Mac?"

A car honked outside. Mac knew it was Roddy, waiting to take him to the airport, though even if they got lucky with the traffic he guessed he'd miss his flight and would have to reschedule.

At the door, Allie turned to hug him goodbye. "Please help me," she said.

And of course Mac promised he would, even if he had to do it long-distance from Rome.

Eight

Allie drove slowly back along PCH lost in her thoughts. The congested highway offered glimpses of the ocean, glinting between low buildings whose doors opened directly onto the road, and which surprisingly were mostly extremely expensive homes.

Revisiting the past was not something Allie did frequently, in fact never, if she could help it, and then only in her dreams when she had no control over the memories that drifted into her mind.

She felt exhausted from the explosion of tears, again something she never did. Nobody ever saw anything but the public Allie, the one smiling for the cameras. She had let her guard down to Mac Reilly and now she was wishing she had not.

The past was the past and that was where she wanted to keep it, locked away in a safe place where nobody could find it. Except Ron, of course, because Ron knew everything there was to know about her. It was as though he'd known right from the beginning, without ever having to ask.

She shook her head, pushing the thought of him away, as she had done physically the night she told him to leave. "Get out of my life," she'd yelled. "Or I'll get out of yours."

"Oh? And exactly how will the famous movie star, America's 'good girl,' manage to do that?" he'd asked.

"Same as all the other women," she'd snapped back, picking up a vase of roses, ready to hurl it at him if he so much as came near her.

He had laughed. "You don't have to go that far," he said. "I'm outta here."

As he'd marched to the door she'd shouted after him, "Back to her, I suppose."

He had turned to look at her. For a long moment their eyes had connected. Then he'd lifted a shoulder in that familiar dismissive gesture of his. "Have it your own way," he'd said. And he'd walked out, closing the door quietly behind him.

After he'd gone Allie had slumped into a chair

in the massive front hall with the double curving staircase and the antique chandelier that had sparkled like Christmas stars on their ugly fight. The chair was a designer *fauteuil* with plaid silk upholstery in soft shades of celadon green and walnut armrests. Expensive of course, as everything in this house was. Still clutching the vase of pink roses, Allie had stared blankly at the door where her life, her future, her very reason for being, had just walked out. Ron Perrin no longer loved her and she did not know what to do about it.

Now, heading home along the coast road, she still didn't know what to do, and what she had told Mac Reilly was the truth. Her very private truth. She liked Reilly. He had something that was rare in her circle. Integrity. She could tell that, even from their brief meeting.

Remembering suddenly why she had gone to see him, she glanced in the rearview mirror. Her heart jumped into her throat. It was there! The black Chrysler Sebring, the kind of inexpensive convertible tourists liked to rent so they could put the top down and enjoy California's rays, soaking up the sun and a lungful of gasoline fumes along with the sea breeze. Except tourist cars didn't have windows tinted so dark you couldn't see the driver, and *this* Sebring driver never put the top down, never stopped to admire the view, and never overtook no matter how slowly she drove. He just sat on her tail a couple of cars back and waited to see what she would do next.

A shiver of fear trickled down Allie's spine.

47

She had experienced stalkers before. Usually they were more insistent, wanting to get next to her, to try to make conversation as she waited at Malibu's Country Mart Starbucks for her double latte, two shots, skinny. Of course she didn't go there anymore because the paparazzi lurked around the place, cameras at the ready, waiting to snag celebrities in their lenses, hopefully doing something naughty. But this stalker was sending letters filled with threats of violence.

She drove faster, to the fringes of Santa Monica. When she got to Topanga Canyon, at the last second she made a quick turn left across the traffic into the parking lot of the Reel Inn, a beach café that served fish in many varieties and almost any form.

She turned to look back. As she had hoped the Sebring driver had been taken by surprise and forced by the traffic to drive on. There were no U-turns on PCH, and he could not come back until he reached Sunset and made a legal turn. She had given him the slip.

She pressed the button to put up the top on her car, then made a left out of the parking lot and a right at the light. She was taking the same road as the Sebring knowing she would pass it coming back the other way in search of her. Then she would take Sunset Boulevard, the long road that led all the way from the beach to Bel Air and Beverly Hills, and to Hollywood and beyond. Meanwhile, she punched in Mac Reilly's number.

"Hi, it's me, Allie," she said when he answered, liking the sound of his strong voice. This man knew who he was. She only wished she could learn from him.

Mac was in his car on his way to the airport. Pirate rode shotgun, head sticking out the window, ragged ears flapping, while Mac's assistant, Roddy Kruger, was in the back seat, negotiating a new flight to Rome and complaining about lack of legroom. Roddy would drive the car and the dog back to Malibu after dropping Mac off.

"So what's up, Allie Ray?" Mac asked, noticing that Roddy fell suddenly silent at the mention of the famous name.

"He's on my tail again. I just lost him at the Reel Inn. I'm on my way home now, via Sunset."

"Okay, no need to panic." Mac's voice was calm. "Your new 'tail'—your personal one hired by me, will be with you by the time you reach home. He will be driving a souped-up black Mustang and he'll have a camera around his neck, looking like the rest of the paparazzi. He's fortyish, bald as a coot, the usual aviator sunglasses, a Tommy Bahama flowered shirt, jeans, sneakers. Six one, in good shape—good enough to take on all comers. You can trust me on that. He's a triple black belt in karate and trained with the Israeli Special Forces. He's also organized round-the-clock surveillance. No need to be afraid, Allie, I promise you. He'll soon find out who the follower is, whether it's the stalker, or some PI hired by your husband to keep tabs on you and dig for any dirt. Not that I expect there is any," he added casually.

"No," Allie said shortly. "There is not."

"Glad to hear it." Mac was smiling. "It makes

49

life easier all around, especially from a divorce lawyer's point of view."

Out of the corner of her eye Allie caught a glimpse of the Sebring with the darkened windows speeding in the opposite direction. Heaving a sigh of relief, she said, "What's his name?"

"Your bodyguard? His name is Lev Orenstein. You can't miss him, and trust me, he won't miss you. You're in good hands," he added gently.

"Okay," she said in a small voice. "See you when you get back from Rome then."

"One week," he said. "We'll get together right away."

"I leave for Cannes a few days after you return," she said. "Please don't forget to call." She was almost begging him, wishing he wasn't leaving, wanting him to stay near her, wanting his strength. It was not often you got a man who understood; a man who listened; a man who saw beyond the façade. A man like Ron had once been.

"Okay, don't worry, I'll call and we'll set a date. You're in my thoughts, Allie."

"And you are in mine," she whispered as he rang off.

Turning in to her street, Allie saw the black Mustang parked discreetly under a tree opposite the gates. She knew Reilly must have informed Security that Lev Orenstein was here for her protection, otherwise the patrol would have moved him on. A couple of other vehicles nosed slowly by, but there was no black Sebring convertible and she breathed a sigh of relief. Slowing opposite the Mustang, she rolled down her window and a tall guy, whippet thin with shoulders like a halfback and, she guessed, probably a full six-pack of abs, got out and slouched over to her.

"Ma'am," he said in a rich dark voice, "I'm Lev, here for your protection. Mr. Reilly probably told you about me."

He leaned an arm lazily on the roof of her Mercedes. "Yes, he did," she said, managing a smile. "I'm very glad to see you, Lev."

"Don't worry about a thing, ma'am. I'm here for you." He stepped back, lifting his hand in farewell. "You need to let me know when you're going out and where you're going. You ever need me, up at the house, wherever, you call this number." He passed a card through the window. "Put it on your cell," he said. "Tuck it in your bra, drill it into your brain. It's your lifesaver, ma'am. Your link to me."

"I will," she promised, shakily. Then she pressed the button that opened the electronic gates and sped down the straight-as-an-arrow driveway that led to the twenty-thousand-square-foot soulless mausoleum she called home.

Nine

Of course Sunny was not waiting for Mac at Rome's Fiumicino airport, as he had hoped, but he took it in his stride. That's women for you, he thought, smiling. Perverse as all get-out. Plus of course, due to his unexpected chat with Allie Ray, he'd missed his original flight and had been forced to make a couple of connections via D.C. and New York to get to Rome. He was late, tired and jet-lagged, but happy.

He took a cab into town which after a lengthy drive deposited him at the venerable Hotel d'Inghilterra, with its charming tearoom, and the wood-paneled bar where Ernest Hemingway used to hang out, and where the driver now relieved him of which seemed to Mac to be a great many euros for his trouble. The bellman took his bag and the desk clerk informed him that the Signorina Coto de Alvarez was taking coffee at Tre Scalini in the Piazza Navona, a short walk away.

He pointed him in the right direction and Mac sauntered happily along the narrow crowded streets. The sun bounced off the ruins in a golden glow, the air smelled of fresh coffee and the chic Roman women, always intent on presenting a *bella figura,* looked like Armani models. Not a bad day in Italy, he thought, pleased. Still, when he stepped from the side street into the vast expanse of the Piazza Navona, it took his breath away.

He stopped to look at the ancient buildings in faded shades of ocher and rose surrounding the arena that, centuries ago, had started life as a stadium, and that now lay buried deep beneath the cobblestones. The many cafés with their striped awnings were crowded, and Bernini's glorious Fountain of the Four Rivers pulsed sparkling jets of water into the air. Tourists milled around taking photographs, while Borromini's Sant'Agnese church, domed and turreted, pedimented and columned, ruled over all.

Mac sauntered past several cafés until he came to Tre Scalini, near the big fountain with a grand view of the church and an even better view of his Sunny, wearing a pale green dress with a neckline that he immediately decided was too low-cut for Rome.

Now Mac knew he might not be your typical detective from the crime-novel genre, but Sunny was another matter. She was your Raymond Chandler woman all right. Long silky black curls brushed smooth from a heart-shaped face, smoky eyes, amber-brown under winging brows; straight-on perfect nose; and the pouty red mouth all Chandler's heroines and villainesses had. Add to that a delicious cleavage and golden legs that went on forever, and Sunny was some kind of woman.

She was sitting in the shade of the café awning, leafing through a copy of Italian *Vogue* and sipping a cappuccino.

"What, no sticky buns?" he asked, depositing a kiss on her sleek dark head.

"You're late," she complained.

Mac sighed as he sank into the chair opposite. "Nice greeting for a guy who's just spent sixteen hours on several planes in an effort to be with the love of his life."

But then she gave him the smile that lit up her face with a thousand candle-watt-power. "I'm glad you came," she said simply and she leaned forward and kissed him. Everything was right in their world again. Temporarily, of course, because that's the way their relationship went.

"I'm sorry," Sunny said, "but I have to go to the studios. It's a longish cab drive out of the city, it's better if you get some rest and I'll catch up with you later."

"Don't worry," Mac said, pushing jet lag away as a memory. "I'm getting my second wind. I'll come with you."

In the car taking them to the studios he slid his arm around Sunny's shoulders. He dropped a kiss on her hair, reaching with his other hand to smooth it from her neck, snuffling her familiar scent.

"I missed you," he murmured. "Do we really have to go to the studios? Can't we just turn around and go back to the hotel, where I can get you alone?"

Sunny was staring nervously ahead at the tangle of traffic that their driver was negotiating with loud honks of the horn and swift sideways maneuvers that seemed typical of Roman driving.

"You seem to forget I'm here on business," she reminded him.

Mac studied her delicious profile. "You're right," he admitted. "Somehow I thought I was here with my lover, enjoying the beauty of Rome, tasting the good red wine and wonderful food, exploring the ancient ruins..."

She turned her head a fraction to look at him. A smile lifted the corners of her pretty mouth. "Is that *really* why you're here?"

He lifted his shoulders in a shrug. "Why else, baby?" he said, as she slid into his arms and began to kiss him. Properly this time. None of that cold shoulder stuff. Just real kissing, like two people in love.

Fifteen minutes later as they drove through the gates at Cinecittà, Sunny quickly reapplied her lipstick and combed her hair. "Do I look okay?" she asked.

Mac's eyes were warm with love. She looked flushed and sparkly, a woman ready to make love and not at all businesslike.

"You look beautiful," he said.

Cinecittà Studios were famous for the years it took to film *Cleopatra,* the Taylor-Burton epic in the early sixties, and for the even more famous love affair between the two stars. Now they were more often used for smaller films, though many of the old sets remained standing.

Sunny's client, a young actor by the name of Eddie Grimes, was making a sci-fi epic produced by the eminent Renato Manzini that, it seemed to Mac, could easily have been made anywhere on the planet. Still, he guessed Rome was as good a place to make a sci-fi as Hollywood or Mars, and the sets were certainly stupendous.

Still, jet lag was taking its toll. He sank a couple of espressos for sustenance, lounging in a chair in the shade while Sunny chatted to Eddie, making a few notes in the yellow legal pad she always carried.

He fell asleep in the cab on the way back to the hotel, leaning dopily against her as the tiny elevator whisked them slowly upward. In their room, he didn't even bother to complain about Sunny's clothes strewn about. He took a quick shower, flopped onto the bed and dropped off the edge of the world into a black abyss of sleep.

So much for romance, Sunny thought tenderly, as she watched him.

She caught him on the rebound though, a couple of hours later. She stretched her long naked body next to his, his hand reached out for her and he turned his face to hers, breathing in the scent of her, his mouth searching for hers.

"This," he whispered, his arms gripping her close, "is what I came to Rome for. I can't do without you, Sunny."

Ten

Mac's assistant, Roddy Kruger, age thirty-five, short bleached-blond hair, good-looking, gay and very popular, was staying at the Malibu house babysitting Pirate. He was sitting on the deck on an old metal lounger from Wal-Mart, which was about in keeping with the rest of the furnishings in Mac's home, a Diet Coke in one hand, the *L.A. Times* sports section in the other.

Every now and then he would glance up from the newspaper to check the Perrin house down the beach. Mac had filled him in on the events and put him in charge of the Allie Ray case, though "case" was hardly the correct term for finding out who was following her, and the anonymous letter writer was more of a problem. Allie had sent Mac a couple of the letters and they were not at all happy about them. Still, Roddy was a longtime fan and the thought that he was working for the star gave him a distinct buzz. There was no activity at the Perrin house though, and he went back to his newspaper.

Half an hour later he glanced at the bright blue rubber-encased diver's watch, waterproof to a depth of three hundred feet, that Mac had given him the previous Christmas. It looked like a piece of junk but he knew it had cost a small fortune, and since he was an avid surfer, he loved it. It was time to polish the Prius. Those pesky seagulls were constantly flying overhead and their droppings could take the paint off a car in no time flat. Twice a day, had been Mac's instructions, and Roddy was conscientious about it because he knew how much Mac loved his customized car. Even more than the black Dodge Ram that had gotten the same treatment, and that had been his previous passion, but now, like most of Hollywood, Mac and Sunny were passionate about ecology.

Malibu Colony might be a beachy suburb grown rich but it still retained its old-world charm. Every house was in a different style, from traditional picket fences to concrete modern. Telephone and utility wires still looped shabbily along the only street, unchanged since the forties, and several cars were usually in the process of being washed, only now it was the detail guys giving the Mercs and the Porsches the tip-top treatment. Kids rollerbladed and uniformed maids walked the dogs, stopping for a chat with the Mexican gardeners who kept the tiny expensive patches of lawn and the floribundas in immaculate shape. Joggers, looking as sweaty as any regular joggers, even though they were movie stars or just plain rich, trotted past, and vans delivering flowers and groceries lurched slowly over the speed bumps. It was like any other upmarket suburb in America.

Roddy carried a bucket of water and a chamois leather out into the street, sloshing off the latest seagull deposits, cursing the birds under his breath. Pirate sat next to him hoping for a ride but today he was out of luck. Roddy dried the car off with paper towels, gave it a quick polish, emptied his bucket down the drain, then checked the car's door. As he'd thought, it was open. He sighed. Mac never locked his car or his house. "Which of my neighbors is gonna steal my Prius?" he'd asked with a grin, and Roddy guessed he was right. Still, he checked the interior to make sure everything was okay.

Smoothing his palm approvingly across the custom black leather, he opened the glove compartment, then took a quick breath.

He was looking at a Sigma .40 handgun. Now he knew Mac never carried a weapon unless he was heading into dangerous territory, and he would certainly never leave one in the car. Anyhow, as far as Roddy knew, Mac's only gun was a Glock semi. He had never seen him with a Sigma .40. Ever.

Roddy put his polishing cloth over the gun, slid it from the glove compartment, put it in the empty bucket and carried it back into the house.

In Rome, Sunny was lying on her back, gazing at the ceiling, a happy post-lovemaking smile on her face, her hand linked with Mac's, when the phone rang. Groaning, she reached for it.

"Pronto," she said, Italian-style. Then, "Oh, hi, Roddy, how are you? Good. Yes, great. It's wonderful. Yes, Mac's here, I'll put him on."

Handing Mac the phone she propped herself on one elbow, watching him.

"Hi, Rod," Mac said lazily.

Sunny saw him frown. She wondered what was going on.

"Okay," he said. "I know where the gun came from. Miss Naughty Angel. So wrap it in the chamois leather and leave it in the bucket under the sink. It's as safe a place as any I guess, until I can give it back to her."

"Crafty woman," he said to Sunny when he'd said goodbye. "Dumping the weapon in my car. Now I wonder why she did that."

Sunny got up. She put on a hotel white waffle-weave robe, took a bottle of water from the mini-bar and climbed back onto the bed. Unmade-up and with her long dark hair all tumbled Mac thought she'd never looked more lovely.

"Why do I get the feeling I don't know *every-thing*?" she asked, giving him the keen amber long-lashed look he knew meant business.

"I was going to tell you all about her, but somehow I got diverted."

She grinned forgivingly at him, upended the bottle and took a slug of the water. "Better tell me now. And make sure you tell *all*."

Mac got up off the bed. "Can't I even take a shower first?"

She shook her head. "After."

"Okay," he said, "so here's what happened." And he told her about the Naughty Angel, about his visit with Perrin, and about the famous Allie Ray Perrin showing up on his doorstep.

"The thing is that both Perrins believe they are being tailed. Allie denies she's having him followed and he denies likewise. Either somebody is lying, or something else is going on. And it

60

just might have to do with the redhead with the gun."

"Miss Naughty Angel," Sunny said. "I'll bet she's gorgeous."

"But not as gorgeous as the famous Allie."

"I leave you alone for a couple of days," she sighed, "and look what you get up to. All these beautiful women running after you."

"Not quite," Mac said with a phony-modest grin, and she snatched up a pillow and whacked him over the head with it.

"No, no," he moaned, pushing out from under the feathers. "No more. I need to take a shower."

She grabbed his hand. "I know a few party games in showers. Oh, and by the way, I hope you haven't forgotten you're taking me out to dinner tonight."

"Right." Mac had been thinking more about room service and sleep but a promise was a promise.

"We're going to Alvaro's," Sunny said, smiling. "Nothing but the best for your girl. Remember?"

Eleven

Tonight Sunny was all spiffied up in an expensive little slip of black chiffon from one of Rome's famous boutiques, that clung where it should and fluttered around her knees in a very feminine way. She wore black pointy-toe stilettos and Guerlain's Mitsouko perfume. She slicked on Dior's Rouge lipstick, a satisfying brilliant red, then smacked her lips together to smooth it out.

The dresses she had tried on and rejected littered the bed and the bathroom was awash in bubble bath and shampoo. After all, it took a lot of effort for a girl to look her best. She wasn't sure whether Mac had gotten it yet, but she was truly a very girly girl.

Anyhow, there she was now in her new designer black chiffon that had cost an arm and a leg and that, looking in the mirror, she thought was worth every cent. She wore little diamond hoops in her ears and a left hand conspicuously lacking in any sort of ring, be it diamond or gold, large or small. That night she planned to use her left hand pointedly, flaunting its nakedness in front of Mac, who in typical fashion probably wouldn't even notice her perfect manicure, let alone that this was her engagement finger. And that it was empty.

After some persuading Mac had temporarily abandoned his favorite tees in favor of a white linen shirt worn open at the neck and without a tie because he couldn't stand to be buttoned up. His Dolce black leather jacket was a concession to Sunny's beautiful dress and the fact that she'd told him chic Romans congregated at the restaurant she had chosen for its authentic atmosphere, as well as for its fine food. Plus the fact that it was only a couple of blocks' walk from their hotel, so no messing about trying to find one of those elusive and horribly expensive Roman taxis, whose drivers, Sunny had found to her cost, invariably quoted the equivalent of forty bucks even though you were only going the shortest distance.

"Ready?" Mac's eyes smiled at her. He pulled her close, burying his face in her fragrant hair. "Why don't we just get room service?" he whispered, nibbling at her earlobe.

She pushed him away, laughing. "Because I want to show off my boyfriend. You put the 'cream of Roman manhood' to shame, baby."

"You too," he said, sincerely. "I've never seen you look so beautiful."

To her surprise, Sunny felt herself blush. Mac wasn't given to paying compliments. He was the kind of man who took it for granted that she knew he loved the way she looked. She supposed she did. Still, it was nice to hear him say it.

Linking her arm in his, they descended in the little cage elevator, then walked up the Via Bocca di Leone, named for the pretty lion fountain in the little piazza.

The restaurant had nicotine yellow plaster walls with ancient blackened beams across the ceiling, and white tablecloths with lavish bouquets of scarlet flowers. It was old-world elegant and filled with a chic crowd, there for the food as well as for the "scene." Their table was along the wall near the center and they settled in, pleased with the place and with each other. A tiny amber-shaded lamp lit Sunny's face from below, turning her into a Latina version of a Botticelli Venus. Mac reached out for her hand. The one without the engagement ring.

"I love you, Sonora Sky Coto de Alvarez," he whispered. And lifting her hand to his lips, he turned it palm up and kissed it, then closed her fingers around the kiss.

It was such an intimate gesture that Sunny felt the little answering shiver in the pit of her stomach.

"I love you too, Mac," she whispered, gazing into his eyes.

But then the waiter broke the spell, bustling with importance as he detailed the night's specials.

"Let's share a small Margherita pizza to start," Sunny said, all a-sparkle with love for her man. "Just to go with the first glass of wine."

"No anchovies though," Mac said, remembering she hated them.

Sunny smiled. This was a big concession on Mac's part because she knew how much he loved them.

Mac studied the wine list carefully, finally

choosing a Montepulciano. When it came the waiter poured a little into his glass. Mac swirled, breathed its aroma, and sipped.

Sunny liked wine, but Mac was an expert. She saw his face light up and he nodded to the waiter. "Good," he decreed. "Excellent, in fact."

They clinked glasses and toasted each other with their eyes. There was no need for words. This was, Sunny knew, going to be one of the best nights of her life. Here in Rome with her lover, who had just told her he loved her.

"I'm glad you invited me to Rome," Mac said, sipping his wine and nibbling on a piece of the small anchovyless pizza.

"Funny, I thought you'd invited yourself," Sunny said.

But to her surprise she realized Mac was no longer listening. Instead, he was looking at something over her shoulder. She turned and followed his gaze to the door.

"Well, well. Would you just look at that," Mac said, sounding astonished.

Sunny stared at the couple standing at the entrance. You could hardly miss them. Or at least *her.* A redhead, on the arm of a rotund, balding man. There was nothing understated about this woman. Tall, with breasts that defied gravity, her waist was tinier than Scarlett O'Hara's when Mammy had finished tying her corset, and her legs went on forever. She was spectacular in a white silk dress that left no curve unturned. Sunny caught a glimpse of the redhead's ring. A *glimpse?* It almost blinded her. A yellow diamond that must have been all of ten carats. *And* it was on her engagement finger.

"Shoot," she said crossly, turning back to Mac, but he was already on his feet.

"Excuse me a moment," he said, then to her astonishment he walked over to the redhead and held out his hand.

"Hi, there," he said to the Naughty Angel. "It's good to see you again. I'm Mac Reilly. Last time we met was in Malibu. Remember?"

The redhead's face turned chalky white. Her hand felt like iced velvet in his.

"Oh, how are you?" she said, in the high, breathy voice Mac remembered calling "sorry" after she'd shot at him.

"Good, thanks. I've gotten over those bruises I acquired tripping over your deck the other night."

"Oh, that wasn't *my* deck." Her voice trailed off uncertainly.

"I believe I have something of yours," Mac said, still with the smile. "You left it in my car."

"Oh, I don't think so," she said too quickly. "I'm not missing anything."

The rotund one gave a discreet cough and she turned her frightened green eyes from Mac to him. "Oh, Renato," she said, "this is Mac Reilly. And this is Renato Manzini. My producer," she added in case Mac might have other thoughts on their relationship.

The two men shook hands. The portly one put a possessive arm around the redhead's waist. "Our table is ready, *carina*," he said, already edging her away.

She glanced apologetically back at Mac.

"Good to see you again," she called as he watched them go.

Sunny was goggle-eyed when he returned. "It was *her*, wasn't it?" she said.

"It was." He took a sip of wine then attacked a plate of antipasto that would have served four.

Sunny stared down at her own little forest of grilled baby artichokes, nonplussed. "How can you just sit there and eat when the woman who tried to kill you is three tables away?"

"I told you she apologized that night. Said it was her mistake." He crunched down the creamy eggplant tart as though he had nothing else on his mind.

"Better watch your waistline," Sunny said.

He glanced up at her, brows raised. "You're the one eating the sugar buns. Two at a time you told me." He winced as her black suede stiletto, Christian Louboutin and *molto* expensivo, caught him on the shin.

"So," she said impatiently. "What's her story?"

"She's with Renato Manzini, her 'producer.' And also, I believe you mentioned, your client Eddie's producer. I still don't know her name."

"That's easy," Sunny said, taking out her cell phone. "I'll call Eddie and find out."

She walked outside to make the call and Mac watched her, smiling at the perfect little twitch of her butt. It was unself-conscious and totally natural and beautiful.

She was back in a flash. "Her name is Marisa Mayne," she said, settling into her chair. "Eddie's seen her around in Hollywood. She's kind of 'a girl around town,' always at the clubs, always on the lookout. He told me she has a walk-on role in the sci-fi movie and that she looks sensational, all bare brown legs and a silver breastplate, with a lacquered silver mask complete with Spock pointed ears.

"Also, apparently at Renato Manzini's insistence, she's been given a couple of lines. Eddie doesn't know where she's staying but assumes, since they appear to be so close, it's with Manzini. His opinion is she's just a girl using her assets to try to improve her status in the movie world. And," Sunny added thoughtfully, "judging by that whopping yellow diamond on her engagement finger, I think she may be succeeding."

Mac took a sip of his wine. "Thanks, babe," he said. "What would I do without you?"

"You'd survive," she said.

He met her cool amber gaze. "No, I don't think I would," he said, leaving Sunny breathless, but just then the waiter arrived to serve the lobster fettuccini, interrupting their moment.

Dinner was delicious and the wine got even richer as the night wore on. They were on to dessert—the *dolce* the waiter called it, making them giggle—and a glass of *vin santo,* when Marisa Mayne made her exit. She stopped by their table en route.

"So good to see you again, Mac," she said, offering her hand as though they were old friends. He shook it, waving nonchalantly at Renato Manzini who glowered from the door, waiting for her.

"We have to talk," Marisa whispered urgently.

"Call me. *Please,* it's important." Then with a quick apologetic smile at Sunny she was gone.

Mac waited until the couple had finally left. Then he opened his hand and took out the scrap of paper Marisa had palmed him. On it was written her phone number.

"She's not joking," he said thoughtfully. "And this time, I think she might be in real trouble."

Twelve

The next morning at the hotel, breakfast was a leisurely affair of endless coffee, sweet rolls, and crumbs in the bed, over which Sunny and Mac made love. Marisa Mayne was temporarily forgotten and they were still rolled in each other's arms at noon when Mac said, "Hey, there's all of Rome outside this window. So why are we just lying here?"

"Because this is more fun." Sunny tossed back her long wild hair and snuggled into his armpit.

"Wait a minute." He tilted her chin, rubbing his nose against hers, the silly way lovers do. "We have work to do."

"The Naughty Angel," she sighed.

"Right." Mac unwrapped her from him and reached for the piece of paper with Marisa's number. Grabbing the phone he punched it in.

She answered right away. "Oh, thank God it's you," she said, sounding tense.

69

"So what can I do for you, Miss Mayne?" Mac asked.

"We need to talk. Please can you meet me, somewhere ... anywhere *anonymous*. You know what I mean."

"You mean a place nobody will recognize you and see you talking to me?"

This time Marisa sighed. "You're so understanding. But I don't know Rome at all, so tell me, where should we meet?"

Mac looked at Sunny, mouthing "Where?"

"The Tazza d'Oro," she said. "A bar in the Piazza della Rotunda."

Mac told Marisa and arranged to meet her there in an hour.

"Better get up, Miss Coto de Alvarez," he said, grabbing her feet and pulling her the length of the bed. He took her by the shoulders and lifted her up and she wrapped her long legs round his waist.

"Shower?" he suggested.

"Of course," she said.

The umbrella-shaded terrace of the Tazza d'Oro was busy with Romans tossing down espresso so dense that Sunny knew it must hurtle straight to their veins, revving them up to face the rest of the day. It was easy to pick out the tourists because they were drinking cappuccino, something Italians only ever drank at breakfast. She had tied her hair back in a glossy ponytail and wore a cool white shirt and a short white skirt, with her trademark red lipstick. She had two favorite lipsticks: the daytime one was a pure red and the

70

night-time one had a touch of blue, making it richer. The sun was shining, the air felt warm on her skin and Mac's hand was cool in hers. The glorious dome of the Pantheon seemed to float toward the blue cloud-spotted sky, and weary visitors took their ease on the imposing flight of marble steps leading up to its massive columned portico.

"The Pantheon was built by the Emperor Hadrian in A.D. 118 to 125," she told Mac as they settled at a shady table.

"That's *old*." He signaled a waiter over.

"*And* it's erected over another, even more ancient temple, built by Marcus Agrippa. Italian kings are buried in there," she added, having done her homework. "As well as Raphael's tomb."

"I want to see it all," Mac said. "But business and a cold Peroni beer come first. What'll you have, sweetheart?"

She gave an exaggerated sigh at his crass dismissal of one of Rome's most important historic monuments.

"Lemonade," she said.

Mac gave the waiter their order, glancing around for Marisa, but as yet there was no sign of her.

"Wait a minute, though." Sunny took off her sunglasses and leaned forward, peering through the crowded square. "There's only one woman here with a body like that."

Mac took another look at the woman with the floppy straw hat pulled over her hair. She wore large dark glasses, jeans, cowboy boots and a loose red linen shirt that barely disguised her assets. It was Marisa all right. He got to his feet and waved her over.

"Oh, thank God you came," she said, sitting down quickly. "I'm so worried."

"Okay, hold on. What would you like to drink?"

"Oh? Campari and soda please."

Sunny was surprised that Marisa was already acting like a Roman, ordering a Roman-style drink. Obviously this woman was adaptable. "Hi." She leaned across the table to shake her hand. "I'm Sunny Alvarez."

"Pleased to meet you." Marisa shook it briefly and Sunny thought for a hot day her hand was exceptionally cold. She really must be frightened.

"You must be wondering who I am," Marisa said to Mac, gulping the Campari and soda as though it were Diet Coke.

"Well, kind of. I mean at least now we know your name."

Marisa took off the dark glasses and took a deep breath. "I'm Ronnie Perrin's fiancée." She held out her left hand with the whopping canary diamond. It caught the light and Sunny quickly put her own sunglasses back on.

"I admired it in Harry Winston's window in New York, so Ronnie bought it for me. But I have to keep our engagement real quiet until after the divorce. He's divorcing Allie Ray you know?" She glanced inquiringly at them and they both nodded.

"Well, anyway when the divorce comes

through I will be the next Mrs. Perrin." She beamed at them and Sunny thought how attractive she was with her green eyes and wide sexy mouth. No wonder Perrin had fallen for her. Or had he?

"How did you two meet?" she asked, taking a sip of her lemonade.

"On an Internet chat room," Marisa said, surprising her. "You can go visit people online, ask who they are, what they are, get to know each other before you even meet. I fell in love with Ronnie before I knew who he was," she added defensively. "The fact that he turned out to be rich was a nice surprise. And Ronnie said the fact that I turned out to be so sexy was a nice surprise too. He loves the Internet, he says you never know who you might meet."

She shrugged, staring down into her pretty pink drink. "The only thing is we can never be seen in public. We never go out together. I go to his Malibu home—he gave me a key. Or else he comes to my place out in the Valley, the suburbs really, where nobody knows what Ron Perrin looks like anyway. To them he's just another guy on a nice Harley."

A Harley girl, Sunny looked interested. "What does he have?"

"Oh, he has a couple, but his favorite is that real old one, not a Harley, the original ... what's it called?"

Sunny drew an envious breath. "The Indian."

"Yeah, that's it. A man like Ronnie can have anything he wants. Including women," Marisa added, a touch bitterly.

"So you were alone at his Malibu house that night?" Mac prompted her.

She nodded, sending the floppy brim of the straw hat fluttering. "It wasn't quite what it seemed that night though." She hesitated, a little frown between her brows, obviously thinking. "I wonder, have you met Ronnie's partner, Sam Demarco?"

"Haven't had that pleasure."

"Hmm," she said, looking doubtful. "Anyway, Demarco told me Ronnie thought he was being followed. He said Ronnie was real worried about it, afraid some nut was going to shoot him, or else it was Allie Ray on the warpath. Or maybe the FBI keeping tabs on him. I asked Ron about it but he shrugged it off. I wanted him to get a bodyguard but he said that would only make him look like a guilty man."

"And is he? 'A guilty man'?"

Marisa's eyes sparked with anger as she glared at Mac. "Why does everybody have to think that just because someone is rich he's guilty of doing something wrong? It's just not fair."

"Okay," Mac agreed mildly.

Then Marisa stunned them by saying, "Ron likes, kind of to be ... dominated, y'know."

Mac remembered that look in Perrin's eyes, like a chastised puppy. "Okay, so you are the dominatrix, he's the subject," he said.

"Kinda like that, yeah," she admitted. "But I really hate to hurt him y'know, I try to go as easy as I can on him and..."

"Still achieve the end result," Sunny said helpfully.

Marisa hung her head. "It's not really my scene," she said. "But, y'know, like, I'm an actress, I can play any role."

Watching her, Sunny wondered why, if she was such a good actress, she could tell Marisa was lying.

Marisa took a large gulp of the bitter Campari, shuddering as she swallowed. "I hate this stuff," she said, "but everybody here drinks it."

"So what happened that night?" Mac asked.

"Ronnie had a meeting and I was in the house alone. I went upstairs to wait for him. I had the TV on but I could still hear the surf outside the windows. I had a bottle of champagne waiting in the cooler, the way I always did. Then Ronnie called, said he was running late, he'd be back in an hour. *That's* when I heard the noise downstairs.

"I thought *no,* I'm imagining things, it's just the waves on the rocks, high tide or something. Anyhow, I turned down the TV and listened. I heard the noise again. *A footstep.*" She shivered. "You know those floors, they're some kind of concrete polished until it shines, but they're hard as hell and nothing you can do can soundproof them. You could hear a petal fall from a rose in that house.

"It was a definite footstep. Someone was moving around downstairs, opening things. *And I was alone.* I was so scared, I grabbed Ronnie's gun from the drawer in the bedside table. I crept to the top of the stairs and peered down."

She stopped with a shudder that this time shook her entire body. She was obviously terri-

75

fied by the memory. "Jeez, Mr. Reilly—Mac—I wanna tell you, my heart was thudding like a friggin' steam engine. But I'd always told myself that in a pinch, in a situation like this, if it was a 'him-or-me' survival, it would be *me*.

"I still couldn't see anybody so I crept further down the stairs. I was standing at the bottom looking round in the darkness when somebody grabbed me. I screamed and he pushed me to the floor. I dropped the gun and I thought, Oh shit this is it ... I was facedown, frantically groping around for the gun. By the time I found it and got to my feet—he was gone."

She looked at Mac. "And then you appeared at the window. I thought you were him, come back again ... I didn't recognize you until after I'd shot at you. And now I just want to say I'm sorry."

Mac grinned. "That's okay, it's happened before, and those other times I never got an apology."

"I was terrified I'd hurt you. I thought you'd send for the cops—and that would have meant the end for me and Ronnie. So I just got out of there as fast as I could. I didn't stop to think— except about the gun. I knew I couldn't leave it there in case the cops came, so I wiped it off on my robe—so there'd be no fingerprints y'see. And then I dumped it in your car. I knew the red hybrid was yours, I'd seen you driving by and it was always parked on the street outside your house. Anyway, that's what I did, and then I went back to wait for Ronnie."

"So tell me," Mac said, "why *didn't* you call

the cops?"

"No cops. Ronnie wouldn't have liked that."

Mac recalled Perrin saying vehemently, "No police" as he'd left him that morning.

"So what happened later?" he asked. "When Perrin came home?"

"I'd already called him, told him what happened. He agreed it was best not to say anything. But I could tell he was scared. He said it must be the guy who was following him, that he must be some nut who wanted to kill him."

"What happened to the FBI theory?"

"That as well. To tell you the truth, Mac, it was a very paranoid situation. And your showing up didn't help things any."

"Thanks a lot," Mac said. "I'll remember that the next time I hear a woman scream."

"Oh, I didn't mean it like that. Really I didn't." She looked away, embarrassed. "It's just that Ronnie was in trouble and I didn't know how to help him. After the shooting incident he said he had to get me out of the country immediately. Ronnie couldn't afford another scandal, after that divorce and ... well you know, the court case about mishandling the funds. And with me out of the way no one could ask me any questions. He called Demarco and told him to 'take care of me.' He meant 'get rid of me.' I knew that.

"Anyhow, Demarco called Renato Manzini in Rome, told him he was sending me over right away, and to make things look legit he should give me a small role in his film. Demarco chartered a private jet and got me to Rome that night. He told Renato to put me in the Hotel Eden and to look after me. And Ronnie said he would join me in a couple of days."

"And?" Sunny was hanging on to every word.

Marisa's face fell. "He's never even called," she said. "I'm still waiting for him at the hotel. But now Renato has found me an apartment. I move in tomorrow. Here's the address and the phone number. You already have my cell." She handed Mac the piece of paper with the information. "I daren't try to call Ronnie because he said never to, his lines might be tapped." She looked helplessly at them. "But he just never showed."

"Where do you think he is?"

Marisa shook her head, sending the floppy straw hat fluttering again. "I don't know. Has he dumped me, or what?" She twisted the enormous ring nervously. "I mean, a guy should tell a girl if there are problems. Not that there were. We were happy as two clams. I knew what he liked, he knew what I liked." She glanced meaningfully at Sunny. "Y'know what I mean."

Marisa sighed again. "It doesn't make sense. And that's why I'm worried about him. Somebody was following him. Somebody broke into his house. He told me somebody wanted to kill him. And now I'm afraid they might have. And that's the truth of the matter."

"And what do you want me to do?" Mac asked.

"I need you to find Ronnie. I want to know he's alive. Tell him I'm still here, waiting for him. At least tell him to have Demarco call me and tell me what's up."

Mac said, "So what do you think the intruder

was after that night? Obviously he wasn't aware you were there, so it wasn't a rapist or a killer..."

Marisa shivered. "Oh, God, don't even say those words. I tremble at the thought of what might have happened. And I really don't know what he wanted."

Mac thought about it. When Perrin had asked him to help he had turned him down, but now Mac needed to know what was really going on. For Allie's sake, as well as for the girlfriend. "Tell you what, Marisa," Mac said. "I'm in Rome for another few days, but I'm gonna call my assistant in L.A., put him onto the case. He'll find out who's following Ron."

"And will he also find Ronnie for me?"

She looked hopefully at him. It was Mac's turn to shrug. "He'll do his best," he said, though he personally felt sure that Perrin had sent Marisa to Rome to get rid of her, and that there was no way she was ever going to see him again.

He thought Perrin's next move would be an offer of a nice little financial settlement. He'd probably also get Manzini to offer her the odd role, keep her here in Rome, out of the way. After all, he had already gotten her an apartment. It would all work out fine for RP. And for Marisa Mayne too. Looking at her, he had no doubt she'd be happy to take the money and run.

Marisa said she had to leave, she was expected on the set. "Just some retakes," she said quickly. "But y'know, it could really lead to something."

She thanked them and Mac promised to call when he had some news. He looked at Sunny who was watching Marisa saunter through the

79

crowd, turning heads along the way, despite the weird hat.

"You're a woman, what d'you think of her story?" he asked.

Sunny looked thoughtful. "It's odd," she said, "but listening to Marisa somehow the word *blackmail* popped into my mind. Y'know the whole S and M dominatrix theme she had going there? I just didn't believe it. Marisa may be lying about what happened that night. Maybe she'd given Perrin an ultimatum, pay up or she'd go to the tabloids and tell her version of 'the truth' about their sexual relationship." Sunny shrugged. "They would have jumped on it."

"But she was onto a good thing," Mac said. "Perrin was generous. Just look at that ring."

"Trust me, I looked." Sunny sighed. "But with playboys like Perrin all good things come to an end. Maybe he was bored with her. On to the next, if you know what I mean. After all, Marisa said he was out that night. I wonder where he was and who with."

Mac took out his cell phone to call Roddy. "Okay, so let's find out where Ron Perrin is. *And* who he's with."

Thirteen

Allie was in her bedroom at the Bel Air house. The same bedroom that used to be hers *and* Ron's, complete with the California king-size bed with the brushed-steel posts Ron had constantly complained about, after getting up in the night to go to the bathroom and cracking his head on them.

"Why can't we have a regular bed? Y'know the kind, with a mattress, box springs, some sheets and a blanket?" he'd yelled. "Why must we have this ... this *glamazon* of a bed?"

Glamazon was the right word to describe the bed's size and flowing draperies. Silk of course. What wasn't silk in this house? If it wasn't expensive limestone or fossil granite or zebra-wood. In fact it was champagne-colored silk with a voile inner lining run through with threads of gold. All in excellent taste, naturally. Ron having chosen the "best" decorator. If you liked that sort of thing. And having finished the house, neither Allie nor Ron had ever admitted to the other that they did not really care for all the opulence.

What the three-thousand-square-foot bedroom suite did have though, were the best closets in the world. His and Hers. They were enormous.

Ditto the bathrooms. Hers larger than His, of course, with golden faucets that spilled long flat streams of water into a jetted tub and with towels thicker than Allie could handle. Secretly, disguised in a dark wig and glasses, she and Ampara, the housekeeper, had slipped into Costco and bought a dozen of their super-sale ones so she could dry herself properly. The "good" ones were just for show. Actually, Allie had been pleased to find that the brown wig and glasses were an effective cover. No one had even glanced twice at her.

Today, Fussy, the Maltese, had as usual parked herself right in the middle of the bed. Her favorite place. She had always slept between them, Allie's legs on one side, Ron's on the other. Anyhow, Fussy just sat there now, barking snappily to let Allie know she was bored and that anyhow she'd rather be in the kitchen with Ampara.

The long room with its floor-to-ceiling windows letting in streams of strong California light was filled with people. There was the stylist who'd brought a rack of gowns from which Allie would choose the ones for her Cannes Film Festival appearances, along with the sexy four-inch-heel shoes neatly laid out in a row, and the expensive little bags, and of course the jewelry that came along with a bodyguard, provided, as were the jewels, by Chopard. A seamstress from the design house waited to pin, a hairstylist hovered, and the makeup girl waited to see what she would choose so they could then decide on a "look." Plus there were a couple of gofers, ready to run to the stores or whatever.

The housekeeper had set up a table with coffee, bottled water and soft drinks, as well as her home-baked cookies and chocolate cake, the smell of which was driving Allie crazy. It reminded her of those rare childhood occasions when, with her mother, she had stirred the Betty Crocker chocolate-fudge cake mix then waited, almost dying with anxiety until the oven door was finally opened and the always-sunken cake removed. She had never been able to wait for it to cool, devouring a chunk smiling her pleasure through warm chocolaty lips. It was one of the few highlights of her youth.

She took a large piece now. The stylist frowned. "Every extra ounce will show in this dress," she warned.

Allie shrugged, uncaring. This was the best she had felt in weeks. Cake was her answer, and maybe about half a pound of M&M's, and how about Starbucks java chip ice cream? Yes! That's exactly what she would have for dinner tonight and the hell with sparkling couture gowns from Valentino and Versace. She needed comfort food.

"Try it," she offered generously. "Ampara makes the best cake you've ever tasted." She put a piece on a plate and gave it to the slender young stylist, who ate it, complaining guiltily she hadn't been this "wicked" in years.

"Go to the gym tonight," Allie said, laughing. "And why should we think it's wicked to enjoy a piece of cake every now and then?"

"I guess it's okay every now and then," the

stylist agreed, albeit reluctantly, as she took another guilty slice.

The others crowded round now, all except the bodyguard, who stood stoically, arms folded, next to the large leather boxes holding several million dollars' worth of jewels.

Allie inspected the rack of gowns, all special, all beautiful and all meant for a grand entrance under lights, a photo opportunity for the magazines and television cameras. *"Allie Ray adorable in Valentino and Chopard diamonds at the Cannes Festival,"* they would say, as she did her job and smiled and waved and stopped to talk to the guy from *Access Hollywood* and the woman from *Entertainment Tonight,* as well as the French TV host, who she always surprised with her ability to speak a little of his language.

"Not fluently," she'd protested, when he'd complimented her last year. "Only enough to get by." It was the compliment that had pleased her the most, though.

She washed the chocolate cake from her fingers and began to try on more gowns, swishing their heavy trains and slinking her thighs together, wondering whether she could even walk. Bored, while they pinned and fussed, she glanced out of the window, thinking of Lev, outside in the black Mustang and probably bored out of his skull too.

What, she wondered, did he do all day to keep himself occupied?

She called him now. "What're you doing?" she murmured into her BlackBerry.

"Isometric exercises," he said, and she heard

the smile in his deep rumbling voice. He was the only man she knew whose voice matched his physique.

"I'll bet you're reading the racing form," she countered, having already divined his weakness for the ponies.

"Possibly."

She grinned. "I'm sending you down a little snack. Homemade chocolate cake. You've never tasted better."

"I don't eat cake."

"Today, you're Marie Antoinette," she said, and heard him laugh again.

Pushing the gown pinner away, Allie went to the table and cut him a slab. Wrapping it in a napkin, she handed it to Ampara and told her to deliver it to the paparazzo in the black Mustang. The others stared at her as though she had gone mad.

She said, "And the hell with these gowns. I'm not wearing any one of them."

There were gasps of horror. "But Allie," the stylist protested. "These are gorgeous, they're perfect for Cannes. They're the latest, right off the runway."

"I'll make my own choices from now on," Allie said firmly. "And that goes for the jewels too," she added. "I won't need any."

"But, Allie..." The stylist was in a panic now. She had to report back to the producers, the director. The hairdresser and makeup girl waited silently, uncertain of what was expected of them.

"Don't worry," Allie said, giving them that sunny grin. "It'll be all right on the night." The plan that had been formulating in her mind began to loom as a reality and suddenly she felt light-years better.

Thanking the stylist and her entourage, she sent the team on their way, still protesting her decision.

Allie knew that most women would have died for the choices she had been offered that day. And of course she was aware of her responsibility. She would do her job. But she had her new plan in mind. She had still to figure it out, but she was about to become a different woman and it had nothing to do with the public. She wondered if she should share her plans with Mac Reilly. But Mac was in Rome and anyhow her future was not his business. Only her present.

Worried, she stared out the window. Beyond the thick greenery and the high wall, Lev, or one of his henchmen, kept guard. She was safe now. Wasn't she?

Her thoughts turned to Ron. In her heart she didn't want to believe he was tailing her, but if he was not, that meant it must be the stalker. There had been more of those letters, the last one smeared, the unknown writer said, with his tears. "Next time it will be with blood. Yours? Or mine?" he'd written.

Allie had refused even to look at the letters, but now she didn't burn them. She'd sent them on to Mac's assistant, Roddy. The game was no longer in her court. They would take care of it.

Feeling guilty about the chocolate cake, she was glad when her trainer arrived to put her through her paces, stretching her body unbearably, urging her on as she sweated on the machines.

"It's worth it, hon," he said, smiling at her. "You've still got the best body in town."

It was the word *still* Allie didn't appreciate. It meant she was no longer eighteen and instead was heading up to forty, a time when actresses were often left in limbo, waiting for those age-appropriate roles that, unfortunately, no matter how good you were, were few and far between.

An hour later, she waved goodbye to him and walked to the window, staring moodily out at the pretty gardens and the deep cobalt blue pool, glinting like a jewel amid the thirsty emerald lawns. She really should think about changing to a desert landscape to save on water, life's most precious commodity. But then, who but she was there to care?

Glancing at her watch, she called her director and canceled their lunch. She would see him later that afternoon at the studio, she said, to do the last of the overdubbing.

After that she changed into jeans, a white shirt and gold flats, put gold hoops in her ears and—after some consideration—slipped her wedding ring back on her finger, and set out for the children's hospital in the Valley, to pay her weekly visit to the young cancer patients.

She called Lev to tell him her plans, watching out for him in her rearview mirror, as he stayed behind her on the freeway. There was no sign of the Sebring convertible.

She'd already spent time at Barnes & Noble choosing picture books and games and had

87

picked up a batch of furry toy animals donated by a caring manufacturer. The kids were always pleased to see her and today they greeted her with smiles and laughter, as though she were Santa on Christmas Day. It made her smile too, and their gaiety in the face of suffering brought her back to her senses and a humble appreciation of the rewards life had offered her.

By four o'clock she was in a darkened Hollywood studio, watching herself on the screen, matching her words to her movements. She was finished by seven, and called Lev again to tell him she was on her way to Giorgio's restaurant on Channel Road in Santa Monica.

She was meeting an old friend there, a woman almost twice her age. Sheila Scott had been good to her when she had first come to town. Sheila was a voice coach and it was she who had taken the Texas twang out of Allie's voice and perfected her sweet gentle way of speaking. And since Giorgio's was also Allie's favorite restaurant, she was looking forward to the evening.

She handed the keys of the Mercedes to the valet parker, who beamed at her, impressed, and said "Good evening, Miss Ray, how are you tonight?" Allie was aware that, as usual, heads turned as she strode through the door and, always conscious of her duty to her fans, even though this was mostly a showbiz crowd, she distributed smiles and stopped to kiss hello to a couple of fellow actors.

She was glad, though, to sink into her chair and share a bottle of Chianti with Sheila, lingering over a plate of fettuccini with langostinos, the house specialty that was her favorite. And also to tell her about her new plan, that was still not a plan. Only an idea.

Sheila Scott, defiantly gray-haired in a town of blondes, her lean face tanned and weather-beaten from years of living near the beach, down-to-earth and motherly, listened in silence.

"I think I've come to the end, Sheila," Allie said quietly. "My new film's no good. I'm about to hit that dreaded—in showbiz anyway—forty. I've lost out in love. Ron has left me, he's found someone else. I have a crazed fan writing scary threatening letters to me, and I'm being stalked. I only feel safe when locked behind my own gates with a bodyguard right outside. I have no privacy, no family. I've reached burnout, Sheila. I need to get a new life."

Sheila nodded, understanding. Allie had been working since she was seventeen and whether a movie lived or died always seemed to depend on her. Not only that, real life had crept up on her. She was a lonely woman trapped by her own fame, abandoned by her husband and stalked by a madman. "Then if that's what you need to do, Allie," she said gently, "go for it."

"There's only one thing—no maybe two—that could stop me," Allie said.

Sheila said shrewdly, "I'm willing to bet that both of those are men. And that one of them is still Ron." Allie gave her a sheepish grin. "So, who's the other?"

"His name's Mac Reilly. The PI. You've probably seen him on TV. But anyhow, like Ron, he's a lost cause. He doesn't seem interested in me, except as a client of course." Her eyes met Sheila's sympathetic ones. "Do you think it's possible to be in love with two men at the same time?"

Sheila patted her hand across the table. "Only if you're trying too hard, sweetheart," she said.

Just then a couple of fans came over with a request for Allie's autograph, and putting on her best movie-actress face she smiled and chatted with them for a minute.

Then the waiter approached. "A delivery for you, Miss Ray."

Allie's heart jumped into her throat as she took the envelope. For a minute she thought she might faint.

"Allie, are you all right?" Sheila's voice seemed to come from a great distance.

"Who delivered it?" Allie asked. "Where is he?"

"It was just some motorcycle delivery service, Miss Ray. He was still wearing his helmet and I didn't get to see his face."

Allie had recognized the writing. "Oh my God," she whispered. "He's found me."

Horrified, Sheila stared back at her. She'd heard all about the letter writer and the stalker, who were probably the same person. It did not sound good. She said, "Where's your body-guard?"

"Outside. Waiting for me. He'll follow me home."

"Call him. Tell him what's happened."

Parked illegally across the street, Lev had kept tabs on the people coming and going at the restaurant. He'd seen the motorcycle arrive and watched the driver go inside. He had thought it odd that the man had not taken off his helmet. It was an automatic reflex: you stopped the bike then took off your helmet. It was that, that had made him take down the bike's license number.

"Don't worry," he told Allie when she called. "Give me the letter and I'll take care of it."

"It's the last straw," Allie said shakily to Sheila. "You see now why I can't go on."

"I understand, sweetheart, but don't let panic send you running away."

"If only it were just that," Allie said, as they kissed good night outside the restaurant.

Lev was right behind her in the Mustang as she drove back along the coast road. At least she knew she was safe. For the moment anyway.

Fourteen

Five days later Sunny and Mac arrived back at LAX. He dropped her off at her place then continued on in the limo, catching up with his phone messages on the way.

Surprisingly, there was one from the supposedly missing Ron Perrin, demanding to know when he was coming back, asking why didn't he pick up his messages anyway and where the hell was he because he needed him. It seemed Marisa was wrong and Perrin wasn't dead after all.

There was also a message from Sam Demarco. "I'm Perrin's right-hand man. I want to talk to you," Demarco said in a voice as crisp and cold as a wedge of iceberg lettuce. "Please call me as soon as possible so we can arrange to meet."

Of course Mac immediately called Sunny to tell her. "Interesting, huh?" he said.

"Which one? Perrin or Demarco?"

"Both. Anyhow, I'm calling them back. I'll let you know what happens. Meanwhile, babe, get some sleep. You looked exhausted."

"Thanks to you." There was a smile in her voice as she said it.

Mac was smiling too as he rang off.

When Mac finally got home, Pirate greeted him with his usual all-over face lick. He smelled like an old sock. Time for the mobile dog groomers whose blond girl-bather Pirate was in love with, if his goofy expression and complete malleability in her hands was anything to go by.

Mac checked his watch. It was still only noon. He showered and put on a pair of comfortable old khaki shorts. Pirate was glued to his heels as he walked out onto the deck and leaned on the rail, taking grateful gulps of the fresh salty air. After the long flights it felt wonderful. The tide was low and the ocean shimmered, flat and steely under the gray sunless sky. Not a surfer in sight. Of course not, they were waiting for the change of tide, ready for those big green rollers that came crashing onto the shore, riding them like circus performers.

Mac had been in touch with Roddy from Rome

and had filled him in on the Marisa situation. Now he called Roddy again and got the news that so far Roddy had no idea who was tailing Allie because, since Lev was on guard, the Sebring had not been seen.

Roddy also told Mac about the latest threatening letter, hand-delivered to the restaurant. "It wasn't written in blood but on a computer. And it was pretty explicit in what he intended to do to Miss Ray. By the way, he never calls her 'Allie,' always the formal 'Miss Ray.'"

"So what are we doing about it?" Mac said.

"Lev got the bike's number and already checked it out. It's a delivery service. Someone hired them and the driver was just doing his job. The person paid in cash. Unusual enough for them to remember, but oddly enough, nobody seems to recall who it was or what he looked like."

Mac sighed. "Par for the course, I guess. I want you to run a check on all Allie's employees, everyone who has intimate contact with her. That means the people who work at the house, gardeners and pool guys included, as well as hairdressers, masseurs, personal shoppers. You know the score."

Roddy did know and it was not a small task.

Mac said, "You ever hear of a guy called Sam Demarco? He's Perrin's partner. Actually his 'right-hand man' is how he described himself in his phone message."

"Not short on ego then," Roddy said. "And yeah, I've heard of him. Kind of a big player around town. Flashier than Perrin. Likes Vegas, the clubs, that kinda thing. Likes to throw big parties at his place. He has a big modern house on one of the 'bird' streets above Sunset, y'know, the ones with the fabulous city views and the 'bird' names, Oriole, Thresher, like that. As well as a new place out in Palm Desert."

"Right. Okay. I'll call Demarco, find out what's so urgent that Perrin's 'right-hand man' needs to talk to me. Marisa wants me to ask him to call her too, she needs to know what to do next."

"Does she want her gun back? If so it's in the bucket under your kitchen sink."

Mac laughed. "Thanks a lot, pal. I'll make sure to get it back to Perrin."

His next call was to RP. Again no answer. He left a message asking him to call him back, then he called Demarco.

After all the hoopla about urgency and the need to talk, Demarco didn't even take his call. Instead his assistant arranged for them to lunch at one o'clock the following day, at the Ivy on Robertson. She also said Demarco needed his help. He wanted to hire him. But she didn't say why.

Mac considered calling the "movie star" but that old jet lag was creeping up on him again as well as hunger, so instead he whistled for Pirate, climbed into the Prius and drove to the Malibu Country Mart, all of five minutes away. It was a small complex of chic boutiques and restaurants set around a grassy square with a sandbox and swings where kids played happily. He bought a take-out ham and cheese panini at the Italian restaurant Tra di Noi and with Pirate breathing heavily at his feet in anticipation of his share, sat on a bench outside enjoying his lunch and watching the Malibu world go by.

As usual, the paparazzi were hanging outside Starbucks and Coffee Bean, hoping to get lucky with the "hot" young set, whose appearances there in search of a Frappuccino, with or without babies or small dogs or underwear, could cause chaos. Mac thanked God that though they recognized him they left him alone. His wasn't the kind of fame—or rather notoriety—they were on the lookout for. There was no scandal around Mac Reilly. Unless of course he was to be seen in the company of Allie Ray. Now *that* would be news.

Walking back to the car, he stopped to look in the window of Planet Blue. There was a white T-shirt with the words "love is all you need" in sparkles on the front. Smiling, he went in and bought it for Sunny.

Back home and out on his deck again, he stared at the ocean. The tide was coming in now. Ruffles of white spray fluttered over the rocks and the sun peeked through the clouds. He called Perrin one more time, frowning as one more time he was asked to leave a message. If RP was around he certainly was not answering his phones.

Lulled by the sound of the ocean, Mac lay back on the old metal chaise and in an instant jet lag claimed him and he was fast asleep.

Fifteen

The next morning as Mac drove through the sluggish L.A. traffic on his way to meet Demarco, he was thinking about the "right-hand man's" choice of restaurant.

The Ivy was an L.A. hot spot. It was *the* place to be seen lunching and there were always famous faces there plus the usual wannabes and of course the paparazzi thronging outside with their intrusive cameras. Still the food was pretty good and it was a buzzing little place, a cottage really with an umbrellaed patio surrounded by a picket fence and with various hokey "country" artifacts substituting for décor. Cute, cheerful and expensive.

Mac gave the Prius to the valet, waving to the paparazzi who must have been having a slow day because they bothered to take his picture.

Sam Demarco was already seated at an inside table waiting. Impatiently, Mac observed. Since he was no more than a couple of minutes late, which was a good deal less than par for the course bearing in mind L.A.'s notorious traffic, Mac thought him distinctly ungracious in his greeting.

"I don't like lateness, especially in a man," Demarco snapped, tapping his watch, a whop-

96

ping gold Breguet that was meant to impress. "I find it discourteous when I made every effort to be here on time."

Mac glanced pointedly at his own watch, a distinctly unimpressive Swiss Army with red numerals and a black rubber strap. "I am exactly three minutes and thirty seconds beyond the appointed hour." He took the seat opposite. "Perhaps in your effort not to be late you got here too early."

Barbed glances shot between them. Demarco was a leonine-looking man, tall, ruggedly built, in his early fifties, lightly tanned and with a mane of thick silver hair. Mac thought he was a little overdressed for lunch in L.A., in a dark blue pin-striped suit from a very good tailor, polished black wingtips, a blue shirt and a yellow Hermès tie. Or maybe it was he who was underdressed, in chinos and a plain denim blue T-shirt from Theodore at the Beach, which happened to be his own personal favorite men's shop. He wore brown suede loafers and no socks. At least *he* was comfortable.

Unlike Perrin, who had eyes like a chastised puppy, Demarco's hard blue eyes told Mac in no uncertain terms to back off.

Demarco offered his hand across the table. Mac reached over and took it, trying not to flinch as it was crushed. Demarco was a physically powerful man and either he was using that power to intimidate, or else he was just unaware of his own strength. Somehow Mac didn't think it was the latter.

The waitress showed up to announce the

specials but Demarco waved her away and they ordered quickly, Mac the salmon and Demarco the burger. Demarco asked for a Perrier and though Mac fancied a smooth, round, mouth-filling Cakebread Chardonnay with the fish, he asked for water also.

"Reilly," Demarco said, in his deep sonorous voice, "I asked you to meet me because I know of your reputation, via the television show of course, as well as your exploits off camera."

Mac nodded. He took a sip of Perrier, already regretting the Cakebread.

Demarco waited for a response, looking at him with those better-watch-out blue eyes. When he didn't get one he said, "I take it that anything I say will be in confidence?" Mac nodded of course and Demarco said, "The fact is, I'm worried about Ron Perrin."

"Your boss," Mac said, letting him know that he knew on just which rung of the ladder of power and fortune Demarco stood.

"First and foremost Ron is my friend," Demarco put him straight. "I started out as his assistant." He shrugged his shoulders, barely wrinkling his immaculate blue pinstripes. "Now we are partners."

"You worked your way up," Mac offered helpfully. Then he thought the hell with it, summoned the waiter and ordered a glass of the house white.

"You might say that." Demarco sat back. His face was a mask but Mac got the feeling he didn't like him. He wondered why Demarco was even bothering. After all, he could hire any PI in town. Anyway he wasn't sure he wanted to work for the guy. In fact he could easily do without both him and RP.

"Reilly," Demarco said again, without benefit of a Mister or even a may-I-call-you-Mac. "I'm worried about Ron. He's been behaving very oddly, claims he's being followed, that somebody wants to kill him."

"So? Is he? And do they?"

"How should I know? That's your department. Didn't he ask you to work for him? Find out what was really going on?"

Mac wondered how Demarco knew that. Perrin must have told him. But then if he had, wouldn't he also have told him why?

He took a sip of the house white. It was okay but he regretted the Cakebread. "Perrin did and I turned him down," he said.

The food came. Mac stared at his poached salmon, artfully presented in a nest of chopped tomatoes and basil with a delicious vinaigrette. He no longer fancied it.

He heard Demarco sigh. Then Demarco said, "I seem to have offended you. I'm sorry, I didn't mean to do that. It's just that I'm upset. I'm concerned for Ron. He's my friend. He's been more than good to me, I can't let him down in what might be his hour of need. I am asking you to work for me and when I tell you why, you'll understand."

"Okay," Mac agreed. "I know these situations can be stressful."

"The truth is I think Ron's going a bit nuts," Demarco said suddenly. "And you know why?

He thinks the FBI is investigating his business dealings."

Mac glanced up from tasting his salmon. This was the second person to mention the FBI. "And is that true?"

"The FBI is always interested in men with multinational billion-dollar businesses, but whether it's true in Ron's case or not, I don't yet know."

"And you want me to find out?"

"As discreetly as possible, of course."

Mac remembered Perrin shredding documents and the overturned shredder box. He'd thought Perrin had simply been hiding financial evidence from his wife's lawyers, but it seemed there was more to it. "Okay," he agreed. "My assistant will let you know about fees and expenses. Meanwhile, have you any idea where Perrin might be?"

Demarco shrugged again, spreading his hands. "I haven't heard from him in over a week. And nor has Allie. Of course, her lawyers are going crazy, calling me at all hours demanding I tell them where he's hiding. Ron was supposed to appear in divorce court this week but he never showed up. Then they tried to serve a subpoena on him and couldn't find him. He's not at any of his houses. My guess is he's hiding out somewhere until he can work things out to his better advantage."

"Or else he's on the run from the FBI."

"It's possible, but I think Allie is the more immediate problem. He doesn't want to part with another cent."

"Tell me, does Perrin have a girlfriend?"

"A rich man always has lady friends."

"Yeah. Anyone special, though?"

"You might as well know that, women-wise, my partner does not have a good reputation. Don't quote me on it."

Mac nodded. "You want me to find Perrin? And find out what the FBI is after?"

"You got it, Reilly. But one thing for sure, no police. Perrin wouldn't like me setting the cops on him. Absolutely no police." He stood up. "I'm late for my next meeting." He shook hands again.

"Let me know how it goes," Demarco said. He paused then added, "I'm really worried about Ron. He's a good guy. *Decent,* y'know. I'm afraid he might do something ... well, foolish. Y'know what I mean?"

Mac did know, but hardly thought Perrin had looked suicidal. In fact quite the opposite. RP definitely did not want to be dead.

"I'll do my best," he reassured him.

He watched Demarco stalk through the tiny room. The man dwarfed everyone in sight. A lion on the prowl was the image that came to mind. Though maybe a kindly lion, deeply concerned for his friend and partner.

He looked at Demarco's plate. He had not touched the burger.

Sixteen

Allie was in her garden when her BlackBerry burbled a tune. She looked at the display to check who it was, but all it said was "Wireless caller."

"Hi, Allie," a familiar voice said.

A smile lit her face. She walked along the terrace overlooking the parterre garden modeled after the ones at Versailles. Not as big but certainly as sculpted. Not a leaf out of place.

"Hi, Mac," she said, her soft voice conveying her smile. "Are you calling from Rome?" She crossed her fingers, eyes raised to heaven, praying he was home.

"I'm back. I wanted to speak to you, make sure you're okay and that Lev and his friends are doing a good job."

"Perfect. Except for the biker with the letter."

"I heard about that," Mac said. "Look, we need to get together. I'd take you out to dinner if it wouldn't cause a scandal in the tabloids."

She laughed. "I could come over to your place," she said, thinking how it would be, just the two of them in his cozy little home. "We could send out for pizza."

"You got it," he said. "Seven okay with you?"

"I'll be there," she promised.

"Oh, just one thing..."

"Yes?"

"You like anchovies on your pizza?"

"Love them," she said, laughing again.

"Seven it is then."

Mac had called Sunny to tell her what was going on. He'd asked her to join them and now she was sitting on his deck. Her hair was pulled back and tied with a scrap of black ribbon and she was wearing the Planet Blue T-shirt with "love is all you need" written in sparkles across the front, topped with a cute little orange and hot pink striped cardigan against evening beach chill. She was holding Tesoro on her lap. Despite the balmy evening, the little dog shivered the way Chihuahuas often did, in what Mac always claimed was a deliberate play for attention.

"It's not cold for God's sakes," he grumbled, keeping a keen eye on Pirate, who was lurking near the steps at the very edge of the deck, ready to run if Tesoro jumped him.

Sunny threw him an exasperated glare. "She's sensitive, that's all." She'd hoped that bringing Tesoro might thaw the cold war between the two dogs, but the Chihuahua wasn't having any, and nor apparently was Mac.

Even though it was not grand like its neighbors, she loved Mac's little house, especially on soft sunlit evenings like this. The house had wood siding painted pistachio green with those cheap aluminum sliding windows that were original and maybe qualified as antiques by now, and there was a touch of gingerbread trim—an afterthought, she guessed, by some previous owner who'd wanted to jazz it up a little. Inside was a tiny wood-floored living room with a picture window overlooking the ocean, a small kitchen, mostly taken up by a large wine cooler; a bathroom at the back; and tacked on at one end and separated by a narrow corridor, the master— and only—bedroom.

She glanced at her watch. Ten minutes before seven. Ten minutes before the fabulously beautiful Allie Ray got here. She wondered what she was like. Mac certainly liked her, and besides she was paying him well to take care of her problems. Of course he couldn't possibly be interested in the beautiful movie star, other than as a client who was in trouble that is. Still, as any woman knew, you couldn't take that kind of high-wattage beauty and fame lightly.

The captain's bell clanged unmusically, making her wince. Nothing she could say could get Mac to part with that cracked old bell. She took another sip of the good red he'd broken out from his best stash, kept in the properly refrigerated cooler that took up a good part of his tiny kitchen. For a wine buff like Mac, wine had priority over food, which after all, could be ordered in and delivered to his door. Just the way the pizzas were being delivered right this minute.

Smiling, she watched him through the window as he turned the oven to high, ready to reheat the pizzas, reaching into the cupboard for the hot peppers and shuffling plates around. He was looking particularly cute tonight in the baggy white linen pants she had chosen for him at the

104

expensive little boutique on the Via Condotti, and an old black T-shirt faded through many washings to carbon gray. His hair was still wet from the shower and she knew exactly how his skin would smell, spicy and sexy and ... well, she wouldn't go there right now.

The captain's bell rang again and she saw Mac hurry to answer it. Pirate was right behind him, barking enthusiastically as he opened the door and welcomed Allie Ray, one more time, into his home.

"Hi, good to see you again," he said as the petite beauty smiled up at him.

"Good to see you too," she murmured, standing on tiptoe putting an arm around his neck and kissing him on either cheek.

"I brought Fussy along." She held up a small bundle of white fur whose black button eyes were half-hidden behind a long fringe. "It's my housekeeper's night off and I couldn't leave her alone. I hope you don't mind?"

"Err ... no. No, of course not." Mac eyed his own dog doubtfully, but Pirate just stared up at the Maltese, seeming stunned to have yet another female invading his home.

"Okay," Mac said. "Let me get you a glass of wine. White or red?"

"Since it's pizza how about red?"

"Perfect. I already opened one of my favorites."

Allie walked with him to the kitchen, still clutching Fussy and followed by Pirate.

"A Nobile—Antinori 'ninety-six," Mac said, pouring her a glass. "I hope you'll like it."

She took a sip. "Hmm, delicious. I didn't know you were a wine expert."

"That's probably because you don't know very much about me, other than the guy you see on TV attempting to solve a few old crimes. Closed cases. With the generous help of the LAPD, of course, without whom none of it could take place."

"I suppose not." Leaning against the kitchen counter she took another sip. "But you know something, Mac. Somehow I feel I *really* know you anyway."

Their eyes met. Surprised, he wondered if he was reading more in her words than she had meant. "There's someone I'd like you to meet," he said quickly. And taking her arm, he walked her out onto the deck.

"Oh, hi." Sunny got gracefully to her feet and found that she stood a good foot taller than the petite movie star. But my lord, she was beautiful. The long straight blond hair fell like a curtain over eyes that were bluer than any she had ever seen. She saw a flicker of surprise cross Allie's face, quickly covered with a smile. It was obvious she hadn't known there would be anyone else here.

Mac introduced them. Clutching their dogs the two women shook hands and said hello. Tesoro extended an aristocratic nose toward Fussy who sniffed back then let out a sudden abused yelp.

"Oh my God," Allie said to Sunny. "Did your dog just nip Fussy's nose?"

"She certainly did not. Tesoro wouldn't stoop to such behavior." Sunny's eyes met Mac's over the top of Allie's head and he grinned. "Your dog just barked, that's all," she added defensively.

"That's all she ever does." Allie sighed.

"Tesoro too." Sunny was suddenly all sympathy. "We should have dogs like Pirate. He's such a good boy, look how well behaved he is."

They both turned to look at Pirate, back at his post near the beach steps, ears down, his one eye wary. Now he had two smart-ass bitches to run from.

"Sunny runs her own PR company," Mac told Allie. "But sometimes she helps me out on my cases." Brows raised, he grinned again at Sunny who looked amazed but pleased.

Allie was taking in Sunny's exotic looks; her glorious body and long slender legs. She didn't see how any man could resist her, especially a sexy guy like Mac Reilly.

She sat on the edge of the metal chair near Sunny, put the Maltese down and took a sip of her wine. "Are you working on my case then, Miss Alvarez?"

"Please, call me Sunny. And actually no, though I do know about your being followed."

Sunny wasn't about to tell the movie star she'd heard all about her storm of tears and confessions. No woman would care to have her life exposed to a stranger like that. Besides when Mac confided his business secrets to her he trusted her to keep them.

The captain's bell jingled again and both women glanced inquiringly at Mac.

"That'll be Roddy," he said, heading for the door, leaving them alone.

"It must be awful, being stalked," Sunny said with a little shudder. "I sympathize with you."

"It's certainly not comfortable," Allie said.

From the house they heard Mac's laugh and then Roddy's voice, lighter than Mac's and excited.

Allie looked expectantly toward the two men as they stepped out onto the deck. She'd thought she would be alone with Mac. Now not only was there another woman, there was also another guy, Mac's assistant, who she knew had been taking care of her problem when Mac was in Rome.

Roddy's spiky hair was bleached platinum. He sported a spray-on tan, white linen shorts, a tight red Gaultier T-shirt and Havaianas flip-flops.

He hugged Sunny enthusiastically. "Missed you when you were in Rome," he said, holding her away from him and smiling into her eyes, and Allie suddenly understood that Sunny had been in Rome with Mac. *And* for an entire week.

Sunny said, "Allie, this is Roddy Kruger, Mac's assistant. And good friend."

He was beaming at Allie, revealing the whitest teeth she had ever seen.

"Allie Ray! Oh ... My ... God!" He sank to his knees in front of her then took her hand and kissed it reverently. "I've loved you since forever," he said dramatically. "You're even more beautiful in person. I'm thrilled to meet you."

He was so genuinely excited Allie smiled. He certainly wasn't Sunny Alvarez's boyfriend though. "I'm glad to meet you, Roddy." She leaned over and kissed his cheek. "There," she

108

added, "now we really know each other."

He scrambled to his feet, beaming back at her, his hand on his cheek. "I swear I'll never wash that spot again," he said, and they both laughed.

"Oh my God," Roddy said again, as Mac handed him a glass of wine. "Will you just look at that dog. It is a *dog,* isn't it?" He glanced at Allie for confirmation and they all stared at her Maltese.

Looking like a white kitchen mop, Fussy was on her belly edging slowly toward Pirate, who sat frozen to the spot, his one wild eye glued on her.

"Oh my God!" Sunny whispered, repeating Roddy's words. "We should do something."

She meant Allie should do something, but Allie simply stared, and Mac held up a hand, watching silently.

Fussy inched closer. A quiver ran through Pirate's body as she drew nearer. There was nowhere for him to run because the tide was already over the rocks.

Everybody held their breath. Fussy was twelve inches away and still Pirate sat transfixed. The Maltese lifted her head, button eyes peering at him through her fringe. A moment passed in silence. Then she rolled over onto her back, paws waving in the air, and peeked flirtatiously up at him.

"Well, the shameless little hussy," Roddy said, breaking the silence. "Will you just look at her, *flirting* with Pirate."

"And take a look a Pirate," Mac added. There was a bewildered look on Pirate's face as he bent his head and the two dogs sniffed, nose to nose. Then he wagged his tail and flopped down beside her.

"How about that? I believe Pirate's in love," Mac said, beaming at Allie.

Sunny's heart sank. In the two years they had been together Tesoro had never as much as acknowledged Pirate's presence, except for the occasional snarl and swipe at his nose. Now Allie Ray's Maltese had Pirate wrapped around her paws like a dog in love. All her theories about Mac not wanting to marry because their dogs were incompatible went out the window.

"I'll take care of the pizza," Roddy said, heading indoors. "We eating out there?" he called back to Mac.

"We are," Mac said. "Unless you're cold," he added, looking, concerned, at Allie.

"Nothing a sweater couldn't fix," she replied. "I enjoy eating outdoors. Californians don't do it often enough. Take advantage of our climate, I mean. I've learned to enjoy Malibu's mists and winter storms as much as our beautiful sunny days, when you wonder why you would ever want to live anywhere else."

"And would you? Ever want to live anywhere else, I mean?" Sunny asked.

Allie gave her a surprised look. "Sometimes I think about it," she said. "Sometimes, I dream of another life." Then she gave a quick shrug and added briskly, "But this is the life I created for myself. I'm a very lucky woman, I know. Millions of women would want to change places with me. Wouldn't they?"

Her turquoise blue eyes fixed on Sunny, who said, surprised, "Yes, I'm quite sure they would. Though of course there would be no way to replace the real Allie Ray."

"I need a magic wand to wave over my life," Allie said softly, as though she were voicing private thoughts, not meant for another's ears. "All I need is that magic wand to make me disappear."

Mac pushed open the rattling screen doors. "Pizza. Come and get it," he said, as he and Roddy put two enormous pies on the redwood trestle table, plonking down bottles of wine and Pellegrino, as well as a container of hot chili peppers. Roddy added a bunch of paper napkins which blew away in the wind, sending him dancing after them. Mac offered Allie his old dark green cashmere sweater and received a smiling thank-you.

Sunny recognized that sweater. She had bought it for Mac a couple of Christmases ago. Buttoning her orange and pink striped cardigan, she took the chair next to Allie.

When they were all seated and their glasses filled Mac said, "Okay, first we have news, Allie. *Good* news," he added. "Well, let me amend that. *In a way* it's good news. The Sebring has not been seen since Lev has been guarding you."

Her shoulders slumped. "But what about when he leaves? And anyway who is it? It's so scary knowing someone is watching you, living your every moment. It's as though they're stealing your life."

Sunny could see she was genuinely frightened.

111

"You'll be all right now," she said gently. "Mac'll sort it out."

"It'll be okay," Mac told her. "We're still working on it." He was slicing the pizza with the expertise of decades of experience. "Allie, I know you like anchovies. Sunny no. And Roddy just a little. You'll have to scrape them off," he added, putting loaded plates in front of Sunny and Roddy.

Sunny was worried. First the Maltese and Pirate and now the anchovies. Maybe she and Mac were not compatible after all. And Allie was so cute, drowning in Mac's big green sweater, looking like a fragile mermaid ready to swim off into the ocean. Even Roddy was under her spell. From under her lashes, she saw Mac smile at Allie.

"So, when do you leave for Cannes?" he asked.

"In a couple of days. Not that I'm ready for it. In fact I'd rather not go, especially knowing what I know about the movie." She shrugged and bit into her pizza. "But it's my job. I'll show up and I'll do my best for them. After all, that's why they pay me."

Sunny took a bite of the pizza. It still tasted of the anchovies. In her lap the shivering Tesoro whinnied like a mini-pony. She got up, went inside, snatched a chenille throw from the sofa, wrapped the Chihuahua in it and went back out again. The wind was definitely chilly now, and like her dog, she shivered. Nobody, meaning Mac, took any notice. They were talking about Allie's new movie, and about Cannes.

"You should come with me." Allie was looking

directly into Mac's eyes. "I could use a friend. And we could talk about the situation with Ron, work out what to do. And about the stalker, and the letters. I simply don't have time before I leave," she added.

"Maybe I will," Mac said.

Sunny's heart sank. She was losing a battle she hadn't even known existed. Scrambling to her feet again, she said, "Sorry, the jet lag is killing me. I have to go. I have an early start tomorrow." Grabbing the whining Tesoro, she dropped quick kisses and called out goodbyes. She was surprised when Allie got to her feet to give her a hug. There was a look of distress on the movie star's familiar face that spelled out her loneliness.

"Listen," Sunny said, suddenly concerned, "if you need someone to talk to, call me. My number's in the book." Their eyes met. "I mean it," she said gently. "Sometimes another woman's opinion can help sort things out."

Allie smiled and hugged her again. "I'm not used to women liking me," she said. "Usually they're jealous."

Sunny smiled, guilty but absolved. Her jealousy had been temporary, even though she was leaving her lover in the company of the famous beauty. Call her crazy, she hoped she was doing the right thing. And anyhow the jet lag was true. She could hardly keep her eyes open.

Mac walked her to the door. He grabbed her shoulder, swung her round to face him. "You okay, honey?" he said.

She pulled the ribbon from her hair and tossed

her head, sending her dark curls cascading in a J.Lo gesture that made her look even more beautiful and made Mac smile.

"Hey, babe, come on," he said persuasively. "You're not jealous of Allie, are you? She's just a lost soul, Sunny. It's nothing personal."

"I know," she said, then added with a grin, "Just be careful, okay?"

Still, with Tesoro zipped safely inside her leather jacket, as she roared the Harley along PCH, heading toward Santa Monica, and Marina del Rey, she did wonder if she had made the right move.

Seventeen

The sound of Sunny's bike faded and Roddy held Fussy on his lap, feeding her morsels of pizza. "It's the anchovies she's after," he said, offering her another. Only this time Fussy bit his finger instead.

He glanced aggrieved at Allie, who sighed and said she was sorry and that Fussy had her problems. "She only has one love and that's Ampara, my housekeeper," she said. "And I can't tell you how many times she's bitten Ron."

Mac took the chair next to her. "Speaking of Ron, have you seen him lately?"

"No, I have not seen him. He was due in court last week, something to do with the divorce proceedings, but he never showed. They issued a subpoena but haven't been able to serve it because nobody can find him."

"Think he's avoiding your divorce issues?"

"Of course he is. Why else would he do a disappearing act? That is unless he's run off with the other woman."

Mac shook his head. "I can reassure you on that. He's definitely not with the other woman. And she doesn't know where he is either."

"Am I allowed to ask how you know that?" Allie said.

"Better not. But I can tell you you don't have to worry on that score."

"This isn't Ron's first extramarital affair. He even hired one as his 'secretary,' and he bought her expensive gifts. The bills were supposed to go to the office but occasionally they would come to me by mistake. He was a generous man," she added drily. "I remember a diamond watch that cost more than the one he'd given me." She smiled. "That hurt. Though to tell you the truth by then I would have been happy with a bunch of daisies."

"You're worth more than that."

She shrugged. "Now I can afford to buy my own diamonds, but you know how it is? It's just not the same."

"And that's how things stand now?"

"That's how things stood as of two weeks ago. Anyway, *where is* Ron?"

"That's exactly what Demarco asked me to-day."

"Sam Demarco?" Her tone was angry. "He

calls himself a friend, but he muscled his way into Ron's good books by persuading him to take it easy. 'Take time off, play with the girls, go on vacation,' he said to him. I put part of the blame for our breaking up on Demarco."

"So Ron seems to have left town with no forwarding address. And since the mistress is eliminated, can you think of any other reason he might want to disappear?"

She shrugged. "Business, you mean? I don't know anything about that."

"If Ron were to die, wouldn't you inherit?"

Allie's long blond hair shifted in the breeze. In a gesture graceful as a ballet dancer's she wafted it out of her eyes.

"All I know is what I'm supposed to get in the prenup."

"Plus whatever else your attorneys can negotiate over and beyond that. Given Ron's rep with women."

"Exactly."

Roddy threw a glance at Mac. It was time for him to leave. "Okay," he said. "I'll call it a night." He took a business card from his wallet and handed it to Allie. "Anything you need, just call. I'll be there."

She smiled as he bent to kiss her cheek. "Thank you again, Roddy. It was lovely meeting you."

"My honor." He backed away, bowing like a commoner before royalty and almost crashing into the plate-glass door, making them laugh.

Eighteen

"He's so nice," Allie said.

"He is," Mac agreed.

Silence fell. The ocean roared in the background as the waves hit the rocks and a final lonely pelican raced home in the dark, wings whirring overhead.

"And so is Sunny," Allie said into the silence. "She's beautiful."

"She is," Mac agreed again.

Their eyes linked and the silence grew deeper. A world of possibilities stretched between them.

It was Mac who finally broke the spell, pouring wine into their glasses, throwing some leftover pizza to Pirate who wolfed it eagerly while Fussy watched from Allie's knee, tossing her fringe like a mini-movie star posing for the cameras.

"So how did you find Pirate?" Allie said.

"I saved him from a fate worse than death. Actually"—Mac glanced at Allie, who was sipping her wine, watching him—"I saved him *from* death."

"Tell me," she said.

"Well, as they say in the old potboilers, 'it was a dark and stormy night.' I was driving over Malibu Canyon when I saw this body in the road.

A frowsy little mutt, just lying there, his head all bloody and one leg crushed so bad it was hanging off. I bent down to stroke his mangy fur, thinking what a way to die, hit by some speedster on a canyon road. But then the mutt opened an eye and looked at me. I'll tell you it gave me quite a shock since I'd imagined he was dead. But there was a kinda hopeful look in that eye." Mac shrugged. "What could I do? Of course I took off my shirt, wrapped him in it, put him in the back of the car and drove to the emergency vet in Santa Monica. I paid the necessary, told them to do their best and went on my way, glad that I'd at least given the mutt a chance. I went out of town and I didn't pick up the vet's message until a week later. The vet said, 'We had to amputate your dog's left hind leg and remove one eye. He's on the mend. You can come and get him. He's ready to go home.'

"'What d'ya mean, get him?' I said when I called him back. 'He's not *my* dog. I just scooped him up off the canyon blacktop, gave him another shot at life.'

"And this is what the vet told me: 'There's an old Chinese saying, that if you save a life you are responsible for that soul forever. He's all yours Mr. Reilly. So come and get him.'"

Mac shook his head, remembering. "So of course I did. And despite his sorry state that dog greeted me as though we had known each other forever. And believe me, now it seems as though we have. I wouldn't be without him."

Allie reached for his hand "And tell me, Mac Reilly," she said, surprising him. "Would you ever be without Sunny?"

Mac took a deep breath. He was looking at one of the most beautiful, the most famous, the most desirable women in the world. Temptation hovered between them, soft as silk.

"I could never be without Sunny," he said quietly.

Allie sighed. Rejection was not sweet. "I like your honesty," she said, gathering her bag and her dog. "It's getting late. I must be on my way."

He walked with her to her car.

"I asked you to come to Cannes with me," she said. "You told me 'maybe.' Is that 'maybe' a promise?"

Mac put his hands on her shoulders.

"A lot depends on your answer," she said. "More than you'll ever know."

He kissed her gently on each velvety peach cheek. "Maybe," he said again.

She turned for the door, then turned back again. "Mac," she said. "Rich men don't just go missing, do they?"

He shook his head. "Particularly ones who owe their wives."

She nodded. "That's what I thought. You will find Ron for me, though?"

"I'll do my best."

She smiled, that heavenly smile that had made moviegoers fall in love with her. "That's all I can ask," she said.

As Allie drove away Mac took Pirate and went back into their little house and closed the door. It was sad, Mac thought, that golden opportunities sometimes missed their mark. It just went to show you, timing was everything.

He went out onto the deck, listening to the surge of the tide and thinking about the missing husband, and about the weird letters and the real stalker. He did not like the scenario. Not one bit.

He dialed Lev Orenstein's number and discussed it with him. "Allie won't bring the police in," he said, "so it's up to us."

"I'll keep her covered," Lev replied, "and keep my eye out for the crazy guy. But the rest is up to you."

Worried, Mac knew he was right. Now, he had three people anxious to find Ron Perrin. His wife, who wanted a divorce; his mistress, who wanted marriage; and his business partner, who wanted his friend back, and possible absolution in case of any financial misdoings. RP was an interesting man.

Mac's thoughts returned to Sunny. Hadn't he said in front of the love of his life that he might consider going off to the South of France with a world-famous beauty? Just him and her? He was lucky she was still speaking to him. It was late and he didn't want to call her because of her jet lag. He knew she was probably already sleeping.

He sent her a text message instead. "hope u slept off the jet lag. miss u like crazy. the marina's not as far as rome. any chance of u inviting me over for dinner tomorrow night? tamales would be good. and no, i'm not going to cannes with the gorgeous movie star. i was just being 'polite.' love U, babe."

Her return message was waiting for him the next morning.

"my place. seven o'clock. forget the tamales. i can cook other things you know."

Nineteen

Sunny had it all planned. Mac was an old-fashioned guy at heart. And she decided to start with butternut squash soup that tasted like sweet velvet scattered with crumbled almond cookies and cinnamon. No one would guess how easy it was to make. Then his favorite chicken cacciatore, which, like the soup, could be made in advance, so she wouldn't be racing around the kitchen at the last minute. For dessert, her own personal favorite, a light-as-a-feather lemon cake from Mrs. Gooch's on Melrose, served with low-fat Dreyer's chocolate fudge ice cream.

She'd thrown in the low-fat as a concession to her own conscience, though when you were romancing a guy you aimed to please. Plus she had bought a good champagne, Henriot, a lesser-known marc but famous in France, and a very splurgy bottle of Bordeaux, a Ducru-Beaucaillou that had cost far too much and which practically had to be opened the day before in order for it to breathe.

Anyhow, that was her man-pleaser menu,

everything carefully planned, the table beautifully set, in honor of her man, with very masculine graphite-gray table mats, plain square white dishes and streamlined silverware. Not a curl or a flourish in sight. Except for a crystal vase of Sterling roses in that offbeat grayish lilac color.

And she was at her most girlish in a sweet-but-naughty silky little dress in the same color as the roses, spaghetti-strapped and with a touch of lace at the dipping neckline. Towering-heeled sandals—just a sliver of silver—Jimmy Choo of course and four years old but she loved them to pieces.

Her dark hair was brushed loose and arranged to fall sexily over one eye, and she wore her favorite Dior Rouge lipstick—the evening one—and of course, the Mitsouko perfume. The fire (gas logs only, but still effective) sparkled in the grate even though the night was mild. Neil Young was singing "Harvest Moon," very softly, and votive candles glimmered in the shadows.

For once the place was tidy, because knowing how Mac hated her chaotic housekeeping, Sunny had shoved everything into cupboards and drawers. Of course this meant she wouldn't be able to find anything for weeks, but tonight would be worth it.

She took a chocolate-covered fig from the refrigerator and bit into it, wondering, at the same time, why she had no self-control when it came to sweet things, when she knew perfectly well that her butt would get bigger by the minute. She sighed, and told herself that after all life was made up of small pleasures. Sweet ones

to find him."

Sunny took a sip of champagne, eyeing him over the top of the glass. "You getting paid for all this?"

"Financial arrangements are being made with Demarco. Allie Ray is paying more than generously to have me on call twenty-four/seven, not only to find her missing husband but also to nail the real stalker, who might have become a major threat. As for Marisa, well I guess she just goes along for the ride."

"Hah!" Sunny sniffed.

"Hah—what?"

"You'll never get rich."

He grinned at her. "But just think how I'm enjoying myself."

Mac changed the subject, admiring the flowers and her dress. He even commented on how neat the place was, then he went onto the terrace and took in the view, while Sunny turned the music up a little and served the soup. As she had hoped, it knocked his socks off, taste-wise, and they were back on romantic course once again. She smiled happily. She definitely knew the way to a man's heart.

The special Bordeaux with the main course mellowed Mac even further. Forgetting about dessert, they took their still-full glasses and, with Mac's arm around her shoulders, hers around his waist, wandered into the bedroom, already artfully arranged with piled up pillows and the old-but-good Frette sheets her mom had given her, as well as a soft cashmere throw. Oh all right, she'd admit it, it was only cashmere *blend*. Still she knew it would warm their naked bodies in its soft folds in the event they felt chilled. Not much chance of that though.

The lamps threw soft golden pools of light, the music was to make love by, and her bed—their destiny—awaited.

She allowed Mac to undress her. Not that there was much to take off, but she loved the way he lingered over the important bits. Then he picked her up and lay her on the bed.

They were both being transported to heaven, or at least that part of paradise you can achieve while still on this earth, when she heard a menacing growl. Opening her eyes she was just in time to see Tesoro launch herself at Mac. All claws extended.

Mac's yell was not the one of passion she had expected. He flung himself upright, cursing the dog, who gave him a contemptuous look then jumped off the bed and stalked out.

Sunny ran to get the Bactine, dabbing it onto the scratch marks that furrowed neatly in four places down his back. He yelled again as it stung.

"Think of the neighbors," she reminded him. "They'll say it's domestic abuse and call the cops."

"Tell them to call Wildlife Control instead," he said, still hurting.

Sunny thought how odd life was. Here was a man who could dodge bullets and killers with impunity, but put him up against a cute little Chihuahua and he was no match. She sighed. So much for her romantic evening.

"Tell you what," she said brightly. "How about a grappa?"

"Sure." Mac was already flinging on his clothes. "At my place. It's safer there."

And so they left poor Tesoro to lick her paws and consider repentance.

Malibu worked its old charm though, and soon they were in Mac's bed. Sunny was carefully avoiding putting her hands on his wounds, and Pirate was a discreet bump in his basket by the window. All was sweetness and light again. And oh God, it was good, she thought, as she fell asleep wrapped in Mac's arms.

No proposal tonight, though. What could a girl do when her love life was sabotaged by her own Chihuahua?

Twenty

Sunny departed early the next morning to pick up her strained relationship with her dog, so Mac decided to wander down the road to Coogies for coffee and pancakes. *Blueberry* pancakes, he thought, whistling for Pirate. Plus enough coffee to float a battleship. His TV show was on hold, with no decision yet made and for once his time was his own.

Feeling good, he waved to the guard at the gate and was strolling out onto PCH when he noticed the car parked a little to the left in the sandy area just off the highway. An old Cadillac. Deep burgundy color. Dusty. It looked as though it had maybe been dumped there, but then he saw a man sitting in the driver's seat. Thin-faced, olive-skinned with a beard that looked like it might be a disguise, and of course, dark glasses.

It flashed through his mind that he'd seen that face, that *man* before, strolling slowly back and forth on the beach, along the surf line.

Calling Pirate to heel Mac walked over to the car. The windows were down and he stuck his head in. "Hi," he said. "What's your problem, buddy?"

The man looked silently at him. The beard was real. He heaved a deep sigh. "I might have known you'd catch on to me," he said. "Of course I know who *you* are." He took a card from the dash and handed it to Mac. "Sandy Lipski," he said. "Private investigator."

Some private eye, Mac thought. He couldn't even conduct a surveillance. He stuck out like a sore thumb.

"We need to talk," Lipski said.

"What about?" Mac said.

"Ronald Perrin."

Mac was surprised but he didn't show it. Of course he could have just gotten in Lipski's car and said okay so talk but he preferred to see people in their own habitats. He found it gave him a clue as to who they *really* were.

"Okay, so we'll go to your office," he said. "I'll get my car and follow you."

Who Lipski was became obvious when Mac saw his office. Small, on a Santa Monica side

130

street. Tired file cabinets; a battered desk with an old leather high-back chair for Lipski and a dingy airport-style chair for his client. Grimy windows; a Sparkletts watercooler with a stack of Dixie cups; a scratched wooden floor and torn screens. No AC but that was usual at the beach where everybody swore you didn't need it because of the sea breezes. It wasn't strictly true, especially today in Lipski's office, but Mac steeled himself against the nicotine-tainted air and got down to business.

"Before we get to Perrin, first tell me who you are," he said, taking the airport chair and making himself approximately comfortable.

Lipski's story was all too familiar: an ex-cop drummed out of the force for drugs, he'd drifted into a seedy underworld life. A few years down the road he'd found a 12-step program, gotten a life back and taken up the investigating business.

"Nothing fancy," he said, lighting up a Marlboro. "Just spying on fiancés for women who want to know if their future husbands have a past. Or else 'a present' they don't know about— like for instance another wife. Following erring husbands to motels. That kinda thing."

He took a long drag on the cigarette. The ash dropped down his shirtfront. Mac waited. His fly-on-the-wall technique never let him down.

"I met Ruby Pearl in rehab," Lipski said. "We kept each other going, encouraged each other, y'know. She was cute, blond, full of life. She always had me laughing. I really fell for her. Then she met another guy. She told me he was really rich. She'd met him on a chat room on the

131

Internet. She started seeing him and soon drop-ped me. He gave her presents—a diamond watch, and like that. Stuff I could never have afforded even if I'd worked twenty-four/seven." He shrugged miserably. "How could I compete?"

This was the second time Mac had heard about a diamond watch.

"But I still loved her," Lipski said. "Y'know how it is? Sometimes there's a woman you can never get out of your system? I would have taken her back in a heartbeat. But then she disappear-ed. Just like they say, 'into thin air.' I didn't know then who the guy was she had been seeing, only that he was rich.

"Months went by. The police put her in the missing persons file. And you know what that means. Nobody was even looking for her. I could not rest, I had to know what happened. A girl like that doesn't just disappear. Somebody had to have something to do with it. And then I found out from an old friend in the LAPD it was Ron Perrin she had been seeing. He'd even given her a job as his secretary.

"I know she's dead," Lipski added quietly. "It's that old gut feeling. Y'know how it is? It just doesn't sit right."

"I understand," Mac said. He was thinking that Ron Perrin was in deep trouble. No wonder he'd done a disappearing act.

"It was me that night in Perrin's house," Lipski said, startling him.

"How'd you get in?"

Lipski shrugged. "Sometimes it's just who you know. An employee with a grudge, a stolen key

132

... y'know how it goes. I made it my business to find out who ... why ... Anyhow, I got the key and the alarm code."

"Jesus," Mac said. "It was that easy?"

Lipski shook his head. "No. I'm that clever."

Mac laughed. There was more to this man than met the eye.

"I saw Perrin drive out the gate. I thought the house was empty. It was quite a shock when the woman came downstairs. And with a gun, for chrissakes. I didn't want to hurt her—and hey, I didn't want to get hurt either and then shoved in jail for burglarizing Perrin's place. I just wanted to get away. So I pushed her to the floor and took off as fast as I could. I figured she'd be too shocked and frightened to come after me with the gun." He shrugged. "I was right. I got away easy."

"So what were you looking for at Perrin's house anyway?"

"Evidence," Lipski said simply. "He killed my girlfriend. There has to be something there, doesn't there?"

Lipski's weary eyes, deep-set like two black coals in his thin bearded face, looked directly into Mac's. "You have to help me, Mr. Reilly," he said. "I'm beggin' you. Please."

133

Twenty-One

Loneliness had Allie in its grip, that kind of strangling sensation when, staring out the window, she felt that the rest of the world was out having a good time, while she was trapped in a prison of her own making. It was exactly the way Sunday afternoons had felt back in that small Texas town when she was a teenager and life was rushing past her and she knew she would never get to participate in it.

She thought about Sunny Alvarez. Now there was a woman who would never allow life to pass her by. Sunny was a driver in the fast lane on her Harley chopper, her black hair crammed under a silver helmet, like the god Hermes in full flight. Allie remembered Sunny's eyes looking directly into hers, that evening at Mac's place, and her saying, "Listen, if you need someone to talk to, call me ... Sometimes another woman's opinion can help sort things out."

Of course Sunny had not meant it. Sunny had a life and she was enjoying it too much to take time out to listen to Allie's selfish tirade of woes. And to any other woman Allie knew her complaints must indeed sound trivial. After all, she was a woman who supposedly had everything.

Still, remembering the concerned look in

Sunny's eyes, her hand hovered over the Black-Berry. She called Inquiries and got her number. After all, she had nothing to lose but her dignity. She punched it in.

Sunny answered immediately. "Hi, Allie," she said, sounding surprised. "I'm glad you called."

"Really?" Allie was also surprised.

"Of course *really*. Listen, you want a cup of coffee? We could meet at Starbucks ... Uh-uh, wait a minute, in a rash moment I forgot you can't do that kind of thing, go to a Starbucks and not get mobbed, I mean. So why don't you come over here instead? Then we can talk."

"You're sure I'm not interrupting your day?" Allie said cautiously.

"Of course you're not," Sunny lied. She gave her the address and said she was putting the coffee on to brew right that minute. "You like espresso?"

"Love it," Allie said, casting aside any worries about caffeine.

Sunny immediately called the potential client with whom she had a meeting and told him she'd been unexpectedly delayed and would get back to him later. So what if it cost her a job? Allie was a lonely woman who needed to talk and she had promised she would be available.

Half an hour later Allie walked in Sunny's front door and stood looking round, taking in the offhand furnishings, the photos of the Harley and the horse and the general chaos.

"Sorry about the mess," Sunny said. "Some-how it's always like this, I don't know why."

Allie saw that Sunny was wearing jeans with

the shirt that said love is all you need, in sparkles. "Do you believe that?" she asked, perching on the edge of the sofa.

Sunny came and shifted a pile of papers from behind her. "Make yourself comfortable," she said. "And no, I don't believe it's all you need, but it's a nice thought."

Allie got up and followed her into the kitchen that she saw was surprisingly neat. "What else do you believe in then?" she asked, taking a seat on a bar stool at the center island, while Sunny poured espresso into two small dark green French café cups.

Sunny thought about it. "Honesty. Loyalty..." Then she grinned. "A good chopper, fun..."

"And love."

"That goes along with the rest." She passed Allie the bowl of sugar and another of sweeteners. "So where are you at, Allie Ray?" she said, leaning her elbows on the black granite island, opposite her, and taking a sip of the deep rich coffee.

"It's not so much where I'm at, I suppose." Allie shrugged. "It's more about the loneliness. It's one of the worst feelings in the world. I was remembering, just before I called you, that this was exactly the way I used to feel when I was a teenager, doomed to be locked into that stifling gray life forever. And now, after all my success, I seem somehow to be right back where I came from."

"But you escaped then," Sunny said.

Allie raised her coffee cup in salute. "I did," she agreed. "I picked myself up and got out of there. I left no trace. I never wanted anybody to find me and drag me back again."

"Kicking and screaming," Sunny said.

"Something like that. Anyhow, I went to Vegas. Where else would a girl who looked like me end up? I worked two jobs, cocktail waitress and like that, skipping from casino to casino. Then I got a job as hostess at a steak house. That's where I met my first husband."

Her eyes met Sunny's. "He was a nice man, y'know. He treated me like a lady—and believe me, by then I was far from feeling like a lady. But I won't go into that now."

"I understand," Sunny said, wondering if she did.

"Those awful tight revealing costumes we had to wear." Allie's eyes were half-closed, remembering. "After that, the steak house felt like a slice of heaven. Safe, you know?"

Sunny nodded, and she went on. "He wasn't really rich, the man I met," she said, "but to me he was. I'd never known anyone who could take you out to dinner at a good restaurant and say, Have whatever y'want, babe. And he bought me presents, flowers, and a bracelet. He was older and I leaned on him. I needed him I guess. So when he asked me to marry him, I did. And I ended up trapped again.

"Oh, I was a good wife. He asked me to give up my job. I stayed home, fixed dinner, watched TV with him. He was in his fifties and I was eighteen, trying to seem older and lying that I was twenty-one. Nobody cared except me. I guess I just wanted to belong."

137

"And did you?" Sunny poured more coffee. She pushed the sugar bowl toward Allie and went to sit on the bar stool next to her.

"Not enough." Allie sighed. "I left him, went to another city ... New York. We divorced a year later. I've never heard from him since."

"Married at eighteen, divorced by twenty," Sunny said, astonished.

"I wasn't lucky enough to get an education like you." Allie was looking at her with that wistful expression in her eyes again. "There was no money for college and anyhow my father wouldn't have allowed it. I was his 'whipping boy' ... me and my mom both." She shuddered, remembering the ugliness of that life.

"I was twenty-two and working as a hostess again, in a fancy brasserie in Manhattan, and living in a cockroach-infested walk-up in Greenwich Village." She shrugged. "It was like history repeating itself, only I was older and a little bit wiser, and I knew I was beautiful now. I wasn't about to throw that asset away again, and when I met the man who became my second husband I made sure he was rich."

She turned her head to look at Sunny. "It didn't make any difference. It ended up the same way. Only this time he was nice about it and settled a little money on me, enough to fly to L.A. and get a small apartment and try to become an actress. Like a thousand other girls just like me."

She shrugged. "I was like all the rest of the pretty girls in town, creating a confident image when I'd never really acted in my life. I went to acting classes, learned my craft, went on auditions, played a little theater here and there, small roles, nothing important. After a while, a couple of years, I was doing okay, getting jobs, minor roles in movies, and TV ... but never really breaking through. And still fending off the Hollywood Romeos that came courting. And then, a couple of years later, I met Ron."

She stopped her confessional monologue and looked at Sunny. "You'll know what I mean when I say it was meant to be. The thing between me and Ron. It was like we had known each other in some other life."

"You were head over heels," Sunny said, and Allie laughed.

"And so was he. We met at a New Year's Eve party in Aspen. We left them all to their Happy New Years and champagne and went back to Ron's log cabin in the woods with the snow piled outside the door. I ruined my expensive shoes that I'd gone without lunches to afford but I didn't care. I just wanted to be with him. And I was lucky, he wanted to be with me.

"Ron was a superb skier," Allie said as Sunny brewed more coffee. "His body's compact but it's hard from all the weight lifting and his legs are strong. In his black Bogner ski suit he skimmed down those mountains, looking like a dark bird of prey. I wasn't nearly as good, in my fur-hooded movie-actress ice-white suit that he made me promise never to wear again.

"I remember him saying, 'Don't you realize that if you're dressed in white and anything went wrong, an accident, a fall, or God forbid an avalanche, the rescue team would never be able

139

to see you in all that snow?' The next day he took me to the store and bought me a bright red suit and boots to match. Then he took me to a jewelers and bought me a diamond ring. An eternity band.

"'It's only the beginning but I feel in my bones, in my heart, this is for eternity,' he told me, holding me by my scarlet shoulders and looking into my eyes."

She looked at Sunny. "It was then I felt our souls connect," she said. "And I knew he was right. We were meant for each other.

"We took the cable car to the top of Ajax Mountain where we celebrated over a mug of hot chocolate, with many soft and gentle kisses. Few people realize that at heart, Ron is a very tender man, because he never allows that side of him to show. He was trained in business and the board-rooms of the world to be poker-faced, unemotional, a hard man who never gives up.

"Ron got me my first really big role, starring in the movie that made my name. I was already well known, of course, but the sexy, glamorous *Good Heavens, Miss Mary,* established me in the kind of fresh comedic romantic role that became my trademark. That role 'branded' me and made my fortune. After ten years I was an overnight success.

"We had celebrated with a trip to Europe, stopping in Paris to shop, and in Saint-Tropez to lie on the beach and drink rosé wine over long lunches. Life was sweet then.

"I owe a lot to Ron," she said. "And that's why I'll never forget him."

"And now you've lost him," Sunny said gently.

Allie's eyes met hers. "Have you ever been heartbroken?" she asked.

Sunny considered. "Once or twice I thought I was. But now I know, never in the way you mean."

"So now you understand why I'm unhappy."

"Because you're lonely," Sunny said, putting her arm around Allie's shoulder. "And you are hurting."

"It's just that I thought I had it made, all my ducks in a row—and now it's all falling apart," Allie said.

She wasn't crying but Sunny could see the held back tears glittering silver in her blue eyes.

"Thank you for telling me," she said gently. "I'll never betray your confidence."

"I'm sorry I used your shoulder to cry on," Allie said wistfully.

Sunny leaned across and kissed her cheek. "That's what girlfriends are for," she said.

But she thought Allie seemed almost embarrassed when she left, as if she had revealed too much of herself. Sunny only hoped that spilling it all out had helped her in some way.

"Call me again, let's get together soon," she said when they kissed goodbye. And though Allie promised she would, somehow Sunny knew she would not.

Minutes after Allie had left, Mac called. Sunny was dying to tell him all about Allie's visit, but he cut her off.

"Tell me later," he said, sounding urgent. "I've got something more important to tell you."

141

And then he told her the Lipski story. And about RP buying an expensive diamond watch as a gift for a woman who was supposed to be his secretary and who was now missing, and that Lipski believed she had been murdered.

"Interesting," Sunny said, thinking of poor Allie, who despite everything, still wanted to believe her husband was a good guy.

"What's even more interesting is I'm on my way to break into Perrin's house myself, just the way Lipski did."

"Why?" she demanded, shocked.

"To look for evidence, of course."

"You can't do that. You'll be committing a crime—"

"No I won't," Mac said calmly. "I'm not breaking in. I have the keys."

"Technically it's a crime..."

Mac was laughing. "I'll let you know how it goes."

"No. Mac, wait. I'm coming right over. Promise me you'll wait."

"Okay, I promise," he agreed.

Twenty-Two

As usual the traffic was hell. Stalled off Surfrider Beach on the throbbing bike, Sunny thought that if you were not in a hurry sometimes driving PCH could be quite a turn-on, what with all those bronzed muscular young surfers stripping off their skintight wet suits behind parked SUVs, or else simply gift-wrapped in skimpy towels.

But she had no time for such erotic thoughts now. Immediately after she'd spoken to Mac, she had called Roddy to enlist his aid in stopping Mac from breaking and entering, but Roddy was in Cape Cod for a long weekend. So now it was up to her to stop him.

You didn't need to be an expert to know that housebreaking was a criminal offense. And besides, she had that gut feeling that not one of the people involved—not Marisa, not Demarco, not even Ruby Pearl, and especially not Ron Perrin—was worth it. It was up to her to use all her arts of female persuasion to stop Mac from making a fool of himself, and maybe ending up in handcuffs, photographed by the paparazzi, disheveled and looking guilty with a two-day growth of beard, en route to the Malibu courthouse.

The traffic unraveled and she coasted to the

Colony, waving to the guard as she drove in. She didn't bother to ring the unmusical captain's bell; as usual Mac's door was unlocked.

There was one of those red sunsets going on where the sun looks like the ball of fire it really is, painting the neon blue sky with a coral and orange glow. Pirate glanced up, no doubt checking to see if the dreaded Tesoro was with her. Satisfied she was not, he gave Sunny a welcoming grin then went back to his snooze.

Mac got up to give her a little more than a mere welcoming grin. "Hello, fellow housebreaker," he said, kissing her soundly.

"What d'you mean?" she gasped, coming up for air. *"Fellow housebreaker?"*

"Okay, so technically, it's not housebreaking. I have the key."

"Where'd you get that?"

"Lipski. I have to give him credit, he even got the alarm code."

"Jesus!" She dropped onto the metal lounger and felt it sink a little even under her modest weight. "You need new chairs," she reminded him while she thought of it.

"Okay. Now listen. So far no police are involved. There's no way anyone will even know we're in the house."

"We?"

"We," he said firmly. "I'll need help. Anyway, there's nothing for the police to be involved in yet. Perrin's just a rich man who's taken off by himself somewhere. Rich men do that all the time, y'know."

"I didn't." She gave him a withering look.

The wind blew her long hair and Mac leaned over and gently brushed it back again. The last of the sun's glow lit her face and he bent again to kiss her. "I love you, Sonora Sky Coto de Alvarez," he murmured, dropping his lips from her hair into that favorite place of his where the pulse beat at the base of her throat.

"You're just smooth-talking me," she said warily, but she was softening. She gave him a smile.

"I am," he agreed. "But maybe I'll save that for later."

"After the break-in."

"Right. Meanwhile, why has Perrin disappeared? Is it because the FBI are after him for fraud? Or perhaps for money laundering? And maybe he killed Ruby Pearl who knew too much? Who knows, maybe Marisa and Allie are next on his list."

"Jesus," Sunny said again. She was a little scared by this time.

Mac took a seat on the end of the lounger. Leaning forward, hands clasped between his knees, he gazed earnestly at her. "I don't know if Perrin is really a killer, but I do believe Lipski is right about one thing. There has to be something, some evidence, *a clue* at least in that house. Remember I told you RP was shredding documents that morning? I'm hoping he didn't get around to all of them. I'm asking you to help because it'll be faster having two of us go through the place." He looked at her, one dark eyebrow raised. "So? Are you with me or not?"

Sunny sighed. It was a foregone conclusion.

They waited until it was dark, then, leaving Pirate at home this time, they walked down the empty beach. The tide was receding and Sunny worried out loud that their footprints in the wet sand would lead incriminatingly to the Perrin house but Mac said to stop being Sherlock Holmes, nobody was looking.

She hurried up the beach steps after him, glancing nervously over her shoulder as he opened the side door. The alarm pinged and, twisting her hands in an agony of fear that they would be discovered, she waited until he'd switched it off.

"Oh my God," she said, shivering. "Tell me, Mac Reilly, why am I doing this? Am I crazy or what?"

"Crazy," he agreed. He was standing by the window almost exactly in the place he had been that night when Marisa had pointed the gun at him. "There's got to be something," he whispered to Sunny. "Some evidence of wrongdoing, something Perrin forgot."

"Okay." She had stopped shivering but was still distinctly nervous.

In an alcove of the enormous living room was a computer. Mac went over and switched it on. Its start page was an Internet chat room with pictures of young women with short bios and even shorter skirts, and messages urging you to get in touch.

Mac whistled. So Perrin really was into chat rooms. Marisa had admitted that's where she'd met him, and Lipski had said the same about Ruby. He guessed that for Perrin it was anonymous and better than going the old-fashioned route via a Hollywood madam who might one day get arrested and spill the beans about your sexual activities and preferences.

The two of them began to go systematically through the house. Mac took the upstairs, Sunny down, grumbling when they found nothing. There were no files and the shredder was gone.

Sunny was in the kitchen when she heard the steel gate leading to the street sliding back.

"Oh my God, Mac," she called in a piercing whisper. *"Somebody's coming."*

Mac raced down the stairs. He grabbed her hand and rushed her through the kitchen door into the garage. He stood for a second until his eyes adjusted to the darkness. He'd wondered what car Perrin would drive and now he knew. A Hummer. Silver. RP's color, it seemed, with windows tinted black so you could not see inside. Next to it was a silver Porsche. Plus a red Harley. And in a corner, the pièce de résistance, an original Indian motorcycle.

"Oh—my—God." Sunny stared reverently at the bike.

Mac was peering through a crack in the door to the kitchen. He could make out someone moving around. A man. He had not put on the lights, so like them, he obviously didn't want it known he was there. It definitely was not Lipski though. The man turned and looked his way.

Mac grabbed Sunny, opened the Hummer's back door and shoved her inside. "Get down on the floor," he said. "Don't say a word, whatever happens."

"Oh my God," she said again, but this time

with a panicked wobble in her voice. "Is it the FBI?"

Mac climbed into the front seat. He got down on the floor and stretched out as best he could. Then he locked the doors from the inside.

"It's Demarco."

"Ohh..." Her agonized moan almost made him laugh.

His shoulders were cramped and his head was stuck under the steering wheel. Above him dangled not just the Hummer's key but a whole set of keys and an electronic opener. He reached up and slipped them into his pocket.

"It's hot as hell," Sunny whispered. "I think I'm dying."

"No you're not," he said confidently. But lying on the floor of the squat Hummer was like being in a hearse without the benefit of a coffin. He was sweating.

In the back of the car, Sunny gripped the side pockets, hauling herself into a more comfortable position. Her fingers encountered a piece of paper. She took it and stuffed it in the pocket of her shorts.

Demarco was standing in the garage, staring around, a baffled look on his face. He was still wearing a pin-striped suit. Not the usual uniform for housebreaking. And unlike most people's garages, this one was not full of stored junk. It was clean as a whistle. There was nowhere to hide anything. Except in the two cars.

Mac ducked as Demarco made for the Hummer, hearing Sunny's little whispered whinny of fear.

Demarco cursed as he tried the Hummer's door and found it locked. Next he tried the Porsche. He opened the door and looked inside it, but obviously did not find what he was looking for. Mac watched him stalk back into the house, allowing the door to slam behind him.

Mac felt in his pockets for the keys.

"Guess what," he said to Sunny. "I left the house keys in the kitchen."

She shot up from the floor in back of him. *"You mean we're locked in this garage?"* she said in a loud whisper.

"Shh." He gestured toward the house. "Actually, yes. That's exactly what I mean."

Sunny moaned. "I'm gonna die in here. I'll leave a note asking that the Indian bike be buried with me. We've got to get out," she added. "Who's gonna give Pirate his dinner?"

"You are." Getting up, Mac helped her out of the car. "See that?" He pointed to the locked side door with the dog flap.

"You mean that *doggie door*?"

"Must have been for Allie's Maltese." He glanced encouragingly at Sunny. "Think you can make it?"

She groaned. "Explain to me why we don't just use the garage door opener and get out the usual way."

"Because we don't want to announce our illegal presence to all and sundry passing by on the street. Especially if Demarco is still around, though I doubt that. Tell you what, why don't you get out, then go around to the beach side. The window should still be open. Then come back through the house and let me out."

Sunny glared at him. "I've a good mind to leave you here."

"Aw come on. You've got to admit it was worth a try."

Sighing, Sunny eyed the doggie door. "I'll never forgive you for this," she said.

In a few minutes she was standing outside breathing the fresh salty night air.

"Oh thank God," she whispered to herself. But she had to be quick and rescue Mac before somebody got suspicious or Demarco came back.

"Thanks," Mac said, when she finally opened the kitchen door and let him out. "Tell you what," he said as he reset the alarm and they exited quickly, locking the door behind them. "I've got a bottle of good champagne chilling just for you. How about it, babe?"

"I hate you," she said, smiling.

After the second glass of champagne, when Sunny's nerves had stopped twitching and she had agreed not to keep looking back down the beach at Perrin's house, she told Mac about Allie's visit, and how she had revealed her very personal life story.

"She just wanted to talk," Sunny said. "And I was the anonymous person who would listen. A 'girlfriend.'"

"So what do you think of Allie, now?" Mac asked.

Sunny took a thoughtful sip. "I like her. I think she's had—is having—a hard time. And I admire her. She came from a tough background and

150

fought her way to the top, even though she says it was Ron who in the end gave her that final leg up to movie-biz stardom. But I get the feeling she's at a crisis point. I don't think she knows which way to turn. And besides, she misses her husband. I got the impression that she depended on him for everything. Ron Perrin was her rock in a very craggy business."

"You sure she misses him?" Mac sounded surprised.

"I'm sure of it," Sunny said firmly. "In fact I'd be willing to bet she still loves Ron Perrin."

Twenty-Three

It was a few days later and Allie was in the South of France, alone on the terrace of her luxurious suite at the Hôtel du Cap. She was clutching a glass of champagne, taking a gulp from it every now and again to steady her nerves, thinking of what she was about to do. Snatches of conversation and laughter drifted from the gardens below, along with the faint slurp of the Mediterranean hitting the shore. Umbrella pines straggled across the skyline as the horizon turned a neon blue to match the sea, and the air felt soft against her skin.

She thought of Malibu, where the Pacific Ocean always let you know who was master, curling in high iced-green waves that slammed against the shore in a torrent of white foam, then receded with a whisper over the rocks. She thought of Ron and their home at the water's very edge, of how, when they had first bought it, they would lie awake listening to the ocean that somehow soothed them into sleep with its noise. And she remembered Mac's humble little place, perched precariously on its wooden pilings, and as charming and casual as the man himself.

A glance at her gold Cartier watch told her it was almost time. She just had one last call to make. She punched in the numbers, hoping Sheila would be there. Luckily, she answered right away.

"Sheila, this is it," Allie said softly. "I have nothing to return for."

"Sweetheart, are you sure?" There was a hint of panic in Sheila's voice.

"I've never been so sure of anything since I was a teenager and wanted to get out of that deadly little town in Texas. Sheila, it's what I have to do. What I *need* to do. I don't know where it will end, but I have to be on my own. I have to try to create a new life."

"But how, what will you do, Allie?"

Sheila was worried, but there was a new lift to Allie's voice as she answered. "I have no idea. I guess I'll find something. I'll let you know, my friend. But you promise to say nothing to anyone?"

"Not even Ron? If he should return that is?"

"Especially not Ron."

"And what about the detective? Reilly?"

Allie hesitated, but she decided quickly she

had to do this alone. "Not even Mac Reilly," she said firmly.

Sheila wished her luck, said she would be thinking of her, and Allie promised to call before too long. Then she walked back into the suite, checked her appearance in the full-length mirror and called for the bellboy to carry her small suitcase to the waiting limo.

Taking a deep breath, she walked to the door. She turned for one last look at the charming room with its view of the sea; at the silver ice bucket with the open bottle of excellent champagne and the massed bouquets of scented flowers; at the piles of expensive clothes that the maid would straighten out for her. At the life of a movie star on her way to her premiere. And then she closed that door and took the elevator downstairs to the lobby where her director was waiting for her.

She caught his slight frown of disapproval at her plain outfit, but still he smiled and said how lovely she looked.

"Sometimes simplicity is better," she said. "It's just a pity we didn't keep that in mind when we made this movie."

They sat in silence for the almost forty minutes it took to drive what usually took only twenty. The traffic was hell and the director was biting his fingernails, afraid they were going to be late. But Allie knew they would wait for her. Everyone always did.

As the limo drew up at the Palais des Festivals, she stepped out and posed smiling for the photographers. Compared to all the glitter and the gowns and the glamour, she caused a sensation. So simple, so different in her narrow black silk pants and plain white taffeta shirt with the sleeves rolled up, her only jewels a pair of gold hoops and, oddly, since it was known her marriage was on the rocks, her gold wedding band. Her blond hair was pulled back into a chignon and tied with a black satin bow, the way Grace Kelly used to wear hers in the sixties, and in fact more than one person commented on her resemblance to Monaco's late princess.

She walked to the enormous red-carpeted flight of steps leading into the Palais, holding hands with her director, smiling and waving to the crowd, posing some more, the complete professional, making sure the photographers had what they needed. Then she strode up the steps, turning at the top for one final wave. No one would have guessed that at that moment she felt she was the loneliest woman in the world.

She sat through the screening of her movie, with its title, *Midsummer's Dream,* half-stolen from Shakespeare. Despite some drastic last-minute cutting it was as slow and emotionally unmoving as she'd suspected it would be from the first week's shooting, when the script had begun to be changed. From then on it had been changed on a daily basis until nothing was left of the charming little love story, which was how it had started out. But anyway, her thoughts were not on the film. That was the past.

She was thinking about Mac Reilly and his phone call before she'd left for France, wishing her good luck. "Sure you won't change your mind and join me?" she had asked wistfully, already knowing his answer. Loneliness had made her try, and despite her brave words to Sheila, she was scared by what she was about to do.

The movie was over. Time to face the press, do the interviews, pose for the photographers one more time. Then on to the cocktail party given by the studio on the enormous yacht moored in the bay, and then to dinner at the famous Moulin de Mougins restaurant, where once again the beautiful Sharon Stone was conducting a live auction to benefit AIDS.

And after that? After that Allie's time was her own.

At the auction, she bid on a luxury cruise for two. Surprised when she won, she generously donated it back to be re-auctioned. Then whispering to her director that she was tired, she said good night and slipped from the darkened room.

Her small suitcase was already stashed in the back of the limo. Allie asked the driver to take her to Nice airport. She opened the case, took out a long cardigan and slipped it on. She pulled a straw hat over her hair and adjusted the brim so it shaded her face. A pair of square-framed glasses hid her eyes and she wiped off her lipstick.

When they arrived, she tipped the driver a generous couple of hundred dollars, said she did not need any help, hefted her suitcase, then walked into the departures terminal and headed for the restroom.

In a stall, she quickly changed into jeans and a

sweatshirt. Then she picked up the suitcase again and walked out to the car rental facility.

This was the test. Would they recognize her? Or would they not?

The woman at Euro-Car was tired and disinterested. Yes, Madam's car was waiting. She just needed to see her driver's license, passport, credit card, and she should sign here.

Allie gave her the new passport with her real name, Mary Allison Raycheck, and the new credit card. She held her breath. Would the woman look at her to check?

"Row C, number 42. Left out of the door. *Et bon voyage.*"

Bon voyage, Allie thought, elated, throwing her suitcase into the trunk of the small baby blue Renault then climbing into the driver's seat. Little did the woman know this was to be the *"voyage"* of a lifetime.

She shut the car door with a solid thud, then sat for a moment, suddenly overwhelmed by fear. Desperate, she took out her BlackBerry and called Ron at the Malibu house. There was no reply. She tried Palm Springs. The same. She called Mac Reilly. Again no reply, only the request to leave a name and number, which she did not.

Tears glittered in her eyes but she brushed them away. There was nobody to even care what she did. Still, there would be no more threatening letters, no more crazy stalkers, no more complicated love life—or rather, lack of one. And no more movie star. She was free. She was Mary Allison Raycheck.

Back to that again.

Twenty-Four

Roddy was having a busy day and one not quite to his liking. First he paid Allie's housekeeper a visit to question her about the staff and the extra cleaners, the pool service, the gardeners. Allie was in Cannes and Ampara was alone.

She was holding Allie's little white dog on her knee while they talked over a glass of iced tea in a rich man's kitchen that could have graced the cover of *Architectural Digest,* and that Roddy thought was big enough to double as a ballroom. *Cozy* was not exactly the adjective that sprang to mind, but he smiled and said how great it was and how happy Ampara must be to be working in such elegant surroundings.

Ampara was from El Salvador and knew what poverty looked like. She had worked for Allie and Ron Perrin for four years and sent money home regularly to her family. Comfortable-looking was how Roddy would have described her, small and round and sort of grandmotherly, though in fact she was only forty-five. She spoke excellent English, which she told him was essential if you wanted a good job like this one because it meant you could take messages.

"And have there been any messages for Miss Ray since she left for Cannes?" Roddy asked.

Ampara shook her head, looking sorrowful. "No, sir. There's been no messages for Mr. Ron either. And with both of them gone and maybe splitting up, I'm not sure where I stand anymore, job-wise."

Roddy looked concerned. "Even though they're away, you still get paid though, right?"

"Oh yes sir, the accountants have always taken care of that. But it gets lonely here, in this big house all by myself. Especially at night. I have my own apartment over the garage and I don't mind admitting that me and Fussy lock ourselves in there and bolt the door. I'm glad of the little dog's company," she added, lifting Fussy to kiss her on her nose.

Roddy could have sworn he saw the dog smile, quite different from the snappy little creature that evening at the beach. And he didn't blame Ampara for being intimidated. This was a huge house that demanded to be filled with people, a party house meant to be exploited and shown off. A bit like Allie herself, he thought.

Ampara told him that all the indoor and outdoor staff had worked there for years. The only casualty was Allie's assistant, Jessie Whitworth, who had worked for Allie for almost a year and who she had "let go" a couple of months back.

"I think Jessie was surprised when Miss Allie told her she didn't need an assistant anymore. Miss Allie said she was cutting back on work and personal appearances, and anyway she wanted to take over her own life," Ampara added.

Roddy's ears perked up. A sacked personal assistant sounded likely to be an angry ex-assistant, one who might want revenge. But when he asked Ampara she said no, Jessie wasn't like that. She was a nice quiet young woman, always polite and with a smile.

So were some serial killers, Roddy thought, writing down Jessie Whitworth's name, address and phone number.

"More iced tea, sir?" Ampara asked.

"Thanks, no. I'll be on my way. You've been more than helpful."

The housekeeper's round face looked doleful. "I surely hope Miss Allie and Mr. Ron gets back together, sir. I'm not happy being here alone. I need someone to look after. That's why I'm so fond of Fussy here."

She saw Roddy out through the massive front hall with its double sweeping staircase and crystal chandelier, standing on the steps, the dog in her arms, watching as he got in his car. She waved as he drove off.

Roddy dialed Jessie Whitworth's number. She answered right away. A pleasant low voice, precise and businesslike. She sounded like the perfect secretary as she agreed to meet him at the Starbucks near Wilshire and Third in Santa Monica.

She was already there when Roddy made his way in. He could have picked her out even if she hadn't waved hello from a corner table. In contrast to the young clientele, who were mostly in lowrider jeans and cropped T-shirts with their hair bubbling down their backs in blond extensions, she was tall and very neat looking in a buttoned-to-the-neck blouse and well-cut brown pants, worn with Gucci loafers. Miss Whit-worth's hair was cut in a neat black bob, and she was pretty in an unobtrusive sort of way. Roddy got the feeling she had spent a lifetime trying to appear unobtrusive. He guessed it was the only way to survive as an assistant to important people who sometimes acted as though they were more important than they were.

"That's what I'm paid for," Jessie Whitworth told him with a smile when Roddy mentioned it, surprising him with a set of expensively veneer-ed, dazzlingly white teeth.

"It's not me up there center stage," she added, and Roddy saw the smile disappear.

"Is that where you'd like to be then?" he said, looking interested as they sat over their low-fat macchiatos.

"About a dozen or so years ago, when I was young and foolish enough to believe I had talent. Hollywood soon robbed me of that illusion," she added. "Not that I minded. I realized I wasn't cut out for the game that had to be played. All I wanted was to act. And you know what, Mr. Kruger? I simply wasn't good enough."

Roddy knew exactly what she meant. He him-self had never had eyes for the acting profession, but he had friends who still cherished the hope of that one role that would change their lives, meanwhile struggling on with a bit part here, a non-speaking part there, even willing to work as extras.

"It's a tough life," he said, all sympathy. He was liking Miss Whitworth and her honesty about herself.

"Allie didn't exactly *fire* me," Jessie said. "She told me her life was changing and she needed to do things herself. Become more independent. Lose all the trappings. That sort of thing. I knew she was unhappy and on the verge of splitting up with Ron and at first I thought it was just a reaction to that. I believed she would get over it, move on. But it seems she hasn't."

"You think she was still in love with Ron?"

Jessie's cool gray eyes met his. "I would say so. Yes, definitely. I mean they fought because ... Well, you know how it is with couples. I don't want to talk about my employers' private lives," she added. "It's not right."

"I understand."

Roddy was on the verge of eliminating her as stalker material when she said, "Of course Allie paid me three months' wages in lieu of notice and gave me glowing references, but the fact is I still don't have a proper job. I'm temping right now, out at Mentor Studios. Just another assistant's assistant. A jumped-up secretary. Quite a comedown," she added bitterly, and Roddy caught the quick flash of anger that crossed her face.

So, he thought surprised, poker-faced Little Miss Goody Two-shoes has emotions after all. And not all of them are good.

"Thanks for talking to me, Miss Whitworth," he said. "You helped clear up a few points."

"Like that Allie was planning on making changes to her life?"

"You believe that, do you?"

She nodded. "I think she might have become

161

tired of being America's darling with no privacy."

Roddy thought she was right. He shook her hand, waving from the door as he left. He thought Miss Whitworth was a dark horse and that an eye should definitely be kept on her.

He waited in the parking lot until he saw her leave. She was driving a bright blue Porsche Carrera. A fancy car for an ex-personal assistant turned jumped-up secretary, he thought, surprised.

He had already checked the other staff on Mac's list, the hairdressers, stylists, et cetera. Now he drove to the studio to snoop around there, see who was what, and what, if anything, anyone had to say about Allie.

He'd gotten personal approval to be on the lot from the producer of her last film, and the guard at the gate checked him out on the computer, made out a visitor pass for him then waved him on. "Visitor parking to the left, sir," he said, so Roddy swung a left and drove down a line of densely packed cars. The studios must be really busy, he thought, turning down another aisle looking for a spot.

He slammed his foot on the brake, threw the car into reverse, backed up, then stopped. He was looking at a black Sebring convertible with very dark windows.

Twenty-Five

Roddy drove back to the gate. From the procedure he had just gone through he knew the guard would have a list of all visitors and their car numbers. He explained who he was, told him what he wanted to know, annoyed but understanding when the guard explained he was not at liberty to give out that information.

Roddy had the number of the production office of Allie's latest movie. He called, explained what he wanted and asked for help. Within minutes the guard had been given permission and Roddy had the information. Or at least some of it.

"That car has been on the lot for a couple of weeks, sir," the guard told him. "It's a rental and the woman driving it told me it had broken down. She said the rental company would come and tow it." He shrugged. "So far they've not shown up. Beats me how they keep in business," he added.

"So who was the driver?" Roddy asked, as casually as he could because he was excited to think he might be on the brink of identifying Allie's stalker.

"A woman by the name of Elizabeth Windsor, sir. I remember because like it's the Queen of England's name."

"The Queen of England right here in your parking lot?" Roddy said. "Imagine that."

The two men laughed together, then Roddy said, "You remember what she looked like?"

"Couldn't forget. Tall, blond and long legs." He made a curving gesture with his hands and they grinned at each other.

"How old?" Roddy said.

"Oh, I dunno—twenties, I guess. Come to think of it, she looked a bit like Allie Ray."

"Better than the Queen of England," Roddy said. "Younger, anyway."

Bristling with excitement, Roddy called Mac to tell him the news.

"I'm sitting here right now, looking at the Sebring," he said. "Of course I know there's probably hundreds like it, but this one was parked on the Mentor lot where Allie was filming. Anyhow, it's a rental in the name of Elizabeth Windsor."

"Like the British Queen?"

"The same, only this one's in her twenties, a tall blond who looks a bit like Allie."

"Check out 'the Queen,'" Mac said. "See if anyone remembers her, and what she was doing on the Mentor lot anyway."

Roddy was weary. It was almost seven and he'd been thinking more along the lines of an iced vodka martini in the bar at the Hotel Casa del Mar in Santa Monica with a soothing view of the ocean. It was close to where he lived in an all-white condo—dogless, thank God—and with a more prosaic view of other people's backyards.

He told Mac about his conversation with Jessie

164

Whitworth, said that he thought she was a dark horse, that she drove a bright blue Porsche, and that she had been fired a couple of months ago. "By coincidence she's working as a temp right here at Mentor Studios," he added.

"She's not tall and blond?"

Roddy laughed. "Quite the opposite. A bit of a plain Jane really, in a nice efficient way. Knows her place and sticks to it."

"So how does the prim Miss Whitworth afford to drive an expensive car?"

Roddy said, "You know L.A. First and last month down and you too can look like a big shot and drive a Porsche."

"Yeah, but that doesn't gel with what you're telling me about the rest of Jessie's image," Mac said thoughtfully. "I wouldn't bet she's the stalker either. Our stalker is really crazy. I'm talking potentially violent crazy and I'm not getting that message about Miss Whitworth."

"Right," Roddy said. "I just thought with her being fired and all..."

"And you're right. We can't dismiss her out of hand. I'll do a little background search on Miss Whitworth myself, okay?"

"Right," Roddy said, relieved that he didn't have to work all night. That martini was getting closer.

"I'll also check out the Sebring," Mac said. "Thanks, Roddy." There was a grin in his voice as he added, "You're the greatest, y'know that?"

Roddy smiled, showing a beguiling pair of dimples. "I always kind of thought so myself," he said, preening in the rearview mirror.

Twenty-Six

It didn't take long for Mac to find out that the rented Sebring had been reported as stolen. The driver's license in the name of Elizabeth Windsor was a fake, and the credit card with which she had paid had a false address in another city.

Driving to the rental facility at LAX, Mac thought about Elizabeth Windsor. Could this really be the stalker? The writer of those filthy abusive letters, filled with explicit threats? Most often a stalker was a man, but this one might also be an expert in using women. Elizabeth Windsor might merely be a pawn in his game.

Planes zoomed low over his head as he parked, merging with bewildered-looking travelers hurrying to pick up cars, only to struggle to find their way out of the traffic into the City of Dreams.

He got lucky. The young guy in charge of the rental place remembered Miss Windsor. "Tall," he told Mac, "with long blond hair. Kind of a looker, if that's your taste."

It was obviously his, which was why he remembered. Mac said, "So where was she from?"

"Wait a sec and I'll look it up for you." He drummed on his computer and within a minute had what Mac had asked for. It tallied with the information the cops had given him. The address did not exist.

"She seemed okay," the young man added. "Pleasant, y'know. Not the sort to steal a car."

"She didn't," Mac said. "Apparently she just forgot to return it."

At eleven o'clock that night the phone rang. Mac was in bed but not yet sleeping. Lying at his feet, Pirate opened his eye. Mac knew it couldn't be Sunny because she was in New York for a couple of nights on business.

He grabbed the phone. "Yeah?"

"Mr. Reilly, sir, it's me, Ampara. Miss Allie's housekeeper."

Mac sat up quickly. "Yes, Ampara?"

"I'm scared, Mr. Reilly. I just noticed that the alarm system has been turned off. Now only I know where that switch is, sir, and I haven't been up in the house for the past five hours. I'm here, all alone, just me and Miss Allie's dog, and I'm scared, sir. I want to call the police, but I know Mr. Ron doesn't want no police here. I don't know what to do, sir."

"Are you securely locked in, Ampara?"

"The door is locked and bolted, and so are all the windows..."

Mac thought quickly. He knew Ampara was safe for the moment and that he needed to get there before he called the cops. If someone really had entered the main house, that person had a key and knew exactly where to turn off the alarm. He might just have his stalker.

"Stay right where you are," he told Ampara.

167

"I'll go into the house and check it myself. You won't see me from the windows because I'll turn off my lights and leave my car at the end of the driveway. I'll call you immediately I get there. Okay?"

"Okay," Ampara said doubtfully.

"And Ampara."

"Yes, sir?"

"If you hear anything at all, anyone near your apartment, if you're scared, call Security and the cops immediately."

"Yes, Mr. Reilly. I'll do that," she said, sounding relieved.

Next Mac called Lev Orenstein. He told him what was going on and arranged to meet him at the house.

Lev was there before him, his black Mustang half-hidden under an overhanging tree. Mac pulled in behind. Lev got out to meet him. He looked every inch the movie-style tough bodyguard, lean and mean and intent on business in a black turtleneck, black jeans and with a weapon tucked handily in a holster under his arm.

Mac was in his usual T-shirt with a pair of shorts he'd pulled on quickly as he leaped out of bed. Pirate sat in the car looking disconsolate at being left but was well trained enough to know not to make a song and dance about it.

"The gate is locked," Lev said. "No car parked anywhere within sight, though he may have parked near the house."

"That would be a very confident move," Mac said, on the phone again with Ampara.

168

"Oh, Mr. Reilly, it's you," she said, sounding relieved.

"Lev Orenstein and I are outside the gates. Can you open them for us, please, Ampara?"

The gates slid smoothly to the sides and Mac and Lev jogged along the grassy verge by the driveway leading to the house. Again, no car was parked outside. Except for the twin lamps illuminating the steps, the house was in complete darkness.

Mac got the housekeeper on the phone again. "Don't you usually leave lights on?"

"Yes, sir, Mr. Reilly. There's always a light in the front hall, as well as in the kitchen, and in the master bedroom. Always."

Eyebrows raised, Mac looked at Lev. "You ready?"

The front door was not locked and no alarm sounded when Mac pushed it open. He slid through, keeping to the wall with Lev right behind him. They paused for a few seconds, waiting for their eyes to adjust to the gloom, listening. There was no sound but Mac felt that someone was here. He thought of Allie, alone at night, unaware that someone had the key and the alarm number. He got the feeling she had left for France just in time.

Lev knew the house and he led the way through the vast rooms to the kitchen. The refrigerator purred and half a dozen green lights flashed the time on various appliances, enough Mac thought to cook for a restaurant. There seemed to be two of everything and sometimes three or four.

Back again in the front hall, they crept silently up the curved staircase. The big double doors at the top obviously led to the master bedroom. Mac turned the handles and pushed them open.

A sudden crash sent them spinning, weapons in hand. It had come from behind a second closed door on the right. They ran toward it, turning quickly, backs against the wall, cop-fashion, as Lev flung it open.

No one was there. Mac switched on the light. The noise they had heard was of a pile of empty hangers crashing from a shelf where they had been clumsily thrown. The clothes they had held lay in a heap on the floor. All Allie's beautiful expensive gowns, slashed to pieces. The perpetrator had done a good job. Nothing had escaped his knife.

"I guess we're too late," Mac said, switching on the lights in the bedroom. "This is an example of what he could have done to Allie."

"Jesus," Lev said, shaken because he knew and cared about her. "I'll make the bastard pay when I find him."

Mac could no longer rule out the police. The crazy guy had to be caught before he did real damage. He called the Beverly Hills PD and informed his contact there what had taken place.

Next he called Ampara, told her that the cops were on the way and that he wanted her to pack her things and move to somewhere safer.

"You have a friend? Someplace to stay?" he said. "If not, we'll get you a rental apartment for the time being."

Ampara said she had friends, she was calling

them now and she and the dog would go there.

The police arrived in minutes; they didn't mess around in Beverly Hills and Bel Air. They surveyed the mess, inspected the alarm system, brushed everything for prints, took pictures and agreed it would be better not to let this leak to the media. "Don't want to scare everybody," was what the detective in charge said to Mac, who knew him well from his guest appearances on his TV show. "What we need to do now is get in touch with Mr. Perrin and Miss Ray."

"Doesn't everybody," Mac said. "Trouble is, she's in France and nobody knows where he is."

"Probably on some tropical island drinking mai tais and getting an expensive tan," the cop said.

Mac didn't think so but he wasn't about to tell the cop that. He was just glad that Allie was away and that Ron Perrin had not been around for the main event.

Or maybe he had? It gave him something to think about.

Twenty-Seven

The next morning, Mac drove to the address Jessie Whitworth had given, on Doheny in West Hollywood. If she was home, he'd ask to speak to her about Allie. If not it would give him a chance to check her out with the apartment manager, find out if she was a good tenant, what the manager thought of her.

The apartment building was not a bad one though he guessed the apartments themselves would be on the small side, studios and one-bedrooms, most likely. Still, it looked well maintained and there was a smart new canopy over the entrance. He pressed the button that said "J. Whitworth."

There was no reply and he pressed again. When he got no answer he rang the bell for the apartment manager.

A woman answered. He told her he had seen the For Rent sign outside and was interested.

"Wait a minute, I'll be right there," she said.

She arrived in a hurry, all dressed up in a fluffy top, cropped jeans and strappy heeled sandals.

"I'm Mila. Gotta be quick," she added with a cheerful grin. "I'm late for my date."

"Sorry to bother you then," Mac said. "It's just that a friend of mine lives here. She told me how much she liked it, said she thought I would too. Jessie Whitworth's her name."

"Jessie?" Eager to show the apartment, she was already unlocking the door to 3J. She stepped aside, waving Mac through. "Wait a minute though, don't I know you from somewhere?" She looked straight at him for the first time. "Oh my God, it's *you*," she said, stunned. "Mac Reilly from the TV show."

Mac smiled. "Got it in one," he said.

"But hey, what would you—I mean a famous man like you—be wanting an apartment like this for? I mean they're nice but not in your league." She caught Mac's rueful glance and said, "Uh-uh, have I put my foot in it?"

"Well, it's really for a woman I know," Mac said. "I just don't want it broadcast around. Right?"

"Right. I mean, of course. I'm the soul of discretion, anyone here will tell you that."

"So how's Jessie anyway?" Mac asked casually. "I haven't seen her in a while."

"Jessie? Oh she and her friend left early this morning. Off on vacation. Cancún, in Mexico she told me. Lucky things."

"Yeah," Mac agreed, walking round the small apartment, opening cupboards, checking out the bathroom. "So who's her friend?"

"Elizabeth, you mean?"

"I don't think I know Elizabeth."

Mila turned out to be far from discreet; in fact she was full of chat and ready to diss anyone and everything.

"A bit haughty, I thought," she said. "Though I
173

guess she's nice enough. Tall and blond, kinda thought she was gorgeous and heading for Hollywood's hot spots. In fact she looked a bit like Allie Ray, the movie star. You know who I mean?"

Mac agreed that he did. "Cancún, eh?" he commented thoughtfully as they walked back outside. "Well, thanks for showing me the apartment, Mila. I think it's a bit small for what I wanted, but if I change my mind I'll let you know."

"Thank *you,* Mac Reilly," she said, giving him a hopeful flirtatious smile. "You can call me any time."

Back in the car, Mac got Roddy and Lev on the Bluetooth in a conference call and filled them in. "Elizabeth Windsor's a blond Allie Ray look-alike," he told them. "A copycat."

"Maybe a *jealous* copycat," Roddy said.

"And I'll bet a *dangerous* copycat," Lev agreed.

"Anyhow, she's Jessie Whitworth's roommate, and Jessie had access to the Bel Air house keys and I'll bet she also knew the code for the alarm."

"Bingo," Roddy said.

"Anyhow, the two of them left for Cancún this morning. Taking a little vacation."

"Are you sure that's their destination?" Roddy said.

"I know what you're thinking," Mac said. "But Allie's at the Hôtel du Cap. And nobody will get in there, not with all the extra security for the Film Festival. In fact, I'll call her right now and

174

tell her what's going on."

But when he called she did not answer. And when he called the Hôtel du Cap he was told Miss Ray had already left.

Twenty-Eight

Mac heard about Allie's disappearance on the car radio, driving north on PCH, on his way to the Malibu Fish Company for a quick lunch with Roddy.

The news reporter said the movie star had left the gala dinner in Mougins alone and been driven to Nice airport. She had not boarded a flight and she had not been seen since.

Since her new movie had received scathing reviews, they said perhaps Allie was simply avoiding the press. But there were also rumors about her marriage being on the rocks, and about Perrin's penchant for another woman, and after all, Allie was about to hit forty. They said there was more trouble in Allie Ray's life than the average fan knew about.

"But hey," the newscaster added with a smile in his voice, "that's Hollywood for ya. On top one minute, down the next. So? Is it goodbye, Allie Ray?"

Mac made a quick right into the parking lot then walked to the wooden shack that sold fresh fish to take out, if you were lucky enough to have a woman at home who could actually cook, that is. Otherwise you sat outdoors at scarred wooden benches and they cooked huge platters of fresh snapper or halibut, or almost any other type of sea creature, with mounds of fries that would satisfy any carb addict's soul.

He ordered the Cajun salmon sandwich, took his number and went and sat on the upper deck with a view of the beach and the pushy gulls begging for scraps and squadrons of brown pelicans zooming past, and the sun casting a golden glow. It was another beautiful day in California. Sheltered from the breeze by a clear plastic awning, he drank his Diet Coke, waiting for Roddy and thinking what to do about Allie.

He wished now that he had said yes when she'd asked him to accompany her to Cannes. But that would have been wrong, it wasn't his place to intrude on her life. Besides, it would have caused havoc with his relationship with Sunny.

He checked his watch. Twelve noon. Nine p.m. in France. He dialed Allie's cell. It rang but there was no reply. Still, her phone worked and if he knew women she wasn't going anywhere without it, so she had to be somewhere around.

He drummed his fingers on the table worried that she had not at least gotten in touch with *him*. She knew whatever happened, he was on her side.

He checked his watch again. Roddy was late. His order number was called and he loped down the wooden steps to pick it up. Biting into his Cajun salmon sandwich he called Sunny.

She was at the spa having a massage but she took his call anyway, to the annoyance of her masseur who grumbled that it ruined the whole aura. Mac could hear new age music whining in the background. He didn't understand why they always had to play Enya to soothe your soul. What was wrong with a little Bach?

"Allie's gone missing," he said, taking another bite of the salmon.

"Where's she gone?" Sunny said.

"If I knew she wouldn't be missing, would she?"

"Ohh. Right. Well, after those reviews I'm not surprised. She probably wanted to get away for a bit of peace and quiet."

"She hasn't contacted anybody."

"Not even you?"

"Right." He waited a minute then he said, "If she doesn't show up soon I might have to go and find her."

Sunny's groan rang in his ear.

"It's not what you think," he said quickly.

"That's what they all say."

"Jesus, Sunny, give me a break. The woman is missing. Her husband is missing. And his girlfriend is still waiting for him in Rome."

"How d'you know that?"

"She e-mailed me yesterday. She's panicked, doesn't know what to do."

"Isn't Demarco taking care of her? Or the Italian producer?"

"I guess so. I might have to go to Rome too. Find out what's going on there."

"I'm coming with you."

177

"Okay."

"Oh." Sunny had thought he would object. "Well, maybe I'll let you go on your own this time," she said. "I've got a job that needs my presence."

"I'll miss you," Mac said, grinning.

"Huh. Right. Of course you will. Anyway, where are you now?"

"Waiting for Roddy. Eating a Cajun salmon sandwich at the fish place on PCH. With the wind in my hair and loneliness in my heart..."

"You bastard," Sunny said. But he could tell she was laughing.

Twenty-Nine

Roddy pranced up the steps, holding a giant-size Coke and a shrimp cocktail.

Mac said, "I keep telling you, you should get Diet. You'll get fat drinking that."

"Fat? Me? I'd poison myself first!" Roddy tossed his blond head, ever the drama queen. "Anyhow you're the one who'll put on weight. Just look what you're eating." He waved a shrimp, minus cocktail sauce, in front of Mac's eyes. "Stick with me, Mac Reilly. I know what's good for you."

"I'm hoping you know something else," Mac said.

"Like who broke in and slashed all Allie's

178

frocks? I wish I knew."

"What else?" Mac asked.

"I've got all the dirt on Perrin. And trust me, it's juicy."

"Just tell me what he's been up to, business-wise."

"Okay! So. Perrin's business dealings are a very tangled web indeed. Multiple companies, multiple transfers, multiple everything. There's no way to trace where money comes from, or where it goes, though the Caymans and the Bahamas are strongly suspected. Perrin flies to both places frequently, on his own jet, always with the excuse of a fishing or gambling trip, and always in the company of half a dozen or so male friends. No women this time."

"So I guess we can assume Perrin took more with him than just his male buddies."

Roddy nodded. "Anyways, the FBI caught on to it, and Perrin found out. That's why he's a frightened man."

Mac said, "Plus Allie's attorneys are demanding a full accounting. Which obviously Perrin couldn't give. *And* he had Marisa lobbying either for marriage or money. Who really knows which? And then there's the case of the missing woman, Ruby Pearl."

"Ruby Pearl?" Roddy cocked his head inquiringly. "Sounds like the poor girl's mother was into jewelry! Am I wrong, or did I miss something?"

Mac told him the Lipski story and about his break-in at Perrin's, and that he'd seen Demarco also looking around the house.

"I can't find anything much on Demarco," Roddy said. "Except like Perrin he seems to have an awful lot of spare cash. He just built a large house in the desert y'know. A very classy area, movie folk and celebs and just plain rich folk. Our Mr. Demarco is mingling with the best."

"I'm not surprised. Which reminds me..." Mac took out his cell and placed a call to Lipski.

Lipski said, "I hope you have some satisfactory news for me, Mr. Reilly."

Mac sighed. The poor guy was desperate. "Not yet. I'm sorry, Lipski. I checked the Malibu house—absolutely zero of any interest. I'm off to France for a few days, but I'll tell you what, when I get back I'll also check out Perrin's Palm Springs place. You got the address?"

He wrote it down, said goodbye and looked at Roddy, who was looking back at him, a question in his widened eyes.

"'Scuse me?" Roddy said. *France?*"

Mac glanced at his watch. "If I move my butt I can be on the late afternoon Air France to Paris."

"Paris?"

"Then the flight to Nice. Be back in a couple of days."

"Thanks very much for telling me." Roddy turned his head away huffily. "I don't suppose you're gonna tell me *why* you're off to France."

"Allie Ray. She's gone missing."

Roddy's head swung back. His eyes opened wide. "No shit. And you're setting off on your charger. The cavalry to the rescue of the poor missing maiden?"

Mac grinned. "Darn right I am," he said.

180

Thirty

Sunny paced her condo with Tesoro nipping at her heels, demanding to be picked up, but for once her mind was not on the Chihuahua. She was wishing she had gone to France with Mac. She had recognized Allie's despair and her isolation, and was concerned about her. Women—especially famous ones—didn't just go missing. But wasn't that exactly what Allie had said about her husband, Ron? And he was missing too.

Before he left Mac had brought Sunny up-to-date on Perrin's possible money-laundering activities. Mac said Perrin had done it before and now it looked as though he was doing it again.

"Once a thief," Sunny had said and Mac had agreed she was probably right.

She stared out at the expensive boats in the marina. Maybe she would go out with a couple of her girlfriends tonight, sink a couple of martinis at one of the local bars, try a little "fine dining"...

She picked up Tesoro, who bit her hand just for the hell of it. Scowling, she walked into the bedroom to check her closet in search of something to wear.

She picked up the pair of shorts lying on the floor and put them into the laundry hamper. As she did so, a piece of paper fell out of the pocket.

Impatient, she threw it into the wastebasket.

Wait a minute though. Those were the shorts she'd worn when they'd broken into Perrin's house. And that must be the piece of paper she'd grabbed from the Hummer's side pocket.

Retrieving it, she smoothed it out. She was looking at a receipt for property taxes received from Ronald Perrin on a dwelling named the Villa des Pescadores, Nuevo Mazatlán, Mexico.

She stood for a minute, letting it sink in. Then with a yelp of joy she grabbed the Chihuahua and swung her high in the air, dancing around the room.

"I think I've got it, Tesoro," she yelled gleefully. "Like Professor Higgins in *My Fair Lady* ... I think I've got it."

If she were quick she might just get ahold of Mac at the airport. She punched in his number but his phone was turned off. He must already be in the air. She tried Roddy next, relieved when he answered. Excited, she quickly spilled out her story to him.

"Sweetie," he said patiently, "I'm in Napa Valley, wine tasting with my boyfriend. Mazatlán's a long shot, not worth ditching my weekend for. I'll be back Monday. I'll check it out then. If RP's really in Mexico we'll go together, have a few margaritas and 'bring him back alive' as they always used to say in the western movies."

Sunny got the strong feeling he wasn't taking her seriously. "But he could disappear between now and then..."

"If he's really *there*. Sweetie, we just don't *know*..."

182

She was getting nowhere. Frustrated, she said goodbye, then paced the floor some more. Time was ticking by. Anything might happen. This was too good a clue to miss. It was up to her to take the initiative, and besides she quite fancied herself in the role of girl detective. Make Mac proud of her, she thought with a grin.

Dumping the dog on the sofa she made a few quick calls, threw some clothes into a carry-on, and packed Tesoro, wailing, into her doggie travel bag. She dropped her at the posh kennel near the airport where the staff knew all Tesoro's likes and dislikes and where she knew the dog would be treated like the princess she was.

In under an hour Sunny was at the airport. She was on the trail of Ron Perrin. *She* would be the one to find him. She would find out what made RP tick and see what he knew about his missing wife.

Thirty-One

STAR CHECKS OUT ON HER NEW MOVIE—AND SO
WILL THE PUBLIC

Allie read the headline sitting in a corner of an autoroute café near the medieval walled town of Carcassonne, looming on the horizon, turreted and battlemented like the façade of a Disney theme park.

She was on her third cup of coffee and her

second croissant with a Michelin map spread across the table in front of her, trying to work out a route. But since she had no clear idea of where she wanted to go, other than simply disappear, it was proving difficult.

She glanced round the café. Nobody was taking any notice of her, everyone caught up in their own breakfast coffee. Anyhow they would not have recognized her. That first night in the small motel off the Autoroute du Soleil she had taken the scissors to her long blond hair, cutting until all that was left was a short untidy mess that she had dyed brown. Unmade-up and with her dark cropped hair and in square-framed eye-glasses she looked like a child's idea of a school-teacher. And in jeans and a baggy T-shirt, she was just another eccentric woman with a bad haircut, driving on her own through France. Nobody had even looked twice at her. It was a first in Allie's life and she liked it.

Draining the last of her coffee she went back outside to the parking lot and the baby blue Renault. Lying next to it in the shade of a tree was a dog. A large dog. It had a German shepherd-type head and a stocky Labrador body, and was shaggy furred and muddy. It looked up as she approached but did not move.

"Hi, dog," Allie said, nervously. "Or should I say, *Bonjour, chien*?"

The dog's eyes were fixed wearily on her. His tongue lolled and he panted even though he was in the shade. She wondered if somebody had dumped him. Thrown him out of their car? No longer wanted? Make it on your own, buddy, they'd probably said.

"Okay ... So ... okay," Allie said. She always said, "so okay," when she was thinking. "I guess you're hungry. You wait here. I'll be right back."

In the café only coffee was available. Lunch was served between noon and two and the rules were the rules. Since she couldn't buy the dog a steak she bought a couple of ham and cheese sandwiches from the dispenser and a bottle of water, then went into the boutique and purchased a pottery bowl with Bienvenue à Carcassonne written on it.

When she got back the dog was still there, his head sunk between his paws. He lifted his eyes and looked at her. He obviously expected nothing and was used to it being that way.

Allie knelt beside him. She poured the water into the bowl and put it in front of his nose. The dog scrambled to his feet and began to lap.

He had not, Allie guessed, had a drink for hours. Maybe even days. Unwrapping the sandwiches, she pulled out the ham and tore it into pieces. She put it on the ground in front of him. The dog took one sniff then, delicately for such a large animal, began to eat. Watching him, Allie marveled. He didn't snatch or wolf the food down. Even under stress, this was a civilized dog.

When he'd finished he sat back on his haunches, looking at her. She thought she caught a glimmer of gratitude in his soft eyes. She put out a hand and lightly touched his fur. It was harsh with ingrained dirt.

"Good boy," she said, refilling his water bowl.

She pulled the rest of the sandwich apart and put it down in front of him, watching as he devoured it.

"So. Okay then..." She gave him a farewell salute. "We're on our own, you and I, boy," she said. "I wish you good luck."

The dog regarded her gravely.

"Okay, so okay. *Au revoir, et bonne chance, chien.*" She climbed quickly into the Renault, glancing at him in the rearview mirror as she drove out of the parking lot and onto the auto-route heading north. The dog was still sitting there, his eyes fixed on the departing car.

"Okay. So it's okay," she told herself nervously for the umpteenth time. "He'll be all right. I mean, he's just a dog, somebody will find him, look after him..."

She slowed down. Cars flashed past her, their drivers hooting angrily. She was remembering Mac Reilly's story of how he'd found Pirate almost dead, and how the vet had told him that once you had saved someone's life you were responsible for their soul forever. She told herself she was a fool, crazy, mad. She was having a hard enough time getting her own life together and nobody was coming along to save *her* soul. Not Ron. Or even Mac Reilly.

She swung the Renault onto the off ramp, crossed under the motorway then re-entered going south.

Back at the autoroute café the dog was still sitting where she had left him, next to his water bowl with Bienvenue à Carcassonne painted on it.

186

The brakes squealed as she pulled up, got out and opened the passenger door. Her eyes met the dog's.

"So okay," she sighed. "Get in."

The big dog was firmly planted on the front passenger seat, eyes fixed on the road in front of him as she drove down the autoroute.

"Sit down and make yourself comfortable," Allie said, giving him a little pat.

His gaze shifted sideways. He looked at her then he slid wearily down until most of him was on the seat, the rest just sort of spilling over.

"You speak English?" she asked, surprised. He gave a little whimper.

"Ah, at least you have a voice," she said, smiling. "I don't know where we're going, you and I," she added, "but I guess from now on we're in it together."

She stopped at the next small town where she found a tiny auberge which, like many places in France, accepted dogs. The owner recommended a salon de beauté for les chiens, where they gave Allie black looks, exclaiming over the dog's condition. "Madame must take more care," the owner said frostily, until Allie explained that she had just adopted him from the side of the road.

The woman recommended a vet, and Allie told him the same story. He gave the dog a thorough examination, said he was badly nourished and had also been mistreated, probably beaten; there were wounds on his back. He gave the dog some shots, gave her an antibiotic gel for the wounds and pills for nutrition, and she bought enough

187

food for a month.

Her dog was now a different animal from the one she had picked up only hours ago. His big shepherd head lifted at a more confident angle; his coat had emerged from the bath as a silky golden brown that almost matched the color of his eyes. His big paws were manicured. His ears were clean. He had his own water bowl and a metal dish that she filled with food which he ate like a perfect gentleman, then lay quietly beside her in a nearby restaurant while she devoured her own bowl of cassoulet, the local specialty, feeding him chunks of the duck meat and sausage, which he accepted with a grateful wag of his bushy tail.

Back at the auberge her dog accompanied her upstairs to her room, nails clattering on the wooden steps, and when she had showered and climbed into bed he lay on the floor, his eyes turned her way.

"Just checking, huh?" Allie said, pleased with him.

When she woke in the night she heard him breathing quietly as he slept. She smelled the clean dog smell of him and loneliness retreated a notch. This dog was all hers and nobody would ever take him away from her. Even though he still did not have a name. She smiled. But now, neither did she.

Thirty-Two

Ron Perrin, hungover from last night's tequila, sat on the deck of the small beach villa, if such a grand word could be used to describe the desiccated concrete building built cheaply many moons ago, and that only he knew about. No one else. Not even Demarco. Or Allie. *Especially* Demarco and Allie.

The Villa des Pescadores, so called because it had once been owned by a Mexican fisherman, was his secret. It wasn't his *only* secret, but certainly now it seemed to be his best kept one.

Sometimes he thought the square ugly little house, with its yellow walls faded to a patchy butter color, was his true home. A place where a man could be alone with his thoughts, where he could be himself, and where, should he need company, all he had to do was drive into Mazatlán town and find solace in a bottle of tequila, while enjoying a local spiny lobster with a decent mariachi band to sing along with. Here, life was simple. Nobody knew him except as the eccentric gringo who kept to himself and liked his tequila.

A CD played in the background. He turned it up louder over the crash of the surf. "Will you still love me tomorrow?" Roxy Music's Bryan

Ferry sang hauntingly. Sighing, he closed his eyes to listen.

In all the years Ron had owned this place he had never brought a girl here. Or, for that matter, brought anyone. Battered and beat up, its saltillo-tiled floors cracked, its plumbing unreliable—sometimes there was water, sometimes not—and with electrical wires sticking here and there out of the walls, it was just a shack on the beach. Forget Malibu and the miniature rolling stock and the expensive art; forget Palm Springs and Bel Air and all the grand rooms and rich décor and the knick-knacks and the gardens. Here there was a terrace just wide enough for a chair and a table, on which he propped his bottle of Corona and his feet. It was the only place that soothed his soul.

He took another slug of the Corona and contemplated the waves pounding in a wall of white foam not too many yards away, thinking of the Malibu home he had shared with Allie. His love. Maybe his one true love. Maybe the love of his life.

Why was it then, he could not tell her that? Why, for fuck's sake, had he treated her the way he did? Why did he always have to show off his power and his masculinity with a series of women he didn't care for? Something was wrong with him, and it was a disease he did not know how to cure.

Sitting here, alone, in a way he never could be in Malibu, where his next-door neighbors' decks overlooked his, with phones ringing constantly, barraged with endless problems, not the least of which was the reason he was here, he tried to get that feeling of peace again. But this evening it wasn't happening.

Why couldn't it all just go away? he thought gloomily. Why couldn't he simply wipe the slate clean and start all over again? How differently he would do it now. How different he would be with Allie. He would eliminate the bitter memories and begin again, crazy in love the way he'd been when he first met her.

The sound of the waves roared in his ears and hunger made his belly rumble. Leticia usually left him food. She came in a couple of times a week to clean the place, if you could call a somnolent flicking of a broom across the tiles and a quick swigging down with a bucket of water that. Still, she did change the sheets every now and again, and she did do his personal laundry, taking it home with her and returning it the following week. Ron figured that since it took her a whole week to wash his simple shirts, her husband was probably wearing them four days while he got the other three. No matter, it wasn't worth worrying about, and people had to live, didn't they?

He put the Bryan Ferry CD on again, scrunching his eyes as if in pain, mouthing the words. "Will You Still Love Me Tomorrow."

His thoughts returned to Allie. He could see her clearly, in his mind's eye, the way she'd been when he first met her. Almost fifteen years ago now. Could it really be that long?

Anyhow, there she was, the petite blond beauty he'd seen on the screen with a skin that glowed like a ripe peach with the pink bloom still on it, and Mediterranean blue eyes that reached into his soul. He'd "recognized" not only who she was, but the person she was, in that way that happens so rarely, when a man instantly understands this woman is for him. But at the back of his mind, even though Allie had always protested that she loved him, was always the nagging worry that how could a beautiful woman like her really love a man like him: unattractive and rough around the edges?

Yet, Allie had said she did, right from that first night together. They had spent it in each other's arms in a forested snowbound log cabin in Aspen, away from all the other New Year's Eve revelers. The Bryan Ferry record had been playing then, as it played in his head now. They had been together ever since. Until lately that is, when the bitterness had risen like bile in his throat, and he had lost her and was verging on losing all his money.

A "shit" was what many called him, and Ron finally believed it was true. And that was the reason he was here, on a lonely stretch of beach outside the funky Mexican tourist town of Mazatlán, hiding from the law and from his own emotions.

This was no time to be alone. His morbid thoughts were getting the better of him. Setting down the empty beer bottle, he walked into the apology of a bathroom, took a sparse shower—water pressure was bad tonight—combed his hair back from his sunburned forehead, put on a faded old T-shirt with Mazatlán printed on the front, flowered beach shorts and flip-flops. He was ready to take on the Mazatlán nightlife.

He knew just the place: a joint on the beach where the booze flowed, the mariachi music blasted to the rafters and nobody knew him. He could get drunk there. Again. In peace.

Thirty-Three

Sunny was glad the Alaska Airlines L.A./Mazatlán flight was a quick two and a half hours. She was itching to get there and see if her theory about Ron Perrin was right.

Arriving at the airport along with the planeload of holidaymakers already in their shorts and tank tops, she picked up the rental car and asked the way to Nuevo Mazatlán.

The sun blazed from a sky as blue as any Raffaello fresco, turning the interior of the little Seat into a furnace. Hitching her skirt to her upper thighs, and gasping for breath, she turned up the air-conditioning. Sweat trickled between her shoulder blades as she drove the airport road, past humble little ranches with thin black cows in sparse fields and lumbering dogs, sniffing for scraps. Past rundown houses and auto repair shops, and cheap street cafés with plastic gauze slung overhead to keep off the sun offering *mariscos* and tacos. And past a yellow-painted school, and lavender and pink and turquoise houses.

The road rambled into the outskirts of Mazatlán, threading through congested traffic out to the marina area, bristling with new condominiums. Then over the new bridge and, at last, into the quiet countryside of Nuevo Mazatlán.

Here development petered out and the scenery reminded Sunny of Provence: stony, dotted with scrub and low-growing shrubs, and with a kind of singing silence in the air.

Following the signs, she came at last to the entrance to the Emerald Bay Hotel. A guard checked her at the gate and she drove slowly down a long avenue, turning finally in to the approach to the hotel, guarded this time by a tall aviary where bright macaws and parrots shrieked a welcome.

The lobby was centered with a large stone fountain set beneath a lofty dome, and its water music immediately cooled her. Slipping off her sandals she walked gratefully across the travertine floor and was checked in by a smiling young woman.

Ten minutes later, in a gauzy white skirt that flowed around her pretty knees as she walked, a black T-shirt and sandals, water bottle in hand, she hesitated at the door to her room. Should she call Mac? Or Roddy? Tell them what was up? She grinned. Nah! Let them wait. They'd find out later what a clever girl she had been.

The door slammed behind her as she hurried along the jungly path leading back to the entrance where her car was already waiting.

194

Pausing only to ask the concierge the names of the most popular bar-restaurants in town and directions, if any, to the Villa des Pescadores, she was on her way, she hoped, to meet the infamous Ron Perrin.

The empty road followed the long curve of the beach as she left civilization behind, or at least the resort version of it, passing small shacklike homes and makeshift outdoor bars. Children stopped their play to wave and a couple of thin brown dogs chased her tires, making her think wistfully of Tesoro, pouting, no doubt, in the fancy kennel with the sofas and cushions and doggie TV. But right now her mind was on bigger things.

As dusk settled over the empty landscape, the road seemed to wind on forever. Loneliness crept around her, almost tangible in the warm air, and for the first time she was nervous. Then suddenly, a house popped into view, right at the edge of the beach. A small square yellow box, very much the worse for wear. She slowed down to read the name painted on a rock by the sandy path leading to it. villa des pescadores.

She took another doubtful look. Could this *really* be a place the worldly, flamboyant billionaire Ron Perrin would stay? Remembering his glamorous Malibu home, she knew she must be on the wrong track. A man like that would never live here. He wouldn't even spend the night here. And neither, she thought, stumbling up the rutted path to the house, would she.

The slatted unpainted wooden door was closed. There was no bell, so she rapped, then waited, glancing anxiously round. It was getting dark and she was in the middle of nowhere. Alone. She was doing everything a woman in a foreign country was not supposed to do. *And* she was on the trail of a criminal. Who knew how he would react when she confronted him?

Uneasy, she rapped again, harder this time, waiting again, sucking on her bruised knuckles. Still no answer. She tried the door. It was not locked. In fact there was no lock.

Calling hello, she stepped inside and found herself in a single small shabby room. There was a narrow unmade bed in one corner. A lamp stood next to it. A couple of cheap woven Mexican chairs fronted the adobe corner fireplace that looked, from the blackened areas around it, as though it smoked badly. The sink and a tiled counter were piled with empty beer bottles and plates, while an open cupboard held a few shirts. Other garments spilled out of drawers in untidy heaps. An old CD player and a Bryan Ferry disc were on the table.

"Is anyone here?" she called hopefully, though she didn't see how anyone could be since there was nowhere else to go, except the primitive bathroom. She checked it, shuddering, then the terrace, if it could fancifully be called that. It overlooked the sea and, in a way, she thought wistfully, had a lot in common with Mac's own place.

Still, out on the terrace she felt the appeal of Perrin's little beach shack. The wind blew coolly through her hair and the only sounds were the thud of the sea and the cries of seabirds. Hard green waves, framed by a couple of blackened mesquite trees, pounded the long crescent of beach, then slurped noisily back again. A squadron of pelicans flew past at eye level, and hanging high in the sky were seabirds with wings like stealth bombers that reminded her of Batman.

Suddenly she understood that Perrin came here in search of peace and simplicity. And to her surprise, she found herself almost hoping he had found it.

Getting a grip, she reminded herself of her mission and also *exactly* why Perrin was here. He must have *something* to do with his wife's disappearance. She was certain he knew where Allie was. Anyhow, he was dodging the law and she was going to find out what was going on and hopefully bring him back.

Tripping over the stones on the path and wishing she had put on sneakers instead of flimsy sandals, she went back to the car. In Mazatlán town, she parked, then hailed a passing minimoke open-air taxi and asked to be taken to the Bar La Costa Marinera.

The bar was down a side street leading to the beach and it was jumping. Impressed, Sunny counted half a dozen Harleys parked outside, and the mariachi trumpets blasted her eardrums before she'd even stepped through the door.

The café was crowded with locals and holidaymakers dressed for a Saturday night out, most already into their second or third margaritas, served in massive goblets. The wooden tables were packed and brawny waiters in yellow shirts lofted enormous platters of seafood over their heads. The aromas of deep-fried red snapper, of shrimp and hot chilies and cheese nachos filled the air, and those seated on the terrace reaped the benefit of the evening breeze while devouring guacamole and spicy salsa. Telling the waiter she was looking for a friend, Sunny wended her way between tables, fending off bantering offers to come take a seat.

A mariachi troupe in tight black pants and short jackets, glittering with silver studs and sequins, were playing familiar Mexican songs very loudly. There were two girls on fiddles, their long hair swaying as they played, warm dark eyes smiling, while an old man hefted the traditional huge Mexican bass. Plus there were four guitars and two trumpets. Sunny stopped to listen, applauding with the others.

In a far corner of the terrace the Harley bikers sat at a big round table, arms around each other's shoulders. Sunny watched disapprovingly as they poured tequila shots down their throats. Bottles of Tecate and Corona littered the table and huge platters of lobsters and rice and beans were being delivered. Sunny hoped they were not riding those bikes home.

She wasn't the only one watching. At his lonely corner table, Ron Perrin sank another tequila shot followed by a slug of beer from a bottle topped with a crescent of fresh lime. The bikers yelled to the mariachis to play "Guadalajara."

"Guadalajara," Perrin yelled with them. It was his favorite.

Sunny turned to see where the American voice came from. And there he was. The rugged, beetle-browed billionaire mogul in a pair of flowered bathing shorts and an old Mazatlán T-shirt.

"Guadalajara," Perrin began to sing along in Spanish, in a firm tenor voice, and the waiters crowded round, joining on the chorus. Ron knew every word and brought it to a fine Mexican-style yipping finale, taking a bow at the applause and whoops of acclaim when he'd finished.

Sunny threaded her way toward him. His head was lowered now and he stared somberly into his glass.

"Ron Perrin," she said.

It was not a question, it was a statement, and he knew it. He lifted his head and looked at her with those molten brown puppy-dog eyes.

"Aw fuck," he groaned, reaching for the bottle. "I'm busted."

Thirty-Four

Perrin did not invite her to join him, but Sunny pulled back a chair anyway and sat down. Her soft white skirt ruffled around her pretty knees and she noticed that Perrin noticed that. He was still the ladies' man, even in a moment of crisis.

Perrin raised his hand to summon a waiter. "What would you like?" he asked, polite despite the circumstances.

"Mango margarita, rocks, no salt," Sunny told

the waiter.

"Are you crazy? Whoever heard of anyone drinking a *mango* margarita?"

"Obviously you haven't traveled in the right circles, Mr. Perrin. Mango margaritas are very popular."

"Hah! I prefer my tequila straight."

"So I notice."

They stared silently across the table, taking each other in. Even though Perrin was drunk, Sunny thought he had an oddly magnetic personality, forceful, drawing you toward him with soft brown eyes that were in complete contradiction to his supposedly tough character. Yet she knew this was a man of steel, a man who did battle in the boardrooms of the world, a dangerous man nobody ever said no to. Except his wife.

"So who the hell are you anyway?" Perrin demanded. "You're not the cops, not the FBI..."

"Is that who you were expecting?"

The waiter brought Sunny's margarita. Her throat was parched by the hot dusty drive and she sipped it through a straw, eyes raised to watch Perrin.

"You're a beautiful woman," he said, avoiding her question. "I came here to get away from that."

"Seems you succeeded." She took another long sip. The trouble with mango margaritas was you could almost forget there was tequila in there. Two and it crept up on you like rocket fuel. Suddenly hungry, she waved the waiter over again and ordered nachos.

"You don't need to worry about your figure

then," Perrin said.

Sunny tried to assess if he was coming on to her, but decided he wasn't, though his eyes still admired her. He seemed suddenly more sober.

"And you speak perfect Spanish," he added.

"My father's Mexican. Other than my grandmother, I make the best tamales you've ever tasted. And since Abuelita wasn't fat, I'm hoping I inherited her genes as well as her recipes."

The nachos arrived: steaming-hot refried beans and cheese on crispy tortilla chips. Sunny dived right in. "Go ahead," she said to Perrin. "Try them, they're good." She stopped in midbite. *What was she doing? This was the enemy, her "prey," and she was acting like they were friends out on a dinner date.* She took another slurp of the margarita and said, "So, anyway, what are *you* doing here, Mr. Perrin?"

He grinned at her, brows beetling. "Well, darn it, I thought you must know. Otherwise why are you here?"

"We're going round in circles," she said, and found herself smiling back at him. She had to admit again that Ronald Perrin had a certain charm. She was meant to be the interrogator, doing Reilly's job, and here she was schmoozing. "Anyway," she said briskly, "I came here specifically to find you. We need to talk."

"So how *did* you find me?"

"The tax receipt in your Hummer for the Villa des Pescadores."

"Should have shredded that," he said with a sigh. "I just couldn't get around to everything, there wasn't time. Anyhow, what were you doing in my Hummer?"

Sunny blushed. "Oh God, now I have to confess," she said, lowering her eyes to avoid his gaze.

"So?" He was waiting for an answer.

"I guess you'd call it 'breaking and entering,'" she said with a sigh. "We were looking for clues."

"Clues to what?"

She glanced up, uncertain. This conversation had gone all wrong. Wasn't she meant to be the interrogator?

She avoided his question. "Don't worry, we didn't find any, except the tax receipt."

They stared silently at each other across the table. Perrin downed his tequila.

"How about that train set?" she said.

He shrugged. "I grew up too poor to have a train set. Call it the child in me."

Sunny smiled back at him, understanding.

"You still have not told me who you are," he said.

"My name is Sunny Alvarez," she said. And to her astonishment he offered his hand across the table.

He held it fractionally longer than necessary, looking deep into her eyes. Then he said, "And exactly who *is* Sunny Alvarez? With the Mexican father and a grandmother who makes the best tamales in town?"

"I'm Mac Reilly's—" Sunny stopped herself quickly from saying *fiancée,* because of course she wasn't, and *girlfriend* sounded too cute. "Assistant," she substituted at the last second.

"I should have known. I asked him to work for me. He turned me down. If he hadn't, maybe I wouldn't be in the fix I'm in now," he added bitterly.

"And exactly what *fix* is that?" Sunny knew she had him nailed. He would tell her everything now.

Instead he summoned the waiter to bring a second mango margarita.

"So, what *really* brings you here?" He gave her that beetling glance.

"Allie Ray," she said simply.

Perrin stared silently into his glass. "Don't tell me you're here to serve me with a subpoena," he said, suddenly turned to ice.

She shook her head. "And don't *you* tell me, Ron Perrin, that you don't know Allie is missing."

Perrin lifted his eyes. He stared at her, his face suddenly devoid of expression.

"You must know she disappeared from the Cannes Film Festival," Sunny prompted. "I thought you'd know where she's gone."

He seemed to pull himself together. "Why should I know where Allie goes these days? She's her own woman."

He was playing it cool but Sunny sensed a thread of despair in the slump of his shoulders, in the suddenly-tired face and the blank eyes that were not willing to show his true feelings. Could he really not know where his wife had gone?

"You care though, don't you?" she said softly.

He lifted a dismissive shoulder again. If he was shocked by the news of his wife's disappearance he wasn't going to talk about it.

"What does it matter? She's going her way, I'm going mine." He called for another tequila and sank it down, then poured the Corona down his throat. "Anyhow, you're not here to talk about caring. You're here to make some kind of deal."

"She's not the only woman missing," Sunny said. "What about Ruby Pearl?"

He stared at her, obviously surprised. "Ruby was a secretary. She helped me out for a couple of weeks. I don't know where she went after that."

"And then there's Marisa. She's still in Rome and still waiting to hear from you. She showed us the canary diamond engagement ring you gave her—no small diamond either, my friend. She told us you'd promised to marry her." She looked hard at him. "She's worried, Ron."

Frowning, he ran a hand through his receding brown hair. "I never talked 'love' or marriage to Marisa. That ring was a token. She admired it in a shop window so I bought it for her. It gave her pleasure, but it was not an engagement ring. Hey, I'm still a married man," he added.

"Pity you didn't think of that before you started an affair."

Perrin leaned in to her across the table. "Let's get this straight, Sunny Alvarez," he said. "Marisa was under no illusions, despite what she said to you about an 'engagement' ring. She knew the score and I wasn't the first rich guy she'd hung out with. Marisa is one savvy chick."

"She also said you were into S and M sex."

"She said *what*?" His face was blank with

204

shock. "That's crap."

"I thought she was lying. I even thought she might be planning a bit of blackmail. You know the kind of thing—she'd sell her story to the tabloids unless you came through. And anyway, what happened that night in Malibu when Mac heard her scream? She *was* there, even though you denied it."

"Okay, so she was there. I just didn't want the world to know about it. Can you blame me? I'm a married man. What happened was, I was at a meeting. She'd gone to the Malibu house to wait for me, said she heard footsteps, got scared. Then Reilly came bursting through the door."

"So she shot him."

"Not exactly."

"She tried."

He lifted his shoulder in a dismissive shrug. "A strange guy comes through your window at midnight you'd shoot him too."

"So why were you with Marisa anyway?" Sunny was suddenly curious. There was more to this strange man than met her eyes and she wanted to dig deeper, find out what he was all about beneath that tough-guy layer, stripped of the glamour of power in his ridiculous flowered shorts and old T-shirt.

He gave her a long dark look. "You want the truth?" he said quietly. "It's love gone wrong. That's all, Sunny Alvarez. *It's love gone wrong.*"

He slumped over the table and put his head in his hands. "Allie doesn't love me anymore. That is if she ever did," he added. "Can I blame her? Of course not. And wouldn't most men in the world have liked to be Mr. Allie Ray? You bet they would. It was what I wanted more than anything, more than all the money, the houses, the possessions, the power. I wanted Allie and now I've lost her. And in answer to your question, Miss Detective, I'm here at my little hangout trying to find my soul again."

Sunny stared at him, stunned into sympathy. She gulped back the tears that threatened. "I'm so sorry," she whispered.

"I've never had a woman feel sorry for me before," Perrin said. "And I don't know that I like it." He lumbered to his feet, swaying slightly. "I'm tired," he said. "That's why I'm talking too much. I've gotta go."

He thrust his hand in his pocket and gave the waiter a sheaf of pesos. "That'll take care of it," he said. And ignoring Sunny, he made for the exit. She followed him out into the street. "How did you get here?"

He searched in his pocket for the car keys. "Drove of course."

"Hah! Well you're certainly not driving now. Not with all that tequila in you."

"Are you implying I'm drunk?" He asked the question with all the pompousness of the inebriated.

"I sure am, Ron Perrin." Sunny hailed a cruising cab. She opened the door and pushed him inside. "Take him home," she told the driver, and she gave him directions.

Slumped in the backseat, Perrin looked at her from under drooping lids. "I'll bet you're in love with Mac Reilly," he said. "A woman like you,

206

you could twist any man round your finger."

"I wish," she replied, smiling. Then, "Look, I'm coming over to see you tomorrow morning. We'll talk some more."

"What about?"

"Well, you know, like about money laundering," she said, then immediately wished she hadn't. "And maybe about love," she added, softening the blow. She slammed the door shut and stood, watching the cab drive down the side street then turn left at the corner, out of sight.

There was no doubt in her mind that Ron Perrin was still in love with his wife. And no doubt he was in trouble. Tomorrow she would see what she could do to help.

The next morning, Sunny was up early. She took a walk along the beach, enjoying the fresh clean air and the early warmth of the sun, watching pelicans drop like dive-bombers into the sea, emerging with glittering silvery fish in their beaks.

She took her own breakfast on the terrace: deep dark coffee with sweet rolls that this morning tasted as good as any she had ever eaten. Then she ordered a thermos of coffee to go and she drove slowly over to Perrin's place.

She knocked on the door but there was no reply. She turned the handle and pushed it open. "Hi, it's me, Sunny," she called. "I brought you some coffee, thought you might need it."

Putting the thermos on the table, she glanced around. The room was empty. The terrace was bare. And the Bryan Ferry CD lay broken in two on the table.

Her heart sank. She wasn't bringing Perrin home in triumph to Mac after all.

Thirty-Five

It was hot in Cannes and Mac drove with the top down on the rental Peugeot, hoping the slight breeze would blow away the cobwebs of jet travel. He checked in at the Hôtel Martinez and went directly to the concierge to ask about limo services.

Armed with a complete list of those in the area, he went to his room, showered and ordered room service breakfast, even though it was one in the afternoon. He pulled on a pair of shorts and sat on his little terrace enjoying the sea view and thinking about Allie.

He had no doubt she had run away from life as she knew it. She'd had enough of being a movie star, enough of being second woman to her philandering husband, enough of the glamour and the riches of the Hollywood lifestyle. Basically, she was a simple woman who, as she had confessed to him, had never felt at home in her skin, and never felt part of the scene in which she played such a major role. Allie wanted her privacy back. She wanted to be anonymous.

He'd had Sunny e-mail the last pictures of Allie, taken at the Festival. She looked beautiful and serene, doing her job, posing for the press and waving to the fans. He thought there was nowhere she could go and not be recognized. She would have to have some sort of disguise, somehow change her look.

He drank the freshly squeezed orange juice that tasted like sunshine in a glass and ate the eggs scrambled with wild mushrooms, still thinking about her.

The most obvious thing would be to cut off her hair. He winced at the thought. Allie's hair was one of her signature features: thick, shiny and naturally blond. Of course then she would need to dye it. She'd go for a simpler look, jeans and T-shirts probably, and she would have to wear glasses. At least if he were in charge of her disguise, that's what she would do. And even then he wasn't sure it would work. Most certainly she would have to leave the glitzy parts of the South of France behind, probably head north, into the countryside.

Taking out the Michelin map he'd picked up at Nice airport, he studied the main routes. One led to Provence and the Luberon, an area filled with movie people, writers and vacationing socialites. The others led toward Toulouse and the west, or north via Agen. Sighing, he folded up the map. France was even bigger than he had thought.

Taking out his list of limo services he began systematically to call each one, trying to locate the service assigned to take Allie to the Festival. He got lucky on the fourth try. Telling the limo company manager he would be right over, Mac threw on a shirt and sandals and drove to the outskirts of Cannes.

The manager was suspicious. "We have already been hounded by too many reporters, monsieur," he said coldly. "We never talk to them about our clientele."

"I work for Madame Ray, I am involved with her security." Mac showed him his card. "I would like to speak to the driver who took her to the airport."

As it happened the man was about to show up for work, and Mac waited under the manager's frowning gaze for him to arrive. When he did, Mac stood up and greeted him warmly, shaking his hand and calling him *"mon ami."* It didn't go down too well. The driver was definitely not his "friend"; he was standoffish, worried that he might be in some kind of trouble. He was a short man with a big nose and beady eyes that stared sullenly at Mac.

"All I need to know is where you dropped Madame Ray, and what she did next," Mac said.

The driver, whose name was Claude, said he had no authority to talk to anyone about Madame Ray and had not said a word to reporters. Mac had to go through his spiel all over again and though still reluctant the driver finally spoke.

"Madame Ray is not a missing person," he said nervously. "There has been no report to the police of her being 'missing.' The cops are not involved."

"True," Mac agreed, knowing he was probably the only person now who might raise questions about Allie's whereabouts. But he still thought she was a runaway and he didn't want the police on her trail.

"I dropped her at Departures," Claude said. "She was dressed up for the Festival, but when she got out she had on a sweater and a hat pulled over her hair. She wore dark glasses. She didn't even let me get her bag—just one small valise. She took it herself. She gave me a good tip, thanked me..." He shrugged. "And that, monsieur, was that."

"Did you watch her go?"

"For a minute, yes. She went straight inside, heading I supposed for check-in. I don't know where she was going, monsieur. That's all I know."

Mac sighed. It had not gotten him much further. All he had was Allie in place, in semi-disguise, at Nice airport on the night she disappeared. She might have done anything after leaving the limo, taken a taxi to the train station for instance, or rented a car.

Thanking Claude, he drove from Cannes back to the airport in Nice, where he found all the flights that had left late that night and their destinations. Next he went to Arrivals and checked out the rental car agencies. None of them had any record of Allie Ray renting a car.

Stymied, and knowing he had wasted his time, he drove back to the hotel. There was an e-mail from Sunny. "Off on a little trip of my own," it said. "I'll call you when I get back."

Of course he called her right away. There was no reply. Mac sighed. The women in his life were giving him trouble. He wondered what Sunny had been up to now.

Thirty-Six

Allie circumnavigated Toulouse, panicked by the spaghetti junction of motorways with signs reading Barcelona, Bordeaux, Paris. She didn't want to go to any of those places.

Sandwiched between cars whose confident French drivers were mostly on the phone, she honked at them furiously, then slid the baby blue car between them, putting her foot down and scattering them honking behind her.

The road sign now said Agen so she guessed that's where she was going. It took longer than she had thought and she was weary of driving. She wanted somewhere rural with fields and trees and maybe even little bubbling streams, the tourist's dream of the French countryside.

The dog snuffled gently in his sleep as she headed north toward Bergerac, through the small town of Castillonnès, where she stopped for a cup of coffee and to walk the dog, and also to ask directions to the scenic route.

Back in the car, she drifted farther into the countryside. Soon emerald green fields rolled away on either side, with caramel-colored cows browsing in the shade of ancient chestnut trees. A small river slid lazily through, making eventually for the big splashy Dordogne. Rocky paths led into hills topped with mysterious turreted castles. Horses grazed in verdant paddocks and long white avenues lined with fluttering poplars led to small peaceful châteaux, while farms with slatted wooden barns looked as though they had been there for centuries.

There was a sudden loud squawking and Allie stomped on the brakes. A bunch of rusty-feathered chickens stood at the gate to a farm, clucking aggrievedly at her. The dog stuck his head out the window to watch as a gigantic rooster stepped into the road. The rooster glanced both ways. Then, squawking and flapping his wings, he sent his harem scurrying back to the gate, out of the way of a small car rushing down the lane in a cloud of dust. The rooster waited till the car was gone, then stepped out into the road again. Again he looked both ways. Getting the all clear, he marched his fluttering flock safely across the road and into the field beyond.

Allie grinned, amazed. She hadn't realized French chickens had road sense. And now her mouth was watering at the thought of a fresh omelet. She pressed on, looking for a place to stay, hopefully near a restaurant.

Quite by accident she found exactly what she was looking for in the back roads around the medieval stone village of Issigeac, where she'd stopped to fill up the car. A red-haired woman was the only other customer and, gathering her courage and adjusting her hat and her dark glasses, Allie asked in nervous French whether she knew a place to stay.

"Why yes," the woman told her, speaking in

English. "My friend Petra's B & B is just down the road." She gave her directions, told her it was reasonable and that Petra had also recently opened a small restaurant.

"It sounds like heaven," Allie exclaimed, smiling.

The woman gave her a penetrating look. "Well, not exactly heaven, but if you've come on a long and difficult journey, it might be exactly what you're looking for."

"Thank you." Allie turned away.

"By the way," the woman said, "my name's Red Shoup."

"Hi." Allie hesitated. Then for the first time she said, "I'm Mary Raycheck."

The woman nodded, still looking quizzically at her. "Be sure to tell Petra I sent you," she said, getting into her car. She took a card from her bag and gave it to her. "Here's my number," she said. "If I can be of any help, give me a call."

Allie watched as she drove away. Did Red Shoup suspect who she was? Or was she just seeing a troubled-looking woman with an unnaturally quiet and far too big a dog, roaming around France on her own?

She got back in the car and following Red's directions found herself crunching up a gravel driveway to a small manor house surrounded by clumps of shade trees, under which more cows lazed. A couple of black and white Border collies raced toward the car, and her own no-name dog cowered worriedly back. The front door was flung open and a tall, plump blonde dressed in what appeared to be a red satin nightgown flew

214

down the short flight of steps toward her.

"Bonsoir, ma chérie," she called in French strongly laced with Brit. "Are you the one looking for a room? Red Shoup just called to say you were on your way. And your dog too. No need to be afraid of this couple of old collies, all they want is to chase sheep. Not that there's many of them here, but we had them on the farm back in Wales, y'know. So come on, darlin', let's have you out of there. I have the best room in the house for you."

Petra stopped her onslaught of words and beamed at Allie, still sitting in the car, stunned by the fiftyish blond and scarlet vision peering shortsightedly back at her.

"I still don't know your name, love," Petra said.

"Oh. Right. It's Mary. Mary Raycheck."

"That's unusual. Polish, is it?"

"Originally, I think so. And you must be Petra."

Allie got out of the car and they shook hands. She put the dog on a lead then walked with her new landlady into the house.

"I'm Petra Devonshire. Posh name for a bit of all right like me, eh?" She nudged Allie, laughing. "Used to be a dancer, TV variety shows, touring musicals, that sort of thing, though everybody said I was more the Benny Hill type. Y'know the one always being chased around the garden in fishnets and a garter belt. Anyway, somehow I ended up here. Remind me to tell you the story, love, one of these nights when we've nothing better to do than natter over a glass of wine."

Petra had not yet stopped for breath and Allie had no desire to stop her. She was charmed with Petra's free-flowing barrage of information, enchanted by her free-form lifestyle, amazed by her uninhibited red satin nightie at four in the afternoon, and by her invitation to hear her life story over a glass of wine.

"Follow me, darlin'." Petra twitched her way up a broad staircase lined with family portraits. "None of 'em's mine," she explained. "They all came with the house." She flung open a door at the top of the stairs. "Best room in the place, love. How does this suit you?"

Dazzled, Allie looked at the gilded Empire bed upholstered in threadbare blue damask; at the battered old pine armoire and the ornate dressing table with three blotchy mirrors and a pair of silver candle sconces; at the fluffy white sheep-skin rug and the lavish once-red satin curtains now faded to a pale pink. A tiled fireplace domi-nated one wall, fronted by a sagging sofa whose flowered chintz bulged at the seams, and a massive gilt mirror looked down over all. On a red tray on the table in front of the big window was a coffeepot and the fixings, and a door led into a blindingly white new bathroom with a plastic shower cubicle barely big enough to hold a grown-up.

All memories of Allie's lavish three-thousand-square-foot boudoir in Bel Air disappeared in an instant. "Petra," she breathed, a hand clutched to her chest. "I love it. You may never get rid of me."

Petra's raucous laugh mingled with her own. "That's good," she said. "Because I could use the money. Now make yourself at home, then come down and join me for a cup of tea. And please, love, take off that awful hat. It doesn't suit you. You'll find plenty of straw hats hanging on the rack in the front hall. I'll be in the kitchen when you're ready."

She disappeared in a flurry of red satin, completely uninhibited about being caught in her lingerie.

Allie walked to the window, opened it and stuck her head out. There was no traffic noise; no sirens; no stalkers. A breeze set the leaves of nearby poplars rustling softly, a cow mooed in the distance and the two Border collies chased each other around the meadow at the bottom of the drive. She could see a horse, black and glossy, nibbling the grass, and a couple of old bicycles lay cast to one side by the front steps, where twin urns held a tumble of geraniums in every color of red, and the fragrance of jasmine twining up the old stone walls mingled with the faint tang of hay.

She sighed happily. Could she have found Paradise at last?

Thirty-Seven

After Allie had showered and changed into a pair of black jeans and a white linen shirt, she walked downstairs, smiling as she passed a suit of armor standing guard draped with a magenta feather boa.

She found Petra in the kitchen, a long room with the kind of plasterwork known as *columbage,* creamy plaster set between a pattern of small beams. Cupboards lined two of the walls while tall windows, inset here and there with stained glass, occupied another. A planked wooden table took up most of the room, big enough to seat at least twenty. On it was piled folded laundry and a basket of knitting wools complete with two sleeping orange kittens. There was an enormous half-finished jigsaw puzzle of the Dordogne countryside and an old radio blasting the latest French hits, several mixing bowls and chopping boards, pottery mugs and plates, together with various magazines and a scattering of papers.

Rickety side tables held tottering piles of books, and coats were thrown over armchairs in front of the enormous fireplace, as if the owners had come in and simply left them there until the next time they were needed. The kitchen door stood open, letting in the breeze and the smell of the countryside.

In the middle of the chaos, Petra, serene, with a pink negligee over her red satin nightie, was fixing tea in a large serviceable brown pot.

"Somehow it always tastes better from a brown pot," she told Allie, pouring boiling water over the tea leaves then clearing a space at the table by leaning her arm along it and shifting the nearest pile to one side.

"There you are, love, you'll be gasping, I'll bet. And here's good English biscuits. McVitie's chocolate digestives. And what about the doggie? What's his name anyway?"

"He doesn't have a name."

Petra's shocked blue eyes were ringed with black and fringed with heavy mascara. "How can that be? We *all* have names, love, even if it's just to differentiate one from the other. I mean, what do *you* call him?"

Allie thought. "Dog dear," she said. "That's all I've called him. So far anyway."

"Well there you are then. Dog Dear he is. Dearie for short. How's that name suit you, old love?" she added, bending to take the newly named Dearie's muzzle in her hand. "I can tell, you're a good dog," she said gently. "You take care of your mum, then. That's your job. All right?" Aiming a critical look at Allie, she added, "Besides, she looks as though she needs it."

Allie took a gulp of the hot tea, burning her throat. She met Petra's mascaraed blue gaze. "Do I look that bad?"

"That haircut's a killer. Whatever possessed you?"

Allie hid her face behind the big blue mug of tea. "Necessity."

Petra nodded. "I've been there myself. A couple of times." She poured milk into her tea from a cow-shaped white jug then added three heaped spoons of sugar, stirring vigorously. "Man trouble was it?"

Allie put her head in her hands, suddenly filled again with despair.

"I left my husband," she said in a whisper so that Petra had to lean toward her to hear. "Or rather he left me. I'm getting a divorce."

Petra sucked in her cheeks and her breath noisily. "Ah, that's bad."

"There was another woman."

"That's even worse!"

"Then he disappeared. Nobody knows where he is."

"Trying to skip out on the alimony, is that it?" Petra heaved a sigh that sent her ample bosom a-tremble. "Men," she groaned. "They never know how good they've got it until it's too late. Trust me, love, if he's got any sense—and since he married you in the first place, I have to credit him with that—he'll come running back, begging you on his knees to let him come home."

"Is that what happened to you then?"

Petra took a biscuit and dunked it into the mug. "I love it when the chocolate melts," she said. "And yes. It did. Twice, in fact."

They were silent as she ate the English cookie, obviously enjoying it.

"So did you take him—both of them—back then?"

Petra's laugh filled the kitchen. "Of course I didn't. I was already on to the next bastard by then. Never could pick 'em, love. Just wasn't in my genetic makeup. Ah well, four husbands and numerous lovers later, here I am on my own again. And I have to admit I'm kind of enjoying it. Though there is a gent I have my eye on. The local squire in fact. Owns a big vineyard hereabouts; tall, dark, good looking. You should see him astride a horse. It turns a girl's knees to jelly."

She threw a penetrating glance Allie's way. "Actually, you're probably more his type than I am. Classier, you know what I mean? Except for the haircut. We have to let our local hairdresser loose on you, see what she can do to tidy it up. Give yourself a break, Mary, just because your marriage is on the rocks doesn't mean you have to let yourself go, now does it?"

Allie recalled standing on the red carpet in Cannes being photographed for the world's press, and she smiled. Her disguise seemed to have worked, even if she did look like hell.

Petra pushed both hands down on the table and heaved herself to her feet, startling the two sleeping orange kittens, who tumbled meowing out of the knitting basket. Rummaging in the table's chaos, Petra found a bowl and filled it with milk from the cow jug.

Just then the two collies bounded through the open door, leaping up to sniff the kittens, who cowered back for a second, then went on calmly lapping. Dearie watched the other dogs nervously, looking ready to run. He turned his big head to look at Allie, and she smiled and gave him a pat and said it was okay.

"Peace reigns," Petra said. "And now, my love, I have to get dressed. My restaurant opens at six and I haven't even started the pastry for the beef Wellingtons." She raised a questioning eyebrow at Allie. "You ever make a beef Wellington? No? Well then don't bother. I don't know what inspired me to try it but I can assure you it's a bitch to get right. Still, nothing ventured, nothing won is what I always say. And this is a fairly new business so I have to offer something a bit different, don't I?"

She made for the door, turning to look again at Allie. "You want to come along, Mary? You must be hungry, though you don't have to order the Wellington. There's simpler stuff on the menu." She hesitated. "Unless you have other plans, of course."

"No! Oh, no. I have no plans." Allie had no plans for her entire life. She was free-falling and right now she wanted to do it in the company of Petra Devonshire.

"You wanna help then? Or are you going to be a customer?"

"Oh, I'll help. I can be a waitress, washer up, anything you like."

"Right. Here's an apron. Put it on, love, and let's get going."

"Can Dearie come too?"

Petra eyed the dog, who was now up on his feet and practically glued to Allie's side.

"Doesn't look like we have much choice, does it?" she said with a cheerful grin.

Thirty-Eight

The Bistro du Manoir turned out to be a small converted stone barn. A graveled pathway led to it, just wide enough for two cars to pass, with a sandy parking area to one side. The front entrance was protected from the elements by a gorgeous fluted glass canopy similar to the art nouveau ones found at some Paris Métro stations, and which Petra told Allie she'd had copied by a local glassmaker.

A spacious flagged pergola shaded by a hundred-year-old wisteria, dripping with purple blossoms, wrapped around the back, where tall French doors stood open to the warm night air. Candles flickered on rosy tablecloths, and the zinc bar was already being propped up by a few die-hard locals who looked very much at home.

"Evening, all," Petra said, floating fast through the room, like a comet with Allie at her sparkling tail. "Jean-Philippe," she called to the bartender. "Don't send those boys out of here drunk, okay? We don't want any accidents."

"Nobody's drunk," grumbled one of the younger customers.

"Fine. Great. Just don't do it here." Petra continued on to the kitchen, grinning as she heard him ask aggrievedly why they even bothered coming here when she didn't want them to drink.

Petra rammed the small bunches of flowers she'd picked from the garden into low glass vases, handed them to Allie and told her to put them on the tables. Then she put her to work brewing up a ratatouille, chopping courgettes and eggplant, onions, garlic and tomatoes, after which she showed her how to make salad dressing, using the good olive oil from Azari in Nice, while she went to start her pastry.

She introduced Allie to Caterine, the teenage girl slowly washing lettuce at the sink, and to her temporary assistant, another Brit, who was preparing chicken for a fricassee, amongst a dozen other things.

All at once Allie found herself doing at least two jobs at once. There was no time to think. Customers were arriving and before she knew it she was discarding her work apron and wrapping herself in a starched white waiter's one and was out there taking orders.

To her astonishment the first customer was Red Shoup, glamorous in a flowing Pucci shirt.

"Ohh, hi," Allie said, smiling a welcome, pencil poised over her pad, ready to write their drinks order.

"Well hello! Petra's put you to work already, has she?" Red laughed. "I should have warned you, she does that to all her B & B guests. Tells them it's 'life experience.'"

"And they fall for it every time," the handsome, silver-haired mustached man with Red said, holding out his hand. "I'm Jerry Shoup. And you must be Mary Raycheck. Red told me all about you."

"I didn't know there was that much to tell."

"Don't worry," Red said. "I told him about the dog. And about the haircut."

"Oh God!" Allie put a worried hand up to her cropped locks. "It was one of those mad moments. My husband had gone off with another woman. It was a kind of retaliatory thing."

"Well, it kind of 'retaliated' on you." Red laughed. "But no need to worry, our local hairdresser will sort you out."

"That's what Petra said. And I can't thank you enough for sending me to her. The Manoir is wonderful, so full of surprises."

"Yeah, well, Petra's known for taking in the waifs and strays," Jerry said. "Not that you are in that category, Mary." He too gave her a long considering glance. "In fact, far from it, I suspect."

Made nervous by his penetrating look, Allie asked about what she could get them to drink, writing their order of a bottle of local red quickly onto her pad.

"I'll be right back," she promised, whisking quickly away, starched apron crackling.

"Excuse me?"

She glanced to her left and saw a man sitting with a tall slender blonde at a table on the terrace just outside the French windows.

"Could we get a bottle of Badoit, please, and two vodka tonics?"

"Of course." Allie made a quick note of their order and the table number, though they were as yet only the second to arrive. "With lemon?"

"Lime, please," the blonde said. In her little

white fitted linen jacket, black tank top and black linen pants, her blond hair pulled back, she looked the epitome of simple elegance.

"Thank you. Yes, of course." Managing a quick smile, Allie hurried back to the bar, placed her order then dashed into the kitchen to alert Petra that the Shoups were here plus an unidentified dark-haired man with a blonde.

"Oh, that'll be Robert Montfort, the local squire. Remember I told you he was dishy. And that's his latest girlfriend, from Paris." She heaved a sigh. "Somehow they are always from Paris."

"She's beautiful," Allie said, heading back to the bar to pick up her orders.

"So is he." Petra's voice floated after her.

Jean-Philippe, the bartender and would-be sommelier, had already set up the bottle of red for the Shoups and when Allie took it out to them the "dishy" squire was standing next to their table, chatting to them.

She hurried past with their vodkas. She placed one carefully in front of the blonde, who was alone at the table. "I've brought extra ice and extra lime, just in case," she said.

The woman nodded. *"Et bien, mademoiselle,"* she said, staring at her. Then switching to English. "Haven't you and I met before?"

Allie thought nervously the woman did seem vaguely familiar. "Oh, no. No, I don't think so. I only arrived today. I'm a guest at Petra Devonshire's B & B."

"Of course you are." The squire was back, looking at her with dark blue eyes under lowering brows. His black hair was brushed back from a widow's peak and his lean face had the hard tanned look of an outdoorsman. "Petra always takes in the attractive ones," he said, making Allie blush. "Despite the hair," he added, and he and the blonde burst into laughter.

Allie hurried back to the kitchen and told Petra what they had said.

"Robert's like that." Petra wrapped a fillet of beef, swathed in pâté, inside a lump of pastry. "There, let's hope the bloody thing doesn't come out looking like an underdone sausage or an overcooked rattlesnake," she said, cutting a series of little V-shaped slits in the pastry then brushing it with a beaten egg mixture. "To add a nice brown glaze," she informed Allie, who was watching interestedly.

"Anyhow, you be careful with her. She's something to do with TV. A journalist. One of those nosey parkers who likes to dig up scandal and gossip about celebrities for the delectation of we plebeian folk with nothing better to do than watch her. Not that she would find anyone to talk about here. Unless it's Robert, of course. Red told me she'd 'set her cap' at him, as the saying goes."

She wiped her hands on a kitchen towel and surveyed her kitchen. "Okay, love, better get out there and start taking orders. The tables are already filling up. Tell them the night's special is the beef Wellington and that it's very good. And remember to keep your fingers crossed behind your back as you say it."

Back outside Allie cast a wary eye at the blond

TV journalist. She was leaning across the table, deep in conversation with Petra's "dishy" squire. They looked as though they didn't need to be disturbed by a waitress asking for their order, and still nervous of the woman's probing question, she decided to ask Jean-Philippe if he would take it instead, since she now had to run around catching up with six more tables that had suddenly filled up.

"That's the way it is, everybody always comes at once," Jean-Philippe told her. "Better get used to it."

Allie rushed from one table to the next, distributing menus, mentioning the night's special, taking drinks orders, then hurrying to the bar to get them filled.

Too soon, Petra was poking her head out of the kitchen and yelling, "Chef here. Or have you all forgotten? The first orders are bloody well ready so get a move on, Mary."

Allie had not worked so hard since the last week of her filming, when she'd had to be dragged by a runaway horse. She'd insisted on doing her own stunts and her body had ached for weeks after, but it had given her the same kind of personal satisfaction she felt now.

By ten-thirty most diners were finished and already drifting away, while others were on to dessert. The squire and his girlfriend were still ensconced beneath the wisteria bower and looked ready to spend the night there, when Petra emerged from the kitchen, wiping her hands on her apron, her perky chef's hat pushed to the back of her fluffy blond head.

"Is that you over there in that dark corner, Robert Montfort?" she demanded loudly, stalking toward him and pulling up a chair.

"It is," Allie heard him say in a resigned tone. "You know Félice de Courcy?"

"I know *of* you, of course." Petra shook Félice's hand. "I've watched your program. I don't think you'll find much scandal and mystery around here, though. But then, you're probably not here for that," she added, with a meaningful smirk at Robert.

Allie hurried back into the kitchen where she began rinsing off plates and stacking them in the dishwashers. She left the roasting tins to soak, wiped down the countertops and put ingredients back in the pantry. The assistant had left long ago and she was alone.

She stepped outside to check on Dearie. He was sitting on the grass. As soon as he saw her he came running and she gave him the big bone from the lamb roast.

Walking back into the kitchen, she poured herself a glass of wine, picking at the leftover Wellington and mulling over her first night as a waitress. All in all, with the exception of the too-perceptive TV woman, it had been a success. She hadn't once thought of Ron or of her world as a movie star. Or of Mac Reilly. She couldn't wait to do it again tomorrow.

Life was pretty good, here in Paradise.

Thirty-Nine

Mac was back in Malibu, having just flown in from Paris. He'd told Sunny he'd gotten exactly nowhere in France.

"I don't believe Allie has come to any harm, though," he said. "My guess is she's temporarily had enough of it all. I think she's gone looking for something better."

"Good," Sunny said, but not as though she meant it.

"Anyhow, the letters have stopped, and the stalker has disappeared into thin air. And so, by coincidence, have Jessie Whitworth and the blond Queen of England."

"No kidding?" Sunny's brows rose in surprise but still, she didn't ask what he meant by that. She was too preoccupied with her own guilt.

They were sitting on the sofa at Mac's place, eating take-out sushi and drinking a Gewürztraminer. It probably wasn't the appropriate wine to accompany spicy tuna hand rolls and yellowtail sashimi, but Mac thought it sure tasted good. Anyhow, he was glad to be home, with his boy, Pirate, lying at his feet gazing adoringly at him. Which was more than Sunny was doing. In fact, she wasn't looking at him at all. He might even have said she looked distinctly nervous.

"So what's up?" he asked, slipping an arm around her shoulders.

She looked sideways at him from under her eyelashes. "I have a confession to make."

He grinned. "Don't tell me you've bought another Chihuahua!"

"I wish..."

She seemed distinctly put out. Serious now, he said, "Okay, so let's have it."

"I found Ron Perrin."

He stared at her. "Go on."

Sunny told him the whole story, from finding the tax receipt in the pocket of her shorts to her talk with Perrin in the Bar Marinera, and the fact that she had let him get away.

Mac heaved a regretful sigh. There was no point in telling her she should have waited, what was done was done. And besides she was obviously upset.

"Hey, maybe you're just not cut out for this detecting business." He squeezed her shoulder sympathetically. "So the man got away. At least now we know he's alive and kicking. Anyhow, we'll be on his trail, don't you worry."

"What do we do next?" she asked, looking hopefully at him, wishing he would say let's forget all this and go to Vegas and get married.

"We'll go pay Demarco a visit in his fancy new desert mansion," Mac said. "Find out what he's all about."

"Be glad to see you," Demarco boomed when Mac gave him a call and told him they would be in the desert that weekend. "I'm having a party

231

Saturday night. Why don't you join us?"

Perfect, Mac thought. It would give him the opportunity to observe the lion in his natural habitat.

"By the way, it's a costume party," Demarco added. "Come as the person you wish you were, is the theme."

With her confession off her conscience, Sunny was looking forward to getting away, just the two of them, no dogs allowed this time. Driving through the Coachella Valley, she was thrilled by the unexpected beauty of the desert, ringed by mountains that turned pink at sunset and fringed with groves of fluffy palm trees, like a storybook oasis. Flowers bloomed everywhere and the many golf courses were dotted with glamorous Mediterranean-style houses.

They checked in to the old La Quinta Resort, which had started as a small adobe getaway for Hollywood's famous in the late twenties. Now it was a wonderful sprawl of coral-roofed buildings surrounded by turquoise blue pools, grassy lawns and sparkling fountains. They had just enough time to get into their costumes for the party.

Demarco's house was in an expensive gated community. The guard took a long look at them in their vampire costumes, then, with a smirk on his face, waved them through.

What's wrong with him? Sunny tugged nervously at her blouse. "Do I look okay?"

"You look fantastic," Mac said. "I'll bet you win first prize."

"I didn't know there was to be a prize," she

said, pleased.

"I was speaking figuratively."

"Oh!" She gave him a glare, but they were already pulling up in front of a massive single-story mansion, complete with marble steps and valet parkers standing to attention.

To Sunny, a party implied some kind of jolly revelry, but here there were just rich older folk in a large overdecorated room, knocking back hefty martinis and making polite conversation. Music droned in the background and a few of the women were in discreet costumes of the twenties flapper era but most looked as though they were wearing Bill Blass or St. John, and all the men, including Demarco, wore black tie.

All eyes turned to look when Sunny made an entrance in her Vampira outfit, flounced peasant blouse hanging off one shoulder, skirt a short sliver of artistically ripped and tattered leather. She wore her tall red Versace boots with the seriously high heels and pointy toes, and a ferocious set of fangs that glittered in the candlelight. Mac was looking pretty outrageous too, in his black leather Lestat outfit with fangs that were a match for Sunny's.

Sunny took in the sedate party group and grabbed Mac's hand for moral support, sucking in her stomach and looking as haughty as a girl could, wearing fangs.

A tall, silver-haired man detached himself from the crowd. "Good to see you, Reilly." Demarco held out his hand. "Though I almost didn't recognize you in that getup."

Sunny noticed Mac held his own hand out

somewhat reluctantly, and she wondered why. That is until their host took her own hand and crunched it in his. She batted her eyelashes in an effort to keep the tears of pain from falling.

"Sam Demarco," he said, apparently unaware of his bone crusher. His smile was jovial, but his eyes were absorbing too much of her. Sunny hitched up her slipping peasant blouse. She felt maybe their roles should be reversed, with him as the vampire and her holding the cross while Mac hammered a silver stake through his heart. But this was just gut reaction and he was her host, so she smiled back and said, "Good to meet you."

"I thought it was supposed to be a costume party," she said.

"Well, of course it is," Demarco said. "It's just that my guests are a little too old to be dressing up. To tell you the truth, it's all some of them can do to get into their normal clothes." He surveyed his guests dispiritedly. "Let me get you a drink and introduce you to some people," he said.

They followed him, shaking various rather limp beringed hands. Sunny sipped a very strong martini and choked down a bite of very good caviar on very hard pumpernickel with a blob of crème fraîche, and unsuccessfully tried to merge with the St. John crowd.

"They're eyeing us like we're the hired entertainment," she whispered to Mac. "I think they're waiting for us to spin into a Fred and Ginger routine or a wild Apache tango."

They slipped out onto the terrace, pretending to be moon gazing, then decided in a quick

234

consultation that Sunny would suddenly feel unwell. They went back inside and Mac told Demarco, who said he hoped it wasn't anything she had eaten there.

"Oh no," Sunny said, attempting to look pale and weak. "The caviar was divine. Thank you so much for a lovely evening and I'm sorry but I really must go."

She avoided Demarco's bone crusher, but to her astonishment, he bent his patrician lion head and kissed her on the cheek. Not an air kiss either, but a real buss that hovered somewhere near her mouth. She smelled his cologne, citrusy, sharp. It suited him.

Leaning pathetically on Mac, she tottered from the house, leaving behind a discreet murmur of conversation, the sound of Andy Williams singing "Moon River" and the scent of Joy hanging like a pall over the room.

"I feel stupid in this outfit," she fumed, waiting impatiently on the white marble steps for the parking valet to bring the Prius. "It wasn't worth holding my stomach in for. Why did we do this anyway?"

"Demarco invited us. I wanted to see how he lived."

"And?"

"RP's assistant lives in maybe even greater splendor than RP himself. This man is earning some serious money simply for being 'the right-hand man.'"

"Maybe RP gives him insider tips." She grinned at Mac. "Y'know like buy Yahoo! for ten dollars a share."

Tires screamed on the blacktop and the Prius stopped on a dime right in front of them. "Thanks a lot," Mac said scathingly to the maybe eighteen-year-old who had gotten off on driving the car with his foot to the metal, just to see how it felt. He tipped the kid, who ran to hold the door for Sunny, grinning down into her peasant blouse. Sunny wanted to trap his fingers in the door but she contented herself with a haughty glare.

"Anyhow, where are we going now?" she asked.

They were heading down a darkened road with nothing but desert rubble on either side. The headlights picked out an animal. Its eyes gleamed like gold mirrors at them for a second before it disappeared.

"Coyote," Mac told her, and in the distance she heard the baying of the pack. "We're going to Ron Perrin's place," he added.

"Great," Sunny muttered, annoyed with her silly costume and the fact that she had made a fool of herself in Desert Society. "Another fun location. Can't I just go and change first? Anyhow, you didn't tell me you had found Perrin. When did he get back?"

"I didn't and he hasn't." Mac swung the car toward a pair of lofty iron gates topped with spikes. The big stucco wall all around the property was studded with shards of glass and a foreboding shiver tickled Sunny's spine.

"What a way to live," she said. "Behind big walls and broken glass and iron spikes."

Mac took the electronic opener he'd filched

from RP's Hummer and pressed the code into it. The gates swung open and they drove through.

"We're trespassing," Sunny said nervously. "There must be dogs, killer Dobermans or something."

"No dogs," Mac said calmly as the gates clanged shut behind them. He parked in front of the pink stucco house that had been built in another era, when glamorous movie stars of the thirties and forties fled L.A. to avoid the media and find solace and sex behind the hidden gates of Palm Springs.

And now it was Ron Perrin's home. Or at least, one of them.

Forty

The moon gazed serenely down. Beyond the walls they could see the distant shimmer of lights in the houses built into the foothills, and above them stars twinkled in an unsmoggy desert sky. Mac had a key in his hand, and in a second they were inside and he had disabled the alarm.

Sunny stood nervously just inside the doorway. She had stepped into a wall of blackness. It pressed against her eyes. The shiver up her spine was no longer a tickle; it was a definite tremor.

"I don't think I like this," she whispered,

groping in the darkness for Mac's hand. She couldn't find it. "Mac," she hissed, frantic.

"Keep quiet, Sunny," he said in her ear, making her jump.

She turned blindly to him. "Don't do that to me," she said, shaken. "I don't think I'm the big strong girl I thought I was."

"Oh yes you are, and for God's sakes, honey, shut up."

Sunny seethed inwardly, wondering why she had agreed to come on this fool's expedition, and looking like a fool in her Vampira outfit. Besides, the pointy-toe boots were killing her.

After a while the darkness seemed to melt a little. Now they could make out the shapes of furniture, heavy-looking carved Spanish pieces. An antler chandelier with crystal drops swung in the tiny breeze they had made closing the front door. Other massive doors led off the hallway and there was a lot of art on the walls.

Sunny squinted interestedly at them. This was not modern stuff like in Malibu, nor the reputedly priceless Impressionist collection of Bel Air, but simple amateur-looking desert landscapes. She wondered whether RP had painted them himself, whenever he took time off from making money, that is. And then there was the wonderful miniature railway track, more elaborate than the one in Malibu, complete with stations and pretty little trains.

Mac walked through a door to the right and she scurried to keep up, heels clattering on the tiled floor. She heard Mac groan again.

"Jesus, Sunny." She caught the glitter of his

238

eyes. "We might as well just turn on all the lights and say, Well, folks, here we are, burglarizing your desert compound."

"Why don't we just do that?" she said wistfully. A little light seemed like a great idea.

She shadowed him, glancing nervously over her shoulder, as he went quickly from room to room. It was not a small house. Sunny counted seven bedrooms, each with bath; plus several main rooms. And through them all ran the metal tracks of the fantastic mini-railway. Kneeling to inspect it, she was so delighted she could have played with it all night.

In the office, Mac switched on the bank of computers, blinking in the green glow from the screens. He looked up puzzled by a sudden roaring noise. It sounded like an approaching express train.

Sunny stared, surprised, at the mini-rolling stock, half-expecting to see a train shoot by. There was a sudden hard jolt. The floor rolled beneath her feet and the whole world was shaking. Things flew off shelves and plaster crashed from the ceiling and she fell backward beneath a heap of tumbled masonry.

"Sunny," she heard Mac yell. Lifting her head, she stared foggily around. The ground began to shake again. She clung despairingly to a heavy table leg.

"Mac, it's an earthquake," she screamed, choking on the dust. *"Mac."*

The scream of rock plate against rock plate as the earth slipped and heaved suddenly stopped. In the eerie silence, the only sounds Sunny could hear were those of her own breathing and of dust trickling in little streams onto the rubble. Then with a sudden rumble and a toot a miniature train scooted tipsily past on its twisted metal track.

"Jesus, Sunny." Mac's arms were around her. "Are you all right, baby? Oh, God, tell me you're all right."

She leaned tearfully against his chest. It was almost worth getting half-killed to hear the tremor in his voice that meant he loved her.

An aftershock rolled through and arms around each other, they staggered through the broken glass and fallen artworks out into the night.

Moonlight dazzled down onto the fabulous cactus garden. Whoever had built the house in the thirties had been a collector and there were many wonderful old species, each with a metal tag, recording where it was native to and its age.

They stood in front of a tall cruciform saguaro cactus planted on top of a small sandy hillock, clinging together, waiting for the earth to stop shaking. The cactus speared upward into the night like a gigantic thorny branch. It looked green and healthy and very well nourished.

The ground shivered again. It was like standing on Jell-O. The sand piled around the base of the cactus began to slide in a miniature torrent. Faster, faster.

As they watched, a second cactus seemed to be growing. It emerged, slowly at first. Then suddenly, it snapped stiffly upright.

It was an arm. No flesh. Just bones. The radius, the ulna, and the hand. A diamond watch clasped around the wrist bone glittered in the

240

moonlight.

"My God, oh my God," Sunny screamed. "Oh my God, there's a body under there. Oh God, Mac, tell me I'm dreaming, tell me this is not really the house of horrors."

Mac was already checking the watch. It was still ticking.

Forty-One

Palm Springs is a cute little town, a leftover from the twenties and thirties with modern-day accents, and its own brand of charm. Sitting in an interview room at the Palm Springs Police Department, Sunny was sure nothing ever happened there, and even though she had removed her fangs she knew that she and Mac still looked highly suspect—she as Vampira and Mac like Johnny Depp playing a psychopath, and both of them battered and bruised and filthy. To say nothing of terrified. At least she was.

A short while later, Mac went back to Perrin's house with the detectives while Sunny sat drinking coffee under the skeptical eye of a young policewoman. They traded stories nervously about their jobs. Eventually Sunny ran out of conversation and coffee, then Mac came back to "rescue" her and tell her they were going back to Demarco's. The cops wanted to ask him some questions too.

Demarco's new house seemed to have withstood the earthquake well, mostly just broken martini glasses and a couple of heart-quakes amongst his more senior citizen guests that had needed defibrillation.

Demarco himself was remarkably cool, unfazed by the questions, polite and enigmatic. He had no idea whose the body was, or where his friend Perrin was. He told the detectives that Mac could testify to that because he'd already hired him to try to find Perrin.

"Feel free to search my house," Demarco said. "Of course you'll not find him."

"But," as Mac said later to Sunny, "this is the Mojave Desert. Perrin could be almost anywhere. Once you are out of the man-made oasis that constitutes the Palm cities, you can drive for miles and all there is, is rocks and rubble, sand and more sand, foothills and gigantic mountains, with occasional small homes and cabins tucked away. It would be like looking for a rat in the desert."

But he knew there was no holding back the police now. A body was buried in Perrin's backyard and Ron Perrin was "a person of interest" to the Palm Springs Police. And everybody knew what that meant.

"He has to be somewhere close by," Mac said. "Remember OJ's friend sheltering him after the murder of his wife? Demarco has a lot to gain from remaining loyal to Perrin. He could be hiding him somewhere."

Forty-Two

Allie was deep into life at the Manoir and the Bistro. Every morning early, with Dearie ambling at her heels, she walked through green-lit birch groves and alongside fields bright with sunflowers. Pale buff-colored bunnies skipped in the hedgerows and the dog chased them, though he'd never caught one. She had avoided reading the newspapers, and the first hue and cry on TV about her disappearance had stopped.

With a tug at her heartstrings, she wondered why Ron had not tried to find her. She guessed he must still be with Marisa. Their affair must have been "love" after all.

Soon she found herself walking along a sandy lane where rows of leafy vines dangled enormous bunches of hard green grapes. A rosebush in full bloom stood at the end of each immaculately groomed row. The roses were so lush and overblown they reminded Allie of Petra and she took out her little Swiss Army knife, bought for use on spur-of-the-moment picnics, thinking she would cut a few to take back to her landlady.

"Hey, what do you think you are doing? This isn't a flower garden open to the public." Robert Montfort's angry blue eyes stared at her. "Don't you know, madame, that the roses are there to protect the vines?"

"Ohh, hmmmmm ... actually, no I did not." He'd spoken in French and automatically so did Allie, somehow better at it when she was agitated and not thinking too hard about conjugating the verbs. "I'm so sorry," she added, "I didn't think."

"Then next time perhaps you will. Those roses serve a purpose. The bugs are attracted to them, and it keeps them off the vines. It also allows us to know what pests might be infesting them."

She nodded, doing her best to look apologetic. He was giving her a long look and she glanced away, but not before noticing that he wore old jeans and a blue open-necked shirt and he looked, to quote Petra, "very dishy."

"The hair looks better," he said, walking toward her.

She put up a nervous hand to touch it. She said, "Jacqui in the village cut it properly for me."

A smile lit his lean face. "Sorry I was so rude about it at the Bistro," he said. "I didn't mean it quite the way it came out."

She nodded again. "That's okay. I probably deserved it."

"Nobody deserves to be laughed at." He stood looking at her as she shuffled the roses from one hand to the other.

"My grandparents were farmers," she said, surprising herself since she had never met them and only vaguely remembered the story passed down in a more sober moment by her mother. "Sharecroppers really. Tobacco. They were from the South."

"Well, I'm a sort of farmer," he said. "Tell me, Mary Raycheck, have you ever seen a winery?" She shook her head, no. "Then would you like to see one now? I'll personally give you the 'Grand Tour.' Come on," he said, walking back down the lane to where a battered old Jeep was parked.

The dog followed them. "His name is Dearie," Allie said, hurrying to keep up with Montfort's long-legged stride. "I found him abandoned at an autoroute café."

"You're a dog lover then?"

Allie thought about Fussy. "Not all dogs," she said. And then she remembered Pirate. "Though there is one other special one I'm in love with."

They took off at a fast clip down the narrow lane. "I've never heard of anyone being 'in love' with a dog," Robert said, swinging onto a smaller road. In the distance a group of pale gold stone buildings rose to meet the sky.

Nor had Allie, and now she wondered if what she had really been thinking of was Mac Reilly. Was she in love with him? Did she still love Ron? And who exactly was this attractive stranger she was drawn to right this moment? She glanced at him out of the corner of her eye. Or was it that she was simply a lonely woman on the lookout for love?

Behind them, balanced on the narrow backseat, Dearie gave a complaining growl as Robert swung the Jeep under a sign that said in elaborate black script, *Château de Montfort*. Underneath were the words *Appellation Contrôlée*.

"Not many wines in this area are designated *appellation contrôlée*," Robert told her. "I'm

245

lucky enough to have one of the best *terroirs,* the best pieces of land in the area. This hillside is perfect for the grapes."

They walked into the winery where he showed her the enormous new stainless steel vats that, he said, compared very well with his older wooden ones. Then he took her into the *cave* where he punctured a cask and drew off a sample of wine for her to taste.

"This is still too young," he said when she tried it, though Allie thought it good. But then he said, "Now, taste this. It will be bottled next month and out on the market."

She tasted again, nodding her enthusiastic approval. Since she had been in France she was beginning to get the hang of this wine thing.

"I'm proud of it. It's one of my best," Robert said, taking her elbow as they walked outside. They stood under a striped canvas awning, looking at each other. Then he said, "Did anyone ever tell you you're a beautiful woman?"

Allie shoved the big square-framed glasses further up her nose. Remembering her other life, when she had been famous for her looks, she smiled. "Not for a long time," she admitted.

"Hmmmm, then whenever I see you, I must remember to tell you." His eyes linked with hers. "And I'll also tell you that behind those glasses your eyes are the bluest I have ever seen. The exact color of the Mediterranean at the very beginning of summer."

Allie felt the blush rise through the back of her neck to the tip of her head. "Thank you, monsieur," she said politely.

His laughter echoed around the paved court-yard, causing Dearie to cock his head wonder-ingly to one side. "After that," he said, "I must ask if you would do me the honor of having lunch with me. There's a café just down the road. It's simple: omelets, salads, that sort of thing."

Soon, they were sitting on the terrace, sipping glasses of the local wine—not Robert's, too expensive for this little café, he told her—and he was asking her to tell him all about herself. Who was she? Where was she from? What did she do before she became a waitress at Petra's bistro?

She looked at him over the rim of her wine-glass. "I hate talking about myself," she said quickly. "I'll tell you only that I'm married, that my husband is in love with another woman, and that I'm getting a divorce."

"Foolish man," he said calmly. "To let a wo-man of your caliber go."

"And how do you know what my 'caliber' is?" She put down the glass. He was, she thought, almost too handsome. He probably had a dozen gorgeous Paris blondes running after him.

He lifted a shoulder in an easy shrug. "I'm not sure. It's just something about you. It's reflected in your eyes ... a kind of simplicity, I think. And of course, there's your beauty." He studied her blushing face a little longer. "An honest kind of beauty I would call it," he said finally. And to her astonishment he leaned across the table and took her hand. Then he bent his head and kissed it.

"Now," he said, releasing her hand, all practi-cality again. "What shall we order? I recommend the *omelette aux cèpes*—the wild mushroom omelet. They're good at this time of year. And a little salad?"

"Sounds great to me," she agreed. "And then it's your turn to tell me all about yourself."

Over their leisurely lunch, sitting on the terrace of the Café Jeannette, Robert told her that he had inherited the Château Montfort from his grandfather when he was only twenty years old. "It's been my home ever since," he said.

"Lucky you," Allie said, thinking of her own soulless house in Bel Air. "I wish I could find a place here I could call home."

"A cottage with wisteria climbing the walls and roses of your own, in a garden with a little brook running through it," he said, and she laughingly agreed.

And then he surprised her and said, "I know just the place. Come on, let's go look at it."

The cottage was hidden down a rutted white lane where brambles and blackberries glistened in the hedgerows. It listed drunkenly to one side and part of the roof had caved in. The gardens had grown wild in a riot of roses and weeds and a rain bucket stood under a crumbling drainpipe leading from the blue-tiled roof. But it fronted onto a small pond fed by the bubbling little stream Allie had dreamed of, and over which glittering, many-colored dragonflies danced.

The cottage was known as Les Glycines, named, Robert Montfort told her, for the wonderful old purple-flowering wisteria that twisted over the stone walls and an arbor in the back, and Allie suddenly wanted it more than anything she'd ever wanted in her life before, except for wanting to be an actress.

She peered through the windows at the dusty old-fashioned rooms, in dire need of restoration, thinking of what she could do to it.

Of course she could not even think about buying it. She was living a lie, and one day soon she would have to move on. No, this cottage was meant for some happy young couple who could breathe new life into it.

She thanked Robert Montfort for showing it to her, but said it was not for her.

Still she found herself returning there on her morning walks, peering again into the dusty windows and sitting by the dragonfly pond watching Dearie chase the fast-jumping frogs that he never caught, though he somehow always managed to end up chest deep in the mud. Later, Allie would have to turn the hose on him, laughing as he shook himself, sending her running and almost as wet as he was.

Finally, she called Sheila and told her about it.

"I've been so worried," Sheila said. "Where on earth are you?"

"In a French village, staying in a B & B manor house, working as a waitress and kitchen help in a simple country bistro, with my new dog, and looking longingly at a broken-down cottage by a pond..."

"Oh my God, you've gone native," Sheila said, but there was a relieved laugh in her voice.

"I think I have," Allie agreed, with that new lift to her voice that made her sound the way she had when Sheila had first met her, when she was young and optimistic and unscarred by life.

"I feel so good here," Allie said. "It's so peaceful and uncomplicated, and nobody cares who I am."

"So where are you exactly?"

"Oh, in the French countryside ... I'm not going to tell you exactly where, Sheila, because then if someone like Ron or Mac Reilly or the tabloids asks, you won't have to lie."

Sheila sighed. "Okay, I understand. So, are you buying the cottage?"

"I wish..." Allie's voice trailed off. Then, "Have you heard anything about Ron?"

Sheila thought quickly; she didn't want to be the one to tell Allie that her missing husband was wanted for questioning in a murder.

"No one knows where he is," she said, evading the issue. "I know Reilly was in France though, looking for you."

"Really?" Allie said, pleased. Then in a burst of confidence she said, "There's a man here, the local squire they call him. He owns a vineyard..."

"Do I interpret that to mean you're interested?" Sheila asked shrewdly.

"Well, not exactly ... At least, I don't think so." Allie was not sure herself about her attraction to Robert Montfort. "I have to go now," she said. "Time to put on my apron, I'm expected at the Bistro."

"Oh my God," Sheila said. "I don't believe it, Allie Ray, back where she started, as a waitress."

Allie laughed. "Hey, maybe I'll be promoted to hostess soon," she said. "I love you, Sheila, just keep on being my friend."

"Of course I will, you know that," Sheila said as they rang off.

Forty-Three

Petra was reclining in her massive brass bed, the one with the huge flying sphinx finials that she'd told Allie came from Egypt and had once been owned by King Farouk. Since Petra had found it cheap in Bergerac's Sunday flea market, this was unlikely, but still Allie was inclined to believe her. After all, who else but Petra would own such a fantastical thing?

Pale green satin pillows were heaped behind Petra's head, while the matching coverlet kept sliding annoyingly onto the floor. Petra told Allie satin was always a slippery problem but she just loved the way it looked. A red bandanna was wrapped around her swollen jaw and tied in a perky bow on top of her head. That morning she'd had an aching wisdom tooth removed. It had hurt like hell and now her face looked like a football.

"Just look at my eyes," she wailed to Allie, as best she could through tight-shut lips.

"They've disappeared," Allie said, offering her a glass of iced orange juice with a straw, which was all Petra had said she could manage.

Petra pushed aside the covers and wobbled to

251

her feet. She sat down again quickly on the edge of the bed. Had she been able to frown, she would have. "I have to get to the Bistro, start prepping the food for tonight."

"Oh, no, you're not." Allie swung Petra's legs back onto the bed. She took off the annoying slippery satin coverlet, straightened the sheet and pulled a blanket over her. Walking to the window, she closed the shutters, turned a lamp on low, then went back and inspected Petra again.

"We'll have to close the Bistro then," Petra mumbled, and despite her slitty eyes Allie could tell she was looking hard at her. "Unless *you* could take over for me, of course."

"What? You mean *me? Run the restaurant?"* Allie was stunned. All she had done so far was follow orders, chopping, slicing, sautéing and serving.

"Why not? You've been there long enough to know how it all works. If you keep the menu simple: chicken, chops, grilled fish, that sort of thing, you'll be fine. And you know how to make sauces now. You can get Caterine to make the salads and the veg. Gazpacho's a breeze, you do it in the blender. That or a goat cheese salad, or quails' eggs, for starters. A fruit pie for dessert—there's a couple in the freezer. With ice cream. Or simply berries and cream. The suppliers will have delivered the fresh produce."

Allie said nothing and despite the swelling Petra managed a frown. "Don't tell me you're afraid," she said. "A woman like you."

"A woman like *me?"* Allie repeated, sounding definitely scared.

"A woman like *you,* who can leave her cheating husband and come to France alone in search of a new life. I would have thought a woman like that could do almost anything. Including running a kitchen in a small local restaurant, where she's worked for the past few weeks."

Sitting up, Petra inserted the straw into her swollen pout of a mouth and took a sip of the cold juice.

Allie said nothing. If she took over the Bistro, everything would depend on her. But Petra needed to make money to keep going. Closing for a few nights would make a severe dent in her budget. And besides, Petra was her friend. Now it was Allie's turn to help her.

"Do it, love," Petra said, sinking back into her pale green pillows and attempting to look fragile, even though she knew she resembled a small hippo. Facially that is.

"So okay," Allie said in a small voice. She hoped she was doing the right thing.

Of course the assistant chef, the young Brit, chose that night not to show up. He'd left a phone message saying he'd gone back to England. "Urgent family business," he'd said.

"Isn't it always?" Petra said resignedly, when Allie phoned from the Bistro to tell her. "Never mind, love, you've got jolly little Caterine to help you."

"Jolly little Caterine" was slow and methodical. Watching her languidly washing lettuces and snipping the tips off *haricots verts,* Allie despaired. There was nothing for it but to plunge in the deep end and prep the food herself.

She took the fruit pies out of the freezer and set them to defrost. She hulled a pile of tiny *fraises des bois,* absently popping a few into her mouth as she went. It was like eating fruity perfume, and she knew they would be wonderful with a touch of Cointreau and maybe some thick rich cream. She found tubs of Carte Noir ice cream in the freezer, the *chocolat gâteau* flavor she already knew was to die for, and *café* as well as vanilla. So much for dessert.

Now for the gazpacho. Checking Petra's recipe book, she peeled and seeded ripe tomatoes and red peppers, previously washed by Caterine, who was now employed slowly setting up the tables. Garlic, tons of it, a bunch of fresh herbs, anything she could get her hands on because she wasn't exactly sure of which ones to use, so she put them all in. Chervil, parsley, basil, chives, tarragon. She contemplated using the blender but then decided she wanted the nuggety texture and chopped all the ingredients by hand instead, sniffing up the herby aroma, and managing not to cut herself. She stirred in lemon juice and the good olive oil from Azari in Nice that Petra preferred. She added thinly sliced sweet onion and cucumber. Salt, a little paprika. And it was done.

Standing proudly back from her handiwork, she called Caterine over to taste. The girl's round brown eyes grew even rounder.

"Mais c'est superbe," she murmured, eyes reverently closed. *"Formidable."*

Allie heaved a satisfied sigh. Telling Caterine

to get the salad ingredients together, she took the goat cheese from the fridge and sliced it into neat rounds. She ground hazelnuts in the blender, added fresh bread crumbs, a touch of nutmeg and a hit of olive oil, then rolled the cheese slabs in them, ready to be toasted under the grill and served on a bed of tiny fresh lettuces, scattered with the edible nasturtium flowers Petra grew in the garden behind the Bistro.

Pleased, she stood back and took a look at the big old railroad clock over the door. With a yelp of distress, she realized it was five o'clock and she had yet to create at least two main courses.

There could be no fresh fish tonight since Petra had not been able to get to the market, but the thin pork chops would grill up crisp and easy. The hanger steak needed a bit of help and she quickly chopped spinach, fried up some bacon, chopped that and mixed in some hearty blue cheese. She beat the steak with the meat tenderizer, spread the stuffing on it and rolled it up. Then she cut it into roulades. It looked terrific. Steak and blue cheese pinwheels. God, she thought, pleased, I'm getting good at this.

Fresh baguettes were delivered to the kitchen door and Caterine, back from setting tables, carried them over to the bread guillotine, where they could be quickly sliced and placed in the waiting red-napkin-lined baskets.

Caterine had already taken out the butter and was making neat little pats out of it, laboriously stamping each one with Petra's favorite cow image. Eyeing the couple of mangoes in the fruit basket, Allie had an idea. She quickly peeled the soft ripe mangoes, mashed them with a fork, then began to blend them in with the butter. She placed the result in little round yellow pots and put them in the fridge to chill. *Mango butter.* She'd had it once in the Caribbean and loved it.

Jean-Philippe arrived, surprised to see her in charge of the kitchen. When she told him what was what, he said not to worry, he'd help with the serving as well as taking care of the bar, and he was sure everything would be okay.

Chopping chickens ready for the fricassee and arranging the piles of already prepped vegetables on the counter in front of her—a *mise en place,* as Allie knew a chef like Wolfgang Puck (a friend of hers) would have called it—Allie was exhausted. And scared. Playing around in the kitchen was one thing. Cooking meals—*many different meals*—and all at the same time scared the hell out of her.

So, okay, you took on the responsibility, she told herself, tying on a clean apron. Petra trusted you with her bistro. It's up to you to take care of things for her.

"Eh bien, what shall I do now, Mary?" Caterine's myopic brown eyes stared anxiously into hers.

Allie took a deep breath and pulled herself together. "Okay ... I mean, *eh bien,"* she said firmly. "Caterine, you will be in charge of cooking the vegetables. You know exactly how many minutes for the *haricots verts* and the baby squash, correct?"

"Correct." Caterine stood up straight, spine stiffened with new responsibility.

"Petra is trusting us to take care of everything for her," Allie reminded the girl. "So we'll both do our best. Correct?"

"Correct," Caterine agreed again.

"First customers," Jean-Philippe yelled from the bar, and despite her resolve, Allie's heart sank. She glanced panicked around the small country kitchen. It was a long way from the Hollywood movie sets, with the catering tents and the professionals in charge of feeding several hundred people every day. And from her own enormous, immaculate Bel Air home, where Ampara ruled over the kitchen. She was on her own.

Jean-Philippe hurried in. "It's Robert Montfort," he said. "And he's with his mother."

"Oh my God," Allie said. Robert of all people. *And* with his mother.

"He'd like the gazpacho, and the lady will have the goat cheese salad to start. One steak pinwheel, and one grilled pork with pepper sauce."

She had forgotten to make the pepper sauce...

Caterine organized the bread and the mango butter and took it out to their table, while Allie got the goat cheese under the grill and toasted the rounds of baguette on which it was to be served, atop a watercress and baby lettuce salad dressed with lemon vinaigrette with a hint of honey. She flung red peppers into the blender with garlic and herbs for the sauce to accompany the pork and added capers and cream for good measure. Then she garnished the gazpacho with a slice of lemon and floated chopped cucumber on top. She checked the goat cheese. It was ready.

Caterine held the plate while she arranged the toasts artfully. First courses done. On to the next.

"More people arriving," Jean-Philippe called out.

Peeking through the bead curtain that divided the kitchen from the restaurant, Allie saw that there were. Lots of them. She glimpsed Robert on the terrace sitting with a handsome older woman. They were tasting their first courses and seemed pleased.

Back in the kitchen, she prepared for a long night.

By ten o'clock Allie was sweaty and tired. Her hair hung in short limp strands around her face and her glasses were pushed on top of her head. At least there had been no complaints.

Robert thrust his way through the bead curtain. "Jean-Philippe just told me it was you, here all alone," he said. "I had no idea you could cook."

"I can't." Allie slid the glasses back onto her nose and ran damp hands through her miserable hair. "I wasn't asked for my culinary ability. I was the only one available."

"The food was excellent," he said. "Ask Maman. She knows good food when she eats it. Come." He held out his hand. "You've finished for the night. There are no more customers. Join us over a glass of wine, and perhaps some more of those delicious *fraises des bois*."

"Oh ... but..." Looking desperate, Allie ran her hands through her ragged hair again, making him laugh.

"You look just fine," he said softly. "Don't you

know by now that you always do?"

"Ohhh..." she said again, but Robert was already untying her apron. "Come on," he said, taking her by the hand and leading her out onto the terrace.

"This is my mother, Céline Montfort," he introduced them. "Mary Raycheck."

Madame Montfort was a still pretty woman, tall, as her son was, with her black hair turning silver at the temples in the most elegant way Allie could have imagined. She wore a blue linen skirt and a white silk shirt with a little scarf at her neck, large pearls, and those chic cream Chanel sling backs with the black toes. She looked, as Allie knew Ron would have said, like a million bucks. While Allie, in her black T-shirt and jeans, felt closer to a mere ten.

"I'm happy to meet a friend of my son's. And such a talented chef." Madame Montfort gave her a long searching look that Allie felt sure missed nothing.

"But I'm only an amateur, madame, standing in for my friend, who had her wisdom tooth removed this morning."

"A painful business," Madame Montfort agreed. And then, over glasses of champagne, she asked Allie a few questions, about how she was enjoying France, and did she find her life here very different from California.

Dearie came wandering over. Madame Montfort caressed his thick shaggy neck, and the dog gazed adoringly up at her. The moon shone down, the little white lights twinkled in the trees and the wine tasted delicious. Allie turned to look at Robert and caught him looking at her. She smiled, feeling good. It was the perfect end to a surprisingly perfect day.

Forty-Four

Half an hour later, after they had said goodbye, Allie found herself alone again, humming softly as she washed off the countertops.

She stood for a moment gazing around the quiet kitchen with its white half-tiled walls, its black-beamed ceiling, its enormous royal blue chef's stove—Petra's favorite color—and the steel grills and cooktops. Battered pots and pans were stacked on wooden shelves, alongside the simple cream plates and dishes stamped in blue with the name bistro du manoir.

Outside, Dearie sprawled on the step and a cool breeze mixed with the aroma of chicken fricasseed in good sweet butter and the perfume of wild strawberries. Leaning against the counter, arms folded across her chest, Allie felt a deep sense of contentment. Tonight she had made a success out of what had promised to be total chaos. On her own, she had fed thirty-five customers and there had been no complaints. Only compliments. Flushed with a new kind of success she thought this kitchen felt like home, in a way nowhere else ever had. She couldn't wait to get back and tell Petra all about it.

But first she and Jean-Philippe had to cash up the night's takings. She put the money and credit card receipts in an envelope and stashed them in her big canvas tote, then walked round the restaurant, turning out the lights, making sure all the doors were locked. She said a fond good night to Jean-Philippe, hauled Dearie into the car and drove home to the Manoir. She liked the sound of that word *home.*

Petra was waiting up for her. Her room smelled of the blue irises in a white pottery jug on her bedside table, and a lamp, shaded with a red silk scarf to prevent the glare bothering her poor swollen eyes, cast a rosy intimate glow. Allie had stopped to brew tea in the big brown pot, making sure to place a packet of the chocolate digestives on the tray before she carried it upstairs.

"Here I am," she said, putting the tray down on the bed.

"Oh, goodie, tea!" Petra tried to beam but her mouth got stuck.

"Do you think you'll need a straw?" Allie said.

"What? Tea through a straw? Never. What are you thinking, girl!" Petra unraveled the bandanna that strapped up her jaw, groaning as the swelling hurt even more.

Allie handed her the Tylenol. "Take some with the tea and biscuits. You need food of some sort," she said as Petra's tummy rumbled loudly.

"So?" Petra said. "Tell *all*! How did it go?"

And, over tea and biscuits in the cozy pinkly lit bedroom, with the faraway song of a blackbird caroling in the woods, Allie described the night's

261

events. She told Petra how panicked she had been by the sous-chef's unexpected defection back to England, and how helpful Caterine and Jean-Philippe were. About the food and her new invention of the blue cheese pinwheel steaks that had, as Petra would have said, "gone down a treat" with the diners. She told her about the fabulous *fraises des bois* steeped in a little Cointreau and served with a huge dollop of fresh cream.

And then she said casually, "Oh, and by the way, Robert Montfort was there tonight."

Through the blue slits that were her eyes, Petra gave her a sharp glance. "Oh? With the Paris girlfriend, I suppose?"

"Actually, he was with his mother."

"Ahhhh! The *maman*!"

"After I'd finished in the kitchen he asked me to join them for a glass of wine."

"And did you?"

Allie grinned. "Of course I did. And Maman was very nice, kind of quietly elegant in that French way, you know with the scarf and the pearls and the Chanel shoes, hair turning silver at the temples."

"Like her son," Petra said, yawning. "I wonder if he'll show up again tomorrow night when he hears you'll be cooking again."

"I will?"

"Well, love, I can't go out with my face like this, can I? The customers would think I'd been poisoned."

Surprised by how thrilled she felt at the news that she was to be chef again, Allie tidied away the tea tray, plumped Petra's pillows, made sure she had a glass of water and kissed her good night. Then she and Dearie drifted down the broad wood-floored landing to her room.

She'd been on such a high she hadn't noticed that her back ached and her feet hurt. Standing in the tiny plastic shower cubicle she let the hot water wash away the smells of the kitchen and her aches and pains.

For once she was not thinking of Ron when she climbed into the soft bed and closed her eyes. She wasn't thinking of Mac, either, nor of Robert Montfort. She was thinking about grilled fresh asparagus with a crust of Parmesan. Perfect for tomorrow's starter.

Forty-Five

Mac and Sunny had managed to dodge the TV camera crews and the paparazzi lurking at the Colony's gates, hot on the news about the body at Perrin's Palm Springs house. They were sitting on Mac's deck, the sun was shining in a clear sky and a soft breeze blew. It was one of those heavenly late afternoons in Malibu.

Sunny was stretched out on the old metal lounger, hands behind her head, gazing skyward from behind large rose-colored aviators. Mac thought the color appropriate. Rose-colored specs matched Sunny's optimistic view of life and people.

She was wearing an orange bikini and her toenails were painted to match. He'd thought she was sensational as Vampira in the red boots, but now she was something else again.

There was no need to keep an eye out for paparazzi because Pirate had stationed himself at the top of the beach steps and, as though he knew what was expected of him, was on the lookout for strangers. Mac gave him a pat then stretched out on the chair next to Sunny. He had no doubt that the skeleton at Perrin's Palm Springs house was that of Ruby Pearl, though it was yet to be confirmed.

"So, what's *your* take on this?" he asked Sunny, catching her hand in his.

Sunny thought about the man she had talked to that night in the Bar Marinera in Mazatlán. She remembered his sad brown eyes and him saying, *"It's love gone wrong..."* Of course with that he'd had her on his side in a minute, and even though he'd disappeared on her, she didn't like to think of him being charged with murder.

"I don't believe it was Ron," she said.

"That's because you don't want to believe it."

"True," she admitted. "But even if Ruby Pearl was blackmailing him, I still don't see him as a psychopath, killing a woman and burying her under his prize cactus. It takes a different kind of man to do something as evil as that. And anyway *why* would he kill her? He's a powerful man with a battery of lawyers. He could simply have given her a chunk of money, had her sign a legal contract, and then he could have said goodbye and thank you very much."

The house phone beeped and Mac got up and went to answer it. He came back a minute later and said, "Demarco's here. He wants to talk."

Sunny sat up quickly. "Why?"

"If I knew I'd tell you."

She slipped on a yellow cotton cover-up. "Do I offer him coffee?"

"If he's coming to talk, my guess is he'll need something stronger than coffee."

He was right. Demarco was looking cool as ever, although this time he was wearing a casual white golf shirt and beige pants. He said he would prefer vodka. On the rocks. He took a long look around the place, then, one disdainful eyebrow lifted, followed Mac outside.

"Good to see you again," he said, though he was obviously surprised to see Sunny. He glanced questioningly at Mac.

"Sunny is my partner," Mac said, thrilling her. "What I hear, she hears."

Demarco nodded. "Then I'd better tell you it's true that the FBI is investigating Perrin's ... *our* ... business."

Demarco wasn't telling Mac anything he didn't already know, but he caught the odd look in Demarco's eyes. He puzzled over it while Perrin's right-hand man talked. What was it exactly? Insecurity? Fear? Surely not, in a man like that. But there was also the matter of the body in the cactus garden.

"I wonder," Mac said. "Do you think Perrin was money laundering?"

Demarco coughed into his drink. "I surely

hope not," he said. "Because as his partner I'm afraid that might implicate me."

"Yes, it might," Mac said with a smile.

"Of course, that would be entirely untrue." Demarco looked Mac in the eye. "If Ron is guilty of something, besides murder, it would be up to you to prove I had nothing to do with it."

"And how will I do that?"

Demarco took a long swig of his vodka. He put down the glass and looked from Mac to Sunny and back again. "I'd pay you well, Mr. Reilly. *Very well.* More than you've ever been paid in your life."

There was a long silence. Mac was aware that Demarco was trying to gauge their reaction. His own face was expressionless, while Sunny looked stunned by such an overt bribe.

Mac's cell rang. He took the call, listening while Demarco sat in silence, staring out to sea, though Mac knew he wasn't watching the brown pelicans doing their high diving act.

He clicked off the phone, then said, "I think you'll be interested to know that the remains found at Perrin's Palm Springs compound have been identified by dental records as those of Ruby Pearl. The diamond watch was traced to a Beverly Hills jeweler. It was purchased by Perrin."

Demarco shrugged his shoulders. "What can I say? Now you see why you have no choice but to help me."

When Demarco had left, with a promise from Mac to try to find Ron and sort out the mess, Mac called Lipski to confirm the news about

266

Ruby Pearl. In a choked-up voice Lipski thanked him. He said now Ruby would be able to rest in peace and he would try to get on with his life. "Just get that killer Perrin for me, will ya?" he begged Mac.

"He's not named as the killer yet," Mac told him. "He's still only 'a person of interest' to the Palm Springs PD. And remember, just because her body was buried in his garden, doesn't mean he killed her."

"Then who else would do it?" Lipski asked.

Mac thought he had a point.

Forty-Six

Ampara was worried. She and the dog had been staying with friends since the scary events at the house, but she was conscientious, and twice a week she went back to the Bel Air house to open up the windows and air out the place, dust the furniture and make sure everything was okay.

Mac Reilly had kept her up-to-date but whoever the perpetrator was, he had worn gloves and there were no fingerprints, other than the normal ones. In Ampara's view there should have been no fingerprints anyway. She kept a clean house and was proud of her work. Anyhow, so far the cops had no suspects and nor did Reilly, though he'd told her he felt sure it was safe for her to go to the house to do her work. "After all, sir, I'm being paid for it," Ampara had said when she called him about it. And besides, she didn't like just doing nothing except walk the dog.

She was there one morning when the usually silent phone rang. Surprised, she stopped her vacuuming and stared at it. It had not rung, at least when she was there to hear it, since that awful night, and now she was scared to answer it. It occurred to her, though, that it might be Miss Allie, and dropping the vac she ran to answer it.

"Perrin residence," she said, cautiously.

"Ampara?"

She recognized the voice. "Miss Whitworth," she said relieved. "I'm glad it's you."

"Were you expecting Allie to call?"

"Well, sort of hoping, y'know how it is..."

"I sure do, and that's why I'm calling. Listen, I know—we all know—that Allie's gone missing and I'm really worried about her. You know how I feel about Allie. How we *both* feel, Ampara. I'm hoping I can help her. She needs someone who knows her, y'know what I mean? And since I just happen to be here in Cannes on vacation, with a friend, I thought if you knew where she was, if she had been in contact ... maybe I could go and help her. Allie needs someone who knows her *well,* Ampara, another woman who really cares..."

"Oh, I agree, Miss Whitworth. Miss Allie's such a lonely woman, and now she's run off and disappeared, and with what happened here at the house..."

"What do you mean? What happened at the

268

house?" Jessie's voice was sharp with anxiety, but just in time Ampara remembered that Mr. Reilly told her not to talk about it to anyone.

"Oh, I just got nervous being on my own, so me and Fussy are sleeping over at a friend's. And anyway, Miss Whitworth, I don't know where she is. Nobody does. And nobody knows where Mr. Ron is either."

"Hmmm, well I'll call back soon, and if you hear anything, Ampara, promise you'll let me know."

"Okay, Miss Whitworth. I sure will."

Ampara went back to her vacuuming. Outside the window she saw the pool guy wielding his long net across the water, sending it rippling like blue silk over the infinity edge, and heard the familiar whine of the gardener's leaf blower and the hum of the John Deere tractor mower. Life went on as normal at the Perrin house. Except its owners had disappeared.

The phone rang again. She stopped and stared at it. Could it be Miss Allie this time? Or maybe Mr. Ron?

She picked it up. "Perrin residence?"

"Oh, Ampara, this is Sheila Scott."

A relieved smile crossed Ampara's face. She knew Sheila Scott and liked her.

"How are you, Ampara?"

"Well, Miss Scott, as good as can be expected, I guess, after what happed here ... Ohh..." Again, she stopped herself just in time.

"What do you mean? What happened?"

Ampara heard the concern in Sheila's voice. She was Miss Allie's best friend, surely she could trust her. Deciding she could, she told her about the break-in, about the beautiful dresses, all slashed with a knife and thrown onto the floor...

"God knows what might have happened if Miss Allie had still been here," she ended with a sigh that was almost a sob.

Sheila was silent for a moment, taking in the full horror of the situation. Then she said, "But surely the police...?"

"They don't know nuthin', Miss Scott, and nor does that Mac Reilly, who was looking after her. And I sure miss Lev, that bodyguard, being around."

"I'll bet you do. Then you haven't heard from her, I suppose?"

"Not a word, miss. And nor has no one else. Not even Mr. Reilly, and I know she trusted him. You too, miss," she added.

Sheila thanked her, and Ampara said she would call her if she happened to hear from Allie.

"You're the second one today calling asking about her," Ampara said, just as Sheila was about to ring off. "Jessie Whitworth called just a few minutes ago. You remember, she used to be Miss Allie's assistant."

"I remember."

"Well, she's concerned too. She thinks Miss Allie must be all alone somewhere and needs another woman, a friend to help her. She said she also happens to be in Cannes on vacation and did I know where Allie was."

"And what did you say?"

"Of course I told her I had no clue. Only that

she was in the South of France when she disappeared."

"Hmm. Quite a coincidence," Sheila said thoughtfully. "Well, thanks, Ampara. You know if you hear from her, to give me a call?"

"I will, Miss Scott. And thank you for calling."

Feeling better now that Allie's friends were rallying round, Ampara went back to her vacuuming. Life at the Bel Air mansion went on almost as usual.

Forty-Seven

Sheila could not get the vision of Allie's gowns slashed by a knife-wielding madman out of her mind. Even in Bristol Farms supermarket buying fruit and flowers and a good French cheese to go with the freshly baked bread, it was still on her mind. The stalker had finally gotten into her house, and it could have been Allie stabbed instead of just those dresses. From Allie's cheerful phone call from somewhere in France, Sheila realized she did not know about the incident and she thanked God for that. Still, she was worried. What if the stalker found her? He was clever enough to get into the house, wasn't he? Scared now, she decided she had to tell Mac Reilly about Allie's phone call.

Mac was surprised to get a call from Sheila

Scott, who described herself as one of Allie's closest friends. As far as he'd known, Allie had no close friends. But when she explained to him that she'd heard about the break-in, that she was worried and needed to talk, he arranged to meet her at home in Venice Beach.

Miss Scott's house was in one of those charming little walk-streets lining the canals that gave L.A.'s Venice its name. It was a cottage, larger than his own and set in a pretty rose-filled front garden, with diamond-paned windows and a sturdy wooden front door. With Pirate at his heels, he opened the wrought-iron gate in the shape of a peacock, stopping en route to sniff the lavender-colored Barbra Streisand rose, which had a spicy, sweet aroma. He wished he could grow roses out at the beach but the salt spray would be too much for them. He climbed the two wide steps and rang the bell, hearing it peal a little song that he recognized but couldn't identify.

When Sheila Scott opened the door to him, she said, "I'll bet you're wondering what the song was."

He grinned. "How did you know?"

"Everyone always does. It's "Nessun dorma," from Puccini's opera *Turandot*. You're probably more familiar with Pavarotti singing it at World Cup finals, or the three tenors, Pavarotti, Domingo and Carreras, in the televised concert from Rome. It's harder to identify it without the words." She waved him inside. "Please, come on in. And the dog too."

She stooped to give Pirate a pat, then, taking in

his injuries, glanced back up at Mac. "I can tell you are a very kind man."

He shrugged. "I only did what anybody else would. Anyhow, I wouldn't be without him."

"You're very fortunate."

She was the second woman to tell him that. Allie had been the first. He liked Sheila Scott already.

She took him into her kitchen, a lovely room, low-ceilinged with French doors thrown open to a vista of more roses and shady pepper trees and eucalyptus and with a narrow flagged terrace overlooking the peaceful green canal. The houses were crammed next to each other in a mishmash of styles, jockeying for space, as they did at the beach. But here, there was also a view of the gardens and houses opposite, with little pleasure boats tied up outside.

"Lovely home you have," Mac said appreciatively.

"I bought it thirty years ago. It was a wreck—as was almost everything else in Venice. Nobody wanted to live here then, too close to the hood, no infrastructure—y'know, no supermarkets, restaurants, boutiques, cafés. Now you can't walk two blocks without falling over all of that."

"And now it's worth a couple of mil, I'll bet," Mac said. "You made a shrewd investment."

Sheila laughed. "There was nothing 'shrewd' —or 'investment'—about it. It was all I could afford, and besides I loved being on the canal. It has its own magic, as you can see. Almost," she added with a twinkle, "as good as the beach.

"Coffee?" She held up the pot. Two mugs

273

already awaited on a pewter tray.

Mac thanked her and they went outside and sat on the terrace in a pair of white basket-weave chairs. Mac took her in as she sat quietly, looking around her garden. She was a handsome woman, very much in charge of herself, but her casual confidence was appealing.

"Are you a musician then?" he said, thinking of the doorbell.

She laughed. "Absolutely not. No. I'm a voice coach. That's how I met Allie, years ago when she first came to L.A. I coached the Texas twang out of her. We've been friends a long time," she added, looking directly at Mac. "And that's why I'm so worried."

Mac sat back, in his usual wait-and-see-what-they-say-to-incriminate-themselves fashion.

"I heard from Allie a while ago," Sheila said, surprising him.

He put the coffee mug carefully down on the small tiled table between them. "Yes?"

"She was still in France but wouldn't tell me exactly where. She said it would save me having to tell a lie if anyone asked me if I knew. She sounded happy, said she had made some new friends, she had changed her appearance and was certain nobody knew who she really was. And that she was working as a waitress. Maybe she'd even met a man..."

"Sounds promising." Mac picked up his mug and took another sip of coffee.

"Let me get you some more." Sheila hurried into the kitchen and came back out with the pot. "It's still hot," she said, pouring it. She looked at him. "I haven't heard from her since, though she promised to call. I was worried, so this morning I telephoned Ampara, the housekeeper. She told me something even more worrying. About the stalker getting into the house, the slashed dresses..."

Mac nodded. "We have to be glad Allie wasn't there."

Sheila shuddered. She didn't want to think about it. "There was something else Ampara told me, though, that I thought was unusual. It's about Jessie Whitworth."

"Allie's personal assistant? The one she fired a few months back?"

Sheila's dark brown eyes met Mac's. "Exactly. And what Ampara told me was that just this morning, she'd had a phone call from her. Jessie told her she was concerned about Allie, that she felt she needed a friend, another woman, someone who knew her, who was close to her. Jessie said she felt strongly that Allie needed help, and since she happened already to be in the South of France, if Ampara would tell her where Allie was, she would go to her aid."

Mac put down the coffee mug and sat up straight. "About what time did she call?"

"Ampara said it was just before I did. So that would make it around eleven this morning."

Mac got to his feet. There was no time to waste. He said, "You have no idea what a big help you've been."

Sheila was also on her feet, looking anxiously at him. "Do you think Jessie has anything to do with it? I know Allie fired her, and that she used to have a key to the house."

"We're certainly going to find out," Mac said. And then, because Sheila's kind face looked about to crumple into tears, he gave her a hug.

"You're a good friend, Sheila," he said, holding her away from him, smiling. "And don't you worry, I have just the man to find out where Jessie is, and exactly what she's up to."

Forty-Eight

Mac was in the car, driving back down Main Street, Venice. As Sheila had said, it was crammed with boutiques and clothing stores, and cafés, with young people toting surfboards and beautiful girls pushing strollers with cute babies. Stalled at the light, Mac called Roddy and told him the news.

"Miss Whitworth, the perfect secretary?" Roddy said. "I always thought she was a dark horse. I wonder if she's still with the Queen of England."

"That's a thought," Mac said, already busy thinking in fact. "I'm on my way back to the beach," he said. "Why don't you meet me there."

"Okay. Maybe you should send me to Cannes to find her. After all, I'm the only one who's actually met her, the only one who knows what she looks like."

Mac laughed. "Maybe," he said, just as he had

276

to Allie when she had asked him to go to Cannes with her. "I'm calling Lev right now, getting him over too. We'll talk then."

He speed-dialed Lev, told him what was going down and asked him to meet him at the Malibu house.

"I'm in Hollywood, I'll be there in forty," Lev said. "God and traffic willing," he added.

In the event, he was there on time. Roddy and Mac were already out on the deck where the velvety sunshine dappled the ocean with sequins of silver. Cold beers were handed round and the three men sat for a moment, enjoying the view of the ocean and the blond girls—somehow they always seemed to be blond—cavorting at the edge of the waves, as well as the surfers "boldly going where few men dare to go," Roddy said, though in fact he happened to be a great surfer himself.

"Okay, so Allie is still in France." Mac laid out the scenario as told him by Sheila and the two men listened attentively.

"The Whitworth woman left her apartment early on the morning after the break-in at the Bel Air house. She told the apartment manager she was going on a vacation to Cancún."

"She and her friend, the blond?"

"Yes. And who, by the way, she said, looked a bit like Allie."

"The security guard at Mentor Studios told me the same thing," Roddy said.

"So maybe Whitworth didn't go to Cancún. Maybe she went to France instead," Mac said.

"Looking for Allie," Lev said.

Mac turned to Lev. "You know your way around that part of the world?"

"I used to work in Paris. I have contacts there. Whitworth will have needed to rent a car, and for that you need a driver's license and credit card. We can check that."

"Okay, I want you to get on to it right away. We don't know where Allie is, but then, neither does Jessie."

Lev glanced at his watch. "I'll be in Paris tomorrow. Trust me, I'll find her."

Roddy looked at Mac. "Can't I go with him?"

Mac laughed. "I think Lev is a man who likes to work alone. Besides, you don't have any contacts in Paris."

Roddy looked aggrieved. "I could make some."

"Okay, so when we find her, you'll go to France."

"I always like celebrations," Roddy said gloomily.

Forty-Nine

Sunny was fixing a salad with mini lettuces, fresh herbs, avocado and sliced strawberries, sprinkled with toasted walnuts, while Mac barbecued a couple of steaks and opened a bottle of Caymus, a deep rich Cabernet that was one of his favorites. Pirate snored loudly, competing with Bryan Ferry's album playing in the background. Sunny had bought it thinking of Ron. They had just settled down to eat when the phone rang.

"Hi," Marisa said. "It's me."

"I know." Mac put her on speakerphone so Sunny could hear. "I recognize your voice."

"I read about the murder in the *Herald Tribune*," Marisa said in a trembly voice. "About Ronnie being suspected of killing that woman, about him still being missing, and about ... oh, everything. Then someone broke into my apartment. Nothing was stolen just everything turned over. Now I'm scared. I think it might be Ronnie."

"Maybe it was the paparazzi," Sunny said to Mac. "They could have found out she was Ron's girlfriend," she added.

He shook his head. "Paparazzi don't break in. And anyhow what could they have been looking for?" He asked Marisa the same question.

"I didn't tell you everything," she confessed. "I took some documents from Ronnie's place that night. They're to do with offshore bank accounts, serial numbers, that sort of things. I know Ronnie wants them. And I think now he's killed one woman and maybe I'm next on his list. I'm scared, Mac. I'm really *really* scared. Please, oh *please*, you have to come out here and help me. I'll give you the papers. And I'll tell you everything I know about Ronnie."

Mac's eyes met Sunny's.

"I'm already packing," she said.

"We'll be there tomorrow," Mac promised Marisa.

Fifty

The following day Sunny and Mac were installed in their usual Rome hotel. There was a message to meet Marisa at her apartment. Mac called to tell her they were on their way. There was no reply but he assumed she had gone out shopping and decided to go anyway.

They took a cab to Trastevere, the old section where artisans and manual workers once lived crammed together in the narrow cobbled alleys and ancient piazzas. Now, though, parts of it had been gentrified and there were smart little bars and cafés with tiny flowered sidewalk terraces.

Marisa's apartment was on the first floor of a tall narrow stucco building whose green-shuttered windows looked out onto the cobbled street. TV aerials sprouted from the roof and a black cat gazed down at them from an ugly iron balcony that was definitely not meant for Juliet.

"Hmm." Sunny sniffed disparagingly. "I would have thought the famous movie producer could have done better for her."

Marisa's apartment was to the left of the hall. A yellow Post-it note was stuck on the door. "Mac, meet me at Bar Gino, in the piazza at the end of the street," was all it said.

They walked to the bar, a long dim narrow

cavern of a place with glass shelves lined with bottles of cheap red wine, and sat on the tiny terrace, sipping a glass each of the red, waiting for Marisa. After a while, Mac got worried and called her again. Still no reply. He called their hotel to see if she had left a message, but there was nothing. They decided to wait a little longer and Mac went back into the bar to order more wine and a pizza. Without anchovies.

Left alone Sunny was drinking the last of her wine, listening to the hungry rumble of her tummy—she hadn't eaten on the plane—when she spotted Marisa at the top of the street.

How could she miss her, even if she was draped in a black pashmina shawl, attempting to look like an old Italian peasant woman and definitely not succeeding? And it wasn't only her Prada platform shoes that were a dead giveaway. A tall man was walking with her, a priest in a black soutane and one of those wide-brimmed flat hats. He was holding on to Marisa's arm and seemed to be guiding her firmly away from the piazza. *Too* firmly, Sunny thought, alarmed. In fact he was pushing her.

Leaping to her feet, she yelled for Mac, then took off after them, trotting in her high heels over the tricky cobbles. In front of her she saw the priest drag Marisa down the dark narrow alley and heard her cry out as they disappeared round a corner.

Panting for breath, Sunny whizzed after them. Her heel caught in between the cobbles, and she went sprawling. A pain shot through her ankle and tears stung her eyes. When she looked up,

Marisa and the priest had disappeared.

She saw Mac at the end of the street, running toward her. "What happened?" he asked anxiously.

Sunny told him the story. "Looks like Marisa knew she was being followed and she tried to lose him, and you almost caught up to them," he said.

Her ankle was swelling rapidly and he helped her up. "At great self-sacrifice," she muttered, clenching her teeth against the pain.

Mac said there was no point looking for Marisa now, she might be anywhere in that maze of alleys, and with his arm around her, they hobbled back to the bar, where a shot of grappa temporarily eased the agony. Then they took a cab to a *farmacia* where they inspected her ankle and prescribed ice packs and an elastic support stocking.

"Terrific," Sunny muttered, surveying the piggy-pink elastic support miserably. "It'll look just great with a little black dress." She had already decided that Marisa Mayne was not worth it.

Mac had called the police and told them what had happened. They said there was not much they could do since Marisa was not yet officially a missing person.

"She'll turn up," the cops told him. "These women always do."

Mac left Sunny at the hotel nursing her swollen ankle, while he returned to Marisa's apartment. The yellow Post-it note was still stuck on the door. He put it in his pocket, then tried the lock. He was surprised to find it open.

Marisa's tiny apartment was immaculate. Her clothes were neatly arranged in the closet, shoes lined up, sweaters stacked. There was a coffee mug on the sink and a couple of magazines on a side table next to the sofa, along with a remote for the TV. And that was about it. No Marisa. No photos, no letters, and no personal documents, not even her passport. And certainly no incriminating papers with RP's offshore account numbers. There was just the yellow Post-it pad near the phone with an address written on it.

"Villa Appia, Gali, Tuscany."

Mac called Hertz, arranged for a rental car, then went back to the hotel to tell Sunny he was off to Tuscany. Of course, despite the injured ankle, she said she was definitely going with him.

Fifty-One

It was Saturday night, Robert Montfort was at the Bistro again, sitting at the same table under the arbor opposite the same Paris blonde. Allie, her crackling starched white apron wrapped twice around her narrow waist, bustled outside, saw them and stepped hurriedly back in again. She asked Jean-Philippe to take their order and ran to the kitchen to tell Petra.

"It's Robert Montfort," she said. "He's out there with the Paris blonde again."

"The TV gal?" Petra raised an eyebrow at her. "Should've thought he'd know better, after having met someone like you. Don't you worry about it," she added, briskly sautéing up chicken pieces in butter with garlic and shallots and pouring in a dollop of good heavy cream. Petra never spared a thought for calories or cholesterol. Good food was good food. "I've no doubt he's saying goodbye to her." She threw Allie a penetrating glance. "That's what you want, isn't it? Robert Montfort, I mean."

Allie stared back at her. An image of Ron flew into her mind: his beetling brows, his powerful frame, his arrogance that concealed the vulnerable man inside. There was nothing vulnerable about handsome Robert Montfort. "I don't know," she said, honestly.

"Well, then." Petra sloshed the chicken around in the sauce, seasoned now with cumin and thyme. "You can't grumble, can you, if he has a blonde here on a date."

"True," Allie agreed. And she strode outside, order pad at the ready.

"Bonsoir," she said, wafting away the new wispy bangs that were sticking to her glasses, and giving them a smile. "Lovely to see you both again. Vodka tonics, isn't it?"

Robert smiled at her. "It is," he agreed.

The blonde took out her cell phone. "Has anyone ever told you you should get rid of those glasses?" she said. "Try some contacts. It would make a difference." And suddenly she reached over and snatched off Allie's glasses, holding her cell phone up to her surprised face.

"There, that's better, isn't it, Robert?" she said. She put down her cell phone, handed Allie back the glasses and said, "I'm dying for that drink."

"Do you have any idea how rude you are, Félice?" Robert's voice was icy. "How dare you do that to Mary."

She shrugged. "It was just a helpful little gesture, that's all. Woman to woman. And you have to admit she looks better."

Allie rammed the glasses on her nose and, furious, hurried back indoors. She knew Félice de Courcy had photographed her and there was nothing she could do about it.

She sent Jean-Philippe out with the drinks. When she complained to Petra, Petra went out and took their order and served them herself.

"There's something about that Félice woman I don't like," she told Allie later, when they were tidying up the kitchen together. "She's too nosy by far, always asking questions about you. I don't know what she's up to, but it's something, you can bet on that."

Allie's heart sank. All was not well in Paradise after all.

Fifty-Two

The drive to the Villa Appia in Tuscany was a long one, and it was dark when Mac finally found the large rose-colored house behind iron gates. A perfectly kept gravel driveway led to the massive front door. No lights were on and it appeared to be deserted.

"It looks like a fortress," Sunny whispered.

Mac tried the gate. "Maybe not," he said, opening it.

He rang the bell. There was no answer. He rang again, waiting. When no one answered, he tried the door. It was locked. They walked around the side of the house until they came to the kitchen door. Surprisingly, this one was open.

Sunny hobbled indoors after Mac. She didn't want to be left behind in that silent garden. There was not even a bird singing, for God's sake.

She hated breaking into places, it gave her the creeps. Like in Palm Springs, she had spooky tremors up and down her spine as they stood waiting for their eyes to adjust to the dark. When they did, she saw they were in an enormous kitchen. Very modern, with everything built in behind dark wooden doors with no handles. It might have been a library there was so much wood. The only way you could tell it was meant for food preparation was the double sink beneath the window and the six-burner stove top. Not a coffeepot, not a canister, not a refrigerator or dishwasher in sight.

"Wait a minute," she whispered. "Aren't Tuscan villas supposed to have nice old-fashioned kitchens, all white tiles and ancient cast-iron cooking utensils and a big old fireplace for roasting wild boar or something?"

Mac was standing at the polished granite slab that served as a table, looking at an envelope by the thin beam of a pencil flashlight.

"Not this one," he said. "This is a movie mogul's country house. Renato Manzini."

"Manzini," Sunny breathed, stunned. "Could *he* have kidnapped Marisa?"

But Mac had already disappeared through a door. It swung silently closed behind him, creating an evil little draft, and Sunny shivered again.

She shifted uncomfortably on her painful foot, hating to be left alone yet afraid to go through that door and try to find Mac in the dark. Why did she always let herself in for these kinds of things anyway? She should have learned by now.

She had a raging thirst and she peered round, wondering which of the doors might be hiding a refrigerator, hoping for some cold bottled water. She tried one, then another. No luck. She stopped and listened, heard the low hum that said fridge, stepped toward it and pulled open the door.

The interior light switched on.

She was staring into the blank green eyes staring back at her. All the shelves had been removed and Marisa Mayne's slender body was folded into the space like a ventriloquist's dummy. A trail of blood streaked from her mouth, and her tumbling red hair sparkled with a coat of frost.

For a numb second, Sunny was spellbound. Then fear surged into her throat, hot as battery acid. A scream gurgled somewhere inside her but she couldn't get it out. She turned to run...

A hand slammed over her mouth. Her arms were pinned at her sides. She felt his breath on her neck...

She bit down on his hand, gagging as her teeth sank into his flesh. She bit harder, teeth seeking bone, red-hot with panic.

The killer ripped his hands away, and now he wrapped them around her throat...

She had not known fighting for your life could feel like this, fighting for every breath.

Her tongue was forced out of her mouth ... She choked and gurgled.

"Sunny?" Mac's voice came from the door. "Sunny, where are you?"

So this is what it feels like to die, Sunny thought, as the killer let go and she dropped like a stone to the floor.

"Oh my God, Sunny." Mac knelt over her, his mouth on hers. "Tell me you're okay. Please, *please,* Sunny..."

She could still feel the painful imprint of the killer's fingers on her neck, and her tongue was twice as big as normal. When she finally managed to speak her voice came out in a hoarse whisper.

She pointed a trembling finger at the wall of dark wooden cabinets. "Look," she managed to say.

"*Who was it?*" Mac demanded.

"Just open it," she whispered... "*Open the door.*"

Mac opened the refrigerator door, the interior light clicked on. And Marisa's icy body slid out and landed at his feet.

Oddly, the one thing Sunny noticed then was that Marisa's ring was missing.

Fifty-Three

If Petra was surprised when Robert Montfort casually dropped by the Manoir, she kept her silence. He pushed through the door calling "*Bonjour*" and strode into her kitchen, making himself at home. He took a seat at the vast table, doing as Petra did and clearing a space with his arm while she brewed up tea in the big brown pot and produced jam tarts fresh from the oven, that along with the chocolate digestives were her favorite snack.

Allie's cheeks were pink from embarrassment as Petra gave her a long inquiring smirk, when she came and sat at the table.

"You two going steady or what?" Petra asked, impatient with all this dodging around the issue. "If not, Robert, then it's time you took her out on a proper date. Tell you what, I'll give her the night off. She's earned it. Take her to Monpazier, let her see how beautiful a thirteenth-century fortified village is. Show her the square and the stone arcades, have dinner at the Hôtel de France. It's always nice there."

Robert laughed. "You should be in the match-making business."

"I thought I was," Petra replied, passing him a hot-from-the-oven jam tart.

Robert looked at Allie. "Would you please accept my invitation to dinner tonight?" he asked with mock solemnity.

"Only if you tell me you weren't bullied into it," she said, and they both laughed.

"And Mary love," Petra said to Allie, "wear something pretty tonight, instead of those ever-lasting jeans."

So Allie put on the black pants and the white taffeta shirt she had worn for the movie premiere in Cannes. Her hair had grown from the Jean Seberg *Breathless* crop into a spiky bob, though she still colored it a drab brown. The heavy framed glasses were not exactly an asset, but she was afraid to go without them. As it was, in her pretty outfit, wearing a little makeup and with gold hoops in her ears, she hoped she would not be recognized.

"But you are gorgeous tonight, Mary," Robert said, his eyes gleaming with appreciation. Actually, Allie thought Robert didn't look so bad himself, in a blue shirt that set off his dark good looks.

As they drove he told her about the history of

the countryside: about the wars when Edward of England, known as the Black Prince because of his dark suit of armor and his black stallion, had ruled over this part of France. Monpazier remained as one of the most beautiful of the fortress villages in the area.

The tiny ivy-covered Hôtel de France was tucked away behind one of the stone arcades. Tables were set outside and the bar was doing good business. Robert had requested a corner table indoors and they were greeted by the owner, who of course knew him, and settled them in with a bottle of Clos d'Yvigne white. A rival vineyard, Robert explained, though he liked their wines very much.

Relaxed, Allie found herself telling him about her Malibu home, and how much she liked the temperamental weather and the sound of the ocean always roaring in the background.

"So tell me the truth, why are you really here?" Robert asked, surprising her.

"So, okay," Allie said, thinking. "I'd lost myself," she said eventually. "I didn't know who I was anymore. Perhaps I never had known. I needed to get away, try something new, in some place where no one knew me, and where I would have to function completely on my own." She smiled with the relief of saying it. "And I did. I found myself a dog. I found Petra and the Manoir. I got myself a job at the Bistro..."

"And tell me, what did you do before you became a waitress and now a chef?"

She could see he wanted the whole truth and nothing but, and he knew he wasn't getting it.

"I guess I was just a Hollywood wife," she said finally. "I loved my husband very much," she added, surprising herself. "He was the only man I ever met who saw the real me."

"Until now, perhaps," Robert said with a meaningful look.

Worried that this might be progressing faster than she wanted, Allie avoided his eyes.

"All my life I've had to make plans, to show up and please people," she said. "When I came here I made a new vow. I would only please myself. I'm happy the way I am. For now," she added.

He lifted his glass in a toast. "Then let us drink to that. I admire a woman who knows her own mind."

Robert didn't try to kiss her on the way home, though he did hold her hands in both his as they stood on the steps of the Manoir, saying good night.

"Tell me we can do this again, Mary," was what he said, and Allie replied that she would love to.

It proved to be the first of several dinners together, each more enjoyable than the last, where Robert taught her the history of the area and they enjoyed the local gourmet produce, until Allie protested that she was getting fat.

"Never," he said, kissing her this time. "You'll always be beautiful."

Allie had kissed a lot of men in her movie career, but she really enjoyed that kiss.

Fifty-Four

In the South of France, Jessie Whitworth was driving a silver Peugeot convertible with the top down. She wore large dark glasses and an expensive designer dress that belonged to Allie. She had taken it from Allie's overstuffed closet a few months ago, because she liked it and saw no reason why she should not have it. After all, Allie had so much, she wouldn't miss it.

She had been taking things for a long time, knowing that Allie was caught up in her work and also in her emotional turmoil. And besides, Jessie knew she was unlikely even to notice. Allie was not into clothes, she was into "people" and finding what was "missing" from her life. Jessie knew exactly what was missing from *hers*. And it was exactly what Allie possessed.

Driving along the Promenade des Anglais in Nice, Jessie thought appreciatively that the Peugeot was a better car than the Sebring she had used in L.A. to stalk Allie, though of course it was not in the same league with the Porsche she'd rented every now and then, when she would get dressed up in one of Allie's outfits, with one of her designer handbags, and shoes. (Jessie preferred Vuitton, because it was so recognizably expensive and she liked people to look at her and admire her and imagine how rich she must be.) Sometimes she would go shopping in Beverly Hills, exploring Neiman's and Barneys and Saks, though she could not afford to buy anything. Still, she'd try things on and the saleswomen were more than nice to her, and for a few hours she'd feel important. She had felt like Allie Ray.

Her own car was a down-to-reality Ford Explorer, five years old and bought used. Somehow, making money had never been one of Jessie's talents.

It was true, what she had told that nosey parker friend of Mac Reilly's. Roddy Kruger, that was his name. She had indeed had ambitions to be an actress. More than mere ambition, she'd wanted it desperately. She was different, with her anonymous half-plain, half-attractive look, and with makeup and clothes she could become almost anyone. But somehow nobody had taken her seriously. Worse, they had rejected her. Time and again they had rejected her. Every audition she went to she faced those same blank dismissive looks, the "Thanks for coming, miss..." They never even remembered her name. The scars of those years were visible now in her tightened mouth and hard eyes.

Jessie so wanted to be Allie, sometimes she believed she really was her. Sometimes she would have her blond hair, her look, her clothes. Then her whole persona became Allie.

But Allie had rejected her too. She had fired her. At first Jessie had thought her boss had found out she had been stealing. But no. It was the same old same. Allie did not want her around anymore. Three months' salary and a reference and that was it.

Jessie had wanted to kill her right there and then, but the timing was bad. And then there had never been the opportunity. And Allie had already left for France the night she went to the house in search of her, the big kitchen knife in her hand. So she'd slashed the gowns instead, taking with her the ones she fancied, and which were now in her luggage ready for her next public appearance.

She was so busy thinking of Allie, she almost missed the turn onto the autoroute. She swerved into it, saw the car in front of her and braked hard. Too late. She plowed into the back of it, saw it lift up into the air and come crashing down on its roof. The Peugeot shuddered to a halt, the air bag burst in her face and she fell back, unconscious.

Fifty-Five

Lev was having lunch at a café in the Marais district of Paris with his old friend from their Israeli Army days. Zac Sorensen was now a French citizen and had for years been a top detective. Like Lev, he was lean and mean and tough, and much too dedicated to his job ever to marry. He rarely even took a vacation.

"Too many crimes," he told Lev over a fast ham and cheese baguette and a beer, keeping an eye on the traffic whizzing past just in case he might spot something of interest.

"Still the same, I see," Lev said with a grin.

Zac glanced at him. "You too. So why are you in Paris anyway? I can tell it's not a vacation."

Lev told him the story and saw Zac's eyes light up.

"You really think Allie Ray is here in France?"

"She might even be here in Paris for all I know," Lev said. And then he went on to tell him the details of the anonymous letters, the stalker, the break-in and slashing of Allie's gowns.

"We're looking for a potential killer," he said, "and I have reason to believe it's a woman named Jessie Whitworth. Seems she's over here now, on vacation with a friend of hers, by the name of Elizabeth Windsor."

Zac glanced at him, one skeptical eyebrow cocked, but he made no comment. "If she's over here the odds are she's rented a car."

"Correct."

"It's a tough job to check the driver's license of every tourist who comes to France," he reminded Lev.

"True." Lev bit into his sandwich, waiting for Zac to come up with an answer.

"Of course, there's always immigration," Zac said thoughtfully. "You said she was in Cannes?"

"We believe so."

"Then that's probably where she rented the car. I know someone there, an old friend..."

Lev grinned at him. Now he was getting some-where.

"Perhaps I could make a call," Zac said, and this time Lev laughed.

"You old bastard," he said, punching him on the shoulder. "I knew I could rely on you."

Lev didn't have to wait long for his answer. He got the call from Zac two hours later. A woman named Elizabeth Windsor had been involved in a crash just outside of Cannes. She had hit a car. It had rolled over and the driver was killed in-stantly. "She's practically untouched, except the face where the air bag hit her. Red and bruised. You know how it is. Her license was false."

"What does she look like?" Lev asked.

"About forty, wearing a blond wig and expen-sive designer clothes, though she was staying in a cheap hotel near the railroad station."

"You might want to check out the name Jessie Whitworth," Lev said. "And by the way, what happened in the crash?"

"She was hospitalized for one night. Currently she's in police custody in Nice on vehicular manslaughter charges."

"Keep her there," Lev said. "I think you'll find she's wanted for more than that."

Fifty-Six

The local Tuscan carabinieri seemed even less thrilled than the Palm Springs PD to have a couple of housebreakers find a body in the refrigerator at an important movie director's villa. They were even less happy with the story Mac told them, but when the paramedics arrived and saw Sunny's throat, they were more inclined to believe them. A search of the area was instigated and Sunny was carted off to the local Cruz Rosa hospital for further inspection.

Following in the rental car, Mac groaned out loud. His Sunny might have been killed. First Ruby Pearl was dead. Had she been blackmailing Perrin? Now poor Marisa. She'd said she had incriminating documents. Had she been trying to blackmail Perrin too? Who next? he wondered.

The name flashed into his head. Allie Ray. Who else would have better access to Perrin's private files than his wife?

The next day, when Sunny was released from the hospital and Mac had completed his questioning by the police, they drove back to their hotel in Rome. After a bowl of soup and half a bottle of wine, with her bruised throat wrapped in a silk scarf (Hermès of course), Sunny was sprawled in front of the TV, watching the news to see if there was any mention of the body in the villa, when to her surprise Allie's face appeared on the screen. She quickly called Mac over.

The Italian newscaster was saying it was a "scoop." A French TV correspondent had discovered Allie Ray, the "lost" movie star, working as a waitress at the Bistro du Manoir near the small town of Bergerac. The Italian station had preempted the French channel and was the first to broadcast the news.

"Jesus," Sunny yelled, then wished she hadn't because it hurt her throat.

But Mac was already dialing the airport in search of a private plane for hire.

Half an hour later, Sunny was ready, dressed in jeans and Mac's green cashmere sweater with cute little Manolo boots into which she'd managed to stuff her swollen ankle. Actually, it felt quite good, she thought, testing it by walking back and forth across the room. The boots supported the ankle, and the scarf hid the bruises on her neck.

"I'm a wreck," she complained. And Mac said yes she was and it was all his fault and he was sorry, and why didn't she just stay here at the hotel and take it easy.

"Room service, TV, anything you want," he added.

"Are you kidding?" Sunny looked scornful.

"Think you're up to it, babe? After last night?"

"Too right I am," she said. She was darned if she was gonna let Mac Reilly go to the rescue of the beautiful movie star all on his own.

They were ready to leave when Mac's cell

rang. With a what-the-hell-can-it-be-this-time look on his face, he answered it. His brows rose.

"Where are you?" he asked.

"Here in Rome. Reilly, we need to talk."

"You bet we do. And—it had better be soon. Like right now."

"The Café del Popolo, on the piazza. I'll be there in fifteen."

Mac clicked off the phone. "You'll have to go on ahead," he said to Sunny. "Make sure she's safe. I'm meeting Ron Perrin in fifteen minutes."

Fifty-Seven

Mac put Sunny in a taxi to the airport then walked to the café in the Piazza del Popolo.

He almost didn't recognized Perrin. He'd shaved his head and was wearing large very dark sunglasses. In a striped T-shirt and a gold earring he looked like a cartoon of an old-time burglar. All he needed was a sack labeled swag slung over his shoulder.

Mac took a seat and ordered an espresso. Perrin was already drinking grappa.

"So, how are you?" Mac sat back, taking him in.

"Not good." Perrin lifted his dark glasses and his sorrowful brown eyes met Mac's. "How could I be? First my wife disappears. Then my girlfriend." His heartfelt sigh shook his strong frame.

"Marisa is dead," Mac said.

For a long silent minute Perrin stared at him. Then he lifted his hand and summoned the waiter. "Another grappa," he snarled. *"Rapido."*

When it came he tossed it down. "How do you know that?"

"I was the one who found her. In Renato Manzini's Tuscan villa. She had been strangled."

Perrin stared into his empty glass. "I want you to know I didn't do it," he said quietly.

He had put back his dark glasses and it was impossible for Mac to read his eyes. Perrin downed the second grappa. "Marisa was like a reincarnation of Rita Hayworth," he said quietly. "All tumbling red curls, flashing green eyes, and that sexy mouth." He signaled for another grappa. "Her real name was Debbie Settle. She's from Minnesota though how that cold state could have bred such a fiery young woman beats me. I'm telling you so you can contact her family out there in Minnesota. God, I feel so sorry for them."

"So what are you doing here in Rome anyhow?"

"What d'ya think I'm doing? Takin' a fuckin' vacation? I'm avoiding the FBI of course. And trying to find out what's happened to my money. A lot of which seems to have gone missing."

"You know we found Ruby Pearl buried under the saguaro cactus at your Palm Springs place."

"Jesus Christ," Perrin, said, white to the lips. Mac hoped that was a prayer, he was gonna need it.

"You're on the hook for two murders now," he told him. "It's only a matter of time, Perrin, so you'd better tell me the truth."

Perrin eyed him. "You on my side?"

"Tell me your version of the story, and then I'll give you my answer."

Despite the grappa, Perrin was sober.

"So I met a couple of women on the Internet," he says. "Look, I don't do drugs, I don't drink to excess—except under special circumstances." He signaled for another grappa. "And so what if I shifted a little money around here and there? So does everybody else in my position, don't they?"

"The FBI claims you committed fraud."

"I'd like to see them prove that," Perrin said angrily.

"Maybe they can," Mac cut through Perrin's bluster. He could see he was a frightened man. He had taken off the sunglasses now and those worried puppy eyes told him so.

"The man following you was not the FBI. It was Ruby Pearl's ex-boyfriend. He told me you gave her the diamond watch. The jewelers confirmed you bought it. He believes you killed her."

Perrin shook his head. "That's not true. I didn't really even know the woman. Demarco got me to employ her as my secretary. Ruby stole some documents from my private files in Malibu, with the coded account numbers for offshore banks. I discovered it by chance when I went to look for one and it wasn't there. When I looked again the next day, it had been replaced. I figured she was working for the FBI and told her goodbye, get out of my life. She'd only been with me a couple of weeks. It was about then I met Marisa." Tears moistened his eyes as he looked at Mac. "I don't have to love her to mourn her, now do I? I'm human, y'know."

"The 'engagement' ring was missing," Mac said.

"You mean somebody *killed* Marisa for the ring I gave her?" Perrin put his head in his hands. "Then maybe in a way I did kill her," he muttered, half to himself.

Mac watched him. He was sure now Perrin had not killed Marisa. Nor Ruby Pearl.

"Why didn't you come to Rome right away, to be with Marisa?"

"I thought if the FBI was after me, they'd be able to trace us. I needed to be 'a lone wolf' at that point, get my affairs sorted out. I made sure, via Demarco, she was okay financially. I didn't want to involve her with the FBI."

"What if it wasn't the FBI?"

"Who the hell else would want to steal my off-shore account numbers? And who else would kill Ruby Pearl?"

"How about the man who employed her?" Mac said.

Perrin jerked back in his chair as though he'd been shot. *"Demarco?"* he said. *"Demarco?* Sonavabitch, you're telling me he's been stealing my money, then laundering it himself?"

Perrin thought for a minute, then he said, "Here's the truth. The missing papers did not have the important account numbers. Only Allie

303

has access to them. I hid them in code on her laptop. She was the only one I trusted. I told Demarco that."

Realization came to them at the same time. They stared at each other across the table. "Then we'd better find Allie," Mac said. "Before Demarco does."

Fifty-Eight

Demarco was in a standard room at a cheap chain motel outside of Florence when he heard about Allie, in a broadcast earlier than the one caught by Sunny and Mac.

The TV news blared in rapid Italian, interspersed with variety revues consisting of almost-naked showgirls and comics he didn't understand. He was polishing off a fifth of vodka and wondering what to do next.

He had not thought he would have to kill two women to achieve his goal. It had almost been three, but he hadn't realized that the woman in the kitchen at the Villa Appia was Reilly's assistant, and that Reilly was with her.

For years Demarco had been committing fraud and laundering the money stolen from the business into his own offshore accounts, leaving a trail that could incriminate only Perrin. But what he'd really wanted was access to Perrin's private offshore accounts. He'd known Perrin kept them in his files in his bedroom safe at the Malibu house where he could never access them. So he'd wooed Ruby Pearl with expensive gifts, culminating in the diamond watch that he'd charged to Perrin. The bills were always sent to the office and Demarco took care of them. Too bad that this time things had gone wrong and the bill for the watch had been sent to Allie by mistake. That had taken a little fancy explaining but he had managed.

Of course he'd used Marisa in the same way. One thing those two women had in common though, they both wanted money. And once they'd got it they wanted more. Marisa had been more than willing to work for him.

Marisa was often alone in the Malibu house and he'd ordered her to access the safe and find the current offshore account numbers. She'd told him later that somebody had come into the house and interrupted her, and that when she finally looked, there were no such papers.

And then, just when he thought he had her neatly tucked out of the way, playing at being a movie actress in Rome, she had pulled the same blackmail trick as Ruby Pearl. The priest disguise had come in handy when he'd followed her in that street in Trastevere, then stunned her and got her into his car. He'd had to kill her of course, she couldn't be left around to tell her story to the world.

Stuffing Marisa into that refrigerator when he'd seen the car's lights approaching the villa had been tougher than actually strangling her. He had strong hands: that was no problem. He had meant to bury her under the chestnut tree on the hill in back of Manzini's villa, but Sunny Alvarez had put paid to that. If she and Reilly had not shown up it would have worked out fine. But he still hadn't won. The papers retrieved from Marisa were the same ones he already had.

Demarco had finished the vodka. The TV was still blaring, only now it was some newscaster talking fast.

Breaking news, he said. *"A woman's body has been found in famous movie producer Renato Manzini's villa."* Demarco couldn't understand the details but he got the picture, and also that Ronald Perrin's name was mentioned several times.

How convenient, he thought, settling back with a grin. They obviously suspected Perrin not only of killing Ruby but now also Marisa. He took the yellow diamond ring from his pocket, twisting it in his fingers, watching it sparkle. He couldn't just leave it on her finger after he'd killed her. It must be worth over a hundred thou. Besides, nobody really knew she had it. He'd be able to sell it secretly, later, when Perrin was doing life for her and Ruby's murders and the fuss had died down.

There was more breaking news, though. *"A scoop, as yet undisclosed on any other show. Not even the as yet unbroadcast show by the French TV journalist who had discovered her.*

"Allie Ray, the movie star wife of Ronald Perrin, missing since the Cannes Film Festival, has been found working as a waitress at the

306

Bistro du Manoir, near Bergerac in France."

A map flashed on the screen showing the region and pointing out the exact village.

Demarco stared blankly at the TV. With Perrin missing and now a prime murder suspect, only one person stood between himself and all the money in Perrin's private offshore accounts. And only that person could know the correct numbers.

He packed his bag, checked out of the motel and drove to the airport. He took a flight to Bordeaux. It was less than a couple of hours' drive from there to Bergerac and the village where Allie Ray was living.

He didn't know it, but he had a good start on the other people on Allie's trail.

Fifty-Nine

Sunny got Mac's text message on the Cessna flying to Bergerac:

Mac to Sunny: demarco is the killer. do not know his whereabouts. allie has account numbers demarco wants. he may be on her trail. take greatest care. in other words sunny please do not do anything scary and risky. when u find allie stay with her. hiring fastest available jet will meet u there. call me and wait till i get there. love u ... mac

Sunny to Mac: since when did i ever do anything foolish other than breaking and entering (three times) at your request; spraining an ankle while on trail of a killer; almost getting myself killed in an earthquake (with u) and opening a refrigerator with a body in it (also with u) and almost getting strangled. what do u expect from glamorous pi (in training)? will call when mission completed. anyway what happened with perrin? and yes since u didn't ask i do love u though there are moments when i wonder why. anyhow how do u know demarco is killer and not perrin?

Mac to Sunny: trust me i know. must get to allie before demarco finds her. urgent and dangerous. i wish i'd never sent u alone.

Sunny to Mac: hah! i'll take care of it don't worry. am calling bistro du manoir soon as i get off this—rather nice—plane. could get used to this. by the way who is paying for it? didn't i tell u you'd never get rich?

Mac to Sunny: be serious. be careful. be mine.

Sunny to Mac: oh my god ... i thought you'd never ask...

Mac to Sunny: i thought u already were mine ... seriously sunny this is dangerous.

Sunny to Mac: forget danger. there's being yours and "being yours." we must talk about this. i'll be careful.

Mac to Sunny: thank god. call me when u arrive.

Sixty

Allie had been invited to dine at the Château Montfort. It was Saturday and Petra had given her the night off, "for good behavior," she'd said. Then she'd winked and added, "Not that I expect you to keep to that."

However, this was not the rendezvous for two Petra and Allie had expected. It turned out that Robert had invited eight other guests.

Allie was in her room, getting ready. Dearie was sprawled on the chintz-cushioned window seat, his favorite place to sleep, keeping a reproachful eye on her, as though he already knew that this time he was not included on the guest list.

Allie twisted and turned in front of the spotty triplicate mirror over the dresser. She had traveled light when she ran away and did not have much choice. Now she was wearing a cream skirt that hit just above the knee and a thin black cashmere sweater that left her shoulders bare. Her only jewelry was the gold hoops and her wedding band. Somehow she still could not bear to take that off. It was too final.

She brushed her hair, which now looked the way Audrey Hepburn used to wear hers, falling in short bangs over her forehead. Then she put on the disguise glasses and sprayed on a little

Chanel. She peered into the mirror again, wondering if she still looked like Mary Raycheck. Feeling suddenly lost, neither one thing nor the other, she went and sat on the edge of the bed, wishing she had said no to tonight and didn't have to go. She was remembering the woman she used to be when she was Ron's lover and then his wife. It seemed a lifetime ago.

Petra had already left for the Bistro and the house seemed too empty. Allie hated to leave Dearie, but she gave him a farewell kiss and made for the door. Of course the dog followed her. She stopped in the kitchen and gave him a chew bone. "I'll be right back," she told him.

It was the first time she had been to the Château Montfort and she found it hidden at the end of a tree-lined drive, emerging like a surprise in all its symmetrical pale limestone glory. There was a columned entry atop a shallow flight of steps and tall French windows that reflected the lights within. Other cars were parked in the gravel circle.

Allie pulled down her skirt, smoothed her hair, took a deep breath and marched up the steps to meet her fate. If Robert Montfort was to be her fate, that is. She still didn't know.

"Welcome, *chérie,*" he said, kissing her three times, first on one cheek then the other, then back again, in that welcoming way the French have for intimate friends. He looked appreciatively at her, then said, "Come with me, beautiful woman. I want to introduce you to my friends. In fact you already know one of them. Félice de Courcy. She surprised me by showing up unexpectedly."

Oh God, the Paris blonde was here. Remembering Félice's behavior last time they had met, Allie's heart sank. So, okay... "I'm happy to meet all your friends," she said.

Taking her hand in his, Robert walked with her into the grand *salon* where the rest of the guests were drinking champagne. He made the introductions and mentioned that Mary might be interested in buying a cottage with a small vineyard attached.

People smiled welcomingly and the talk was general and mostly, for her sake, in English. Allie relaxed. Nobody was looking at her like she was anything special, just another pretty woman of which there were at least two others that night. Not counting the Paris blonde, who had taken up a stance near the fireplace, vodka tonic in hand, and who was watching her through narrowed eyes.

Fortunately, Robert had placed Félice at the far end of the table, with Allie on his right, and all seemed well until the end of the evening, when they assembled once more in the beautiful pale-paneled *salon* for coffee.

"So, Madame Raycheck." Félice was quickly at Allie's side. "Tell me, how are you enjoying the quiet of the Dordogne? After Hollywood it must come as quite a culture shock."

"Actually, it's the other way round," Allie said quietly. "Hollywood is always a culture shock."

"And do you miss it? That other life?"

"Not especially."

There was a cunning look in Félice's narrowed

311

eyes and a tight smile on her lips that made Allie nervous. Félice glanced at her watch, then turned to face the room, clapping her hands for silence.

"Messieurs et Mesdames, I have a surprise for you. Normally, I would not disrupt a party but this is special. It is time for my TV show."

She pressed the button and a panel slid back revealing a TV set. Switching it on, she went to stand by Robert. He glanced at her, puzzled, then at Allie who was watching the lead-in to the program. The Félice de Courcy Show was imprinted over the journalist's face and then she came into view.

Allie thought Félice looked pretty good on TV, blond hair swinging free, eyes narrowed in that habitual knowing stare, elegant in a low-cut black silk jacket showing plenty of cleavage.

"Tonight, my friends, I have something very special for you. A 'scoop' you might call it. In fact two 'scoops.' Like ice cream only better."

The other guests glanced at each other, smiling, but Allie didn't understand completely what she was saying, only the word *scoop.*

"Missing billionaire Ronald Perrin is now wanted for questioning in the murders of two women, both reputed to be his ex-girlfriends."

Allie's face drained of color. She stood rooted to the spot, not even hearing as Félice's voice droned on.

"The first woman is Ruby Pearl." A picture of a pretty dark-haired woman came to the screen. *"The second is Marisa Mayne."* It was the glamorous redhead's turn.

It wasn't Ron, Allie was thinking ... *It couldn't*

be him ... .Ron could never kill a spider ... he wouldn't do that ... she'd swear to it...

Then suddenly her own face flashed onto the screen. *"Ron Perrin's wife, the movie star Allie Ray, glamorous at the Cannes Festival on the arm of her director,"* Félice said.

"This is the last picture taken of the famous movie star before she too disappeared. Some said forever. And after the critical reviews of her last movie"—Félice shrugged dismissively— *"who could blame her? Or could Ronald Perrin have killed her too? But then..."* She was smiling into the camera now as another picture flashed onto the screen. *"Take a look at this. This is Mary Raycheck, a waitress at the Bistro du Manoir in the Dordogne."*

Allie gasped. It was the photograph Félice had taken with her cell phone that night at the Bistro. "Oh God," she said, turning to run.

"Wait." Robert grabbed her hand, glaring at Félice.

"So, my friends, who is Mary Raycheck? Well you and I and most of the world know her as Allie Ray. The 'missing' movie star. So Ronald Perrin did not kill her after all."

The stunned faces of the other guests swung Allie's way, but she didn't wait for more.

The last thing she heard was Félice's laugh as she fled, and Robert calling out to her to wait and that it was okay.

It was not okay. She was Allie Ray again and now everybody knew it. And Ron was wanted for murder.

Paradise was lost.

Sixty-One

Allie drove back through the narrow country lanes as thunder rumbled all around. Then quite suddenly the rain came down, sloshing across the windshield in a mini-waterfall the wipers had trouble keeping up with. Allie's tears matched the rain and she was forced to a crawl.

Lightning lit up the beautiful valley bright as a carnival fairground, then darkness settled over her again and she peered through the windshield, looking for the safe lights of "home."

Dearie heard the car and was waiting for her, tail wagging enthusiastically as she rushed in through the kitchen door, brushing rain and tears from her face. She stopped, surprised.

Petra and another woman were sitting at the kitchen table, drinking wine, deep in conversation. Their backs were toward her and their heads swiveled as they heard her come in.

"Oh, hi, Allie," Sunny Alvarez said, sounding relieved. "Am I glad to see you." But then Sunny's face fell. "Oh my God," she said in a kind of breathless way that sounded scared.

Allie stared at them puzzled. Both women were looking past her. She turned to look and saw Demarco standing there.

She said, astonished, "What are you doing here?"

Sixty-Two

Demarco took a step toward her. "Ron asked me to find you, Allie," he said. "He's my friend and now he's in trouble. I'm helping him. He wants me to get his private account numbers, the ones you have on your laptop. He needs them now more than ever. If you give them to me, I'll be on my way back to him."

Allie looked at Sunny and Petra. They were sitting perfectly still, eyes glued on Demarco. She looked back at him and this time noticed the hunting rifle slung over his shoulder. She took a quick wary step backward, still not quite understanding.

"That's my ex-husband's hunting rifle," Petra said suddenly. "Where did you get it?"

Demarco shrugged. "You should not leave your doors open, madame. And rifles should be kept in locked cupboards." He turned to Allie.

"Come on, Allie, let's just go get them," he said.

"Where's Ron?"

He sighed. "I'm afraid Ron's wanted on two counts of murder. That's why he'll need his money. It's better if you and I cooperate, my dear. We'll sort out all the problems together. All I want from you are those account numbers."

Allie knew what he was talking about now.

Ron had put the coded numbers on her computer a long time ago. So long ago, in fact, that she had erased them.

"I erased them," she said truthfully.

Demarco's cold eyes told her he didn't believe her. He said, "Well isn't that too bad. Then I suggest we go look again." In a quick movement he grabbed her arm.

Sunny screamed and Dearie gave a warning growl.

"He's the killer, Allie," Sunny yelled. "He almost killed me a couple of days ago, and now he'll kill us all if necessary. He's *crazy*, Allie—"

Demarco took a step toward Sunny and back-handed her so hard her head snapped.

"Shut up, you interfering Mexican slut," he snarled.

Dearie gave a warning growl and jumped to his feet. Sunny bit her lip hard in an effort not to cry, and Petra clutched her hand under the table.

"You can't do that," Allie yelled and Demarco turned and smacked her head back too.

Dearie leaped for his throat. Demarco had the rifle at the ready. He didn't even have to aim, the dog was so close.

The shot cracked through the room, and Dearie slid to the floor.

"Oh, God, oh God..." Allie screamed. She hurled herself at Demarco. *"Bastard,"* she screamed. "You *bastard.*"

She'd learned what to do at self-defense classes and now she jabbed her fingers at his eyes. He dodged her, caught her arms, held them in a tight grip behind her back.

316

The rifle clattered to the floor and in a second Sunny had grabbed it. Now Sunny held the rifle and Petra hefted a handy meat cleaver.

"One more move, you evil louse, and I'll slit you in two," Petra said in a tone that spelled business.

Demarco let go of Allie. He began to back toward the door.

"Stay right there," Petra warned.

Demarco had his hand on the doorknob when the wail of police sirens cut through the silence. The women's heads shot up expectantly.

Demarco flung open the door. The rain was still slicing down and lightning lit the sky. And in that second, Demarco was gone.

Outside, gravel spurted as the police cars squealed to a halt.

"Here comes the cavalry," Petra said calmly.

A few seconds later, Ron Perrin burst through the door, followed by Mac.

"Allie, Allie, are you all right?"

Ron's strong arms were around her and she was pressed to his fast-beating heart. "Oh, Allie, what did I do to you? How did we ever let things get to this?"

Mac looked at Sunny. "I'm okay," she said, but she could see he was shocked. "Demarco just ran out the door," she added urgently, as the police swarmed into Petra's kitchen. "He has a rifle."

Mac and the cops ran back outside, leaving two detectives with the women and Perrin. Mac heard a car start up near the bottom of the drive. Demarco was getting away. He leaped into the cop car and they took off after him. It was just

317

like when he was that city reporter in Miami, all those years ago.

Allie was on the floor, kneeling next to Dearie. The dog's eyes were rolled up in his head but when she put her face to his mouth she felt a faint breath.

"Get me a big towel," Ron said to Petra. "And one of you who speaks French tell this detective that he has to get us to the nearest vet."

Petra gave Ron a towel and he carefully wrapped the dog in it. Then she rang the vet, woke him up and told him it was an emergency.

Ron and Allie took off with the cop driving and the dog on Ron's lap, and Sunny and Petra were left alone again under the watchful eye of the second detective.

Sunny spotted something sparkling on the floor. She picked it up. It was Marisa's ten-carat yellow diamond ring. She put it in her pocket to give to Mac later. Demarco must have dropped it.

Petra gave an aggrieved sigh, and put the kettle on to boil. "All I thought was Mary was going to a nice dinner party at Robert Montfort's," she said. "Will someone please tell me what's going on?"

"I'm sorry," Sunny said. "I was in the middle of telling you when Allie got back and then Demarco showed up. He's the killer you see. In fact he almost killed me the other night and ... Ohh." She shuddered. "It's just too much to tell."

"Of course I knew she was Allie Ray," Petra said, pouring the boiling water onto the tea leaves (Darjeeling, her favorite in moments of

318

stress). "Everybody did. Well, those who counted anyway. Nobody else really cared, they just
knew her as Mary. You know, the new waitress."

"And you never told Allie?"

"Of course not. She'd come here seeking
sanctuary, and until Félice got the story and then
Mr. Demarco showed up, she had found it. Now
she'll probably lose her dog and regain her
identity."

"And maybe even her husband," Sunny said
thoughtfully. But she was worried. Mac was out
there with the killer and anything could happen.

"How about a nice cup of tea?" Petra said,
pouring out.

Sixty-Three

Demarco saw the police car's lights behind him.
He swung off the main road and onto a narrow
lane that ran alongside the river. The signpost
read Trémolat. The road was difficult at night,
muddy and completely dark, but that was in his
favor. He doused his own lights and sped on. He
could no longer see the police car's and he
sighed with relief. He'd given them the slip.

He stared ahead into the blackness and the rain.
Over the roar of thunder he could hear the Dordogne River rushing past and the trees cracking
in the gale-force gusts of wind.

He had been a fool. He should never have risked it. He would have been home free with Ron guaranteed to be accused of the murders. Now he had blown it.

He slowed down. No matter how hard he ran there was no way out. And anyway there were the police sirens again, *blah blah-blah blah,* that up-and-down wail that meant they were coming closer. He could see the blue lights flashing now.

The muddy road widened as it merged into a corner. Next to him the Dordogne roared into a weir, white foamed and swirling. A power-generating plant loomed a hundred yards ahead.

The sirens were coming closer ... the lights were turning the corner behind him...

Demarco swung the car suddenly to the left. He put his foot down and headed directly into the surging river.

Mac heard the thud as the car hit the water. He was out of the police vehicle before it had even stopped. He ran to the edge of the river, staring down at the vortex caused by the car's descent into the depths.

He nodded. It seemed an appropriate ending for an evil man.

Sixty-Four

Allie walked wearily back into Petra's kitchen, followed by Ron. The two women looked hopefully at her.

"So, okay ... Dearie didn't make it," she said in a choked voice. And then she sank into a chair and put her head in her hands and wept.

Petra quickly took the seat next to her. She put her arm around Allie's shaking shoulders. "Poor Dearie," she said softly. "And poor Allie. There's only one way to look at it though, love. Dearie came to you at a time when you needed him. It's as though he were meant for you, just for that moment. Now he's gone, but he did his work. He gave you the love and companionship you needed. And then he gave you his life. He was a noble fellow and we'll miss him. So cry all you want, love, if it makes you feel better."

She got up and went to pour the tea. She put the cup in front of Allie and said, "A nice cup of tea. They say it's good for all that ails you but this time I'm not so sure." And throwing Perrin a grim look, as though daring him to say anything, she sat next to Allie again, waiting for her to stop her sobbing.

The door opened and Mac strode in, followed by the two cops and two plainclothes detectives who had pulled up next to them.

Mac was soaked. He ran his hands through his wet hair, taking in the scene. He walked over to Sunny and she got up and went into his arms. Tears were also running down her face. "It's okay, Sunny honey," he said, not minding the awful rhyme. "It's all over now. Demarco's dead."

The two detectives strode over to Ron Perrin, who was standing near the big Welsh dresser that held about a hundred blue and white plates and a collection of teapots and carved wooden Welsh marriage spoons, as well as Petra's usual junk.

"Ronald Perrin, we have a warrant for your arrest," the first detective said.

Just like in a play, Sunny thought. She stopped crying and watched, amazed as the two collies came bustling in from the rain. They ran to the detectives and shook themselves, spattering the two men with about half a gallon of muddy rainwater.

Fastidious, they exclaimed with horror and took a step back.

"It's just the dogs," Petra explained.

Allie's head was up. Her eyes were lost behind two red swollen circles and her nose was running.

The kitchen door slammed back and Robert Montfort strode in. He stared, stunned, at the collection of people. He looked at Allie's blotched face; at the big bald man in the tight striped T-shirt, the earring and the handcuffs; at Petra pouring tea and the handsome couple staring back at him amid an assortment of cops and detectives.

Puzzled, he spread his hands wide. "What's going on?" he said.

"You're too late to join the cavalry, Montfort," Petra said. "It's all over."

Sixty-Five

A week later, they were all back in L.A. Ron Perrin was in a downtown jail awaiting trial on tax evasion, but the FBI had not pursued the allegations of fraud. Demarco was the one guilty of that. Allie was cloistered in her Bel Air mansion dodging the press, with Lev back in charge of security, and her friend Sheila for company. And Mac was busy giving depositions and being interviewed by the police, and walking Pirate along the beach at midnight. Sunny was incommunicado in an expensive spa, having her frazzled nerve ends soothed by hot stone massages and mud baths, the bill for which she was sending to Mac since she said it was all his fault she was in this state anyway.

Right now though, Mac was on his way to the pet rescue center in Santa Monica. Leaving Pirate in the car, he explained what he needed then walked along the rows of sad-eyed caged animals. He wanted to take them all home, but he could take only one.

He spotted the dog halfway down the line, but walked on, still checking. Its soft taupe-colored eyes followed him. He thought they were not so different in expression from Ron Perrin's when he'd last visited him in jail. "Get me outta here," the dog's eyes seemed to say. Which is exactly what Perrin had said.

The assistant took the dog out of the cage for Mac to see. It was young and battle-scarred. A line where stitches had sewn its head together lay unfurred and pink from ear to ear, one of which stuck up, the other down. It was a sort of taupe brown, short haired, with maybe a bit of Weimaraner. That explained those soft taupe eyes that almost matched its coat.

"I'll take him," Mac said. And apologizing to all the other rescue animals for not taking them as well, he made his way quickly out of there.

He put the new dog on its lead in the backseat and Pirate turned for a quick suspicious sniff. He needn't have worried. The dog immediately curled up, closed its eyes and went to sleep.

Mac drove back to Malibu, smiling at the blue and gold beach scene as he descended the incline onto PCH. It felt good to be home.

He punched a number into his cell. "Hey," he said when Allie answered. "Can you escape? Come out to Malibu for lunch?"

"I'll do it," she said, sounding relieved. "I'm alone, Sheila's gone to the hairdresser, but Lev will get me out from under the paparazzi's noses."

An hour later she was there. Almost the old Allie Ray this time, only with short blond hair and no glasses—well, only the de rigueur shades.

"It's you," Mac said with a grin.

"The original," she said. "Back to me again."

"That's funny," he said. "Somehow I thought you were always just you."

She laughed as they walked out onto the deck. The two dogs were sitting next to each other inspecting the beach. They turned to look as Allie stepped through the door.

"Ohh, hi, Pirate," she said.

"Meet Frankie," Mac said, and the dog came running over.

"He's sweet," Allie said. Then with a catch in her throat, "He has that same look in his eyes..."

"As Dearie and Pirate you mean."

"Yes." She sighed, still stroking the dog's smooth short fur.

"That's why I got him for you." Mac was holding his breath. If she didn't want the dog then it was his and though Pirate was okay with Frankie, his home was a bit crowded for two people and three dogs. He was counting the Chihuahua in that group.

"Fussy's not your kind of dog," he said referring to Allie's snippy Maltese. "You told me yourself she's happiest living with the housekeeper. I thought you needed Frankie to take care of you."

She looked up at him, surprised, and then she was laughing. "You sure know the way to a girl's heart," she said.

He'd brought in some sandwiches and they sat on the deck enjoying them with cold beer drunk from the bottle. "What's happening with Jessie

Whitworth?" she asked.

"She's still in jail in France, facing vehicular manslaughter charges, as well as driving with a false license. Seems she'd also run up a few quite hefty credit card debts."

"She wanted to be me more than I wanted it," Allie said. "The blond wig, wearing my clothes."

Mac felt Allie's eyes on him. He looked at her. "That night when she cut up my gowns, did she ... I mean...?"

"Was it you she meant to slash? Yes, I believe it was. And once the French police are through with her, it's our turn. You'll have to press charges against her, you know. She's guilty as hell, and I've no doubt she'll do time in France and then here."

She nodded. "I'm just glad it's over."

"You can go back to living again."

She smiled. "I guess I can," she said.

"What'll you do next?"

"I've decided to go back to France. Petra's keeping my job open, and there's a sweet little cottage I could buy."

"You won't be lonely?"

She shrugged. "Perhaps. I don't know. There's someone I'm friendly with..."

"Montfort," Mac guessed with a grin.

She shrugged again, grinning back. "Maybe," she said.

He didn't ask her about Ron. He figured it was her business.

He took the yellow diamond ring from his pocket and gave it to her. "I guess you should have this," he said. "It was Marisa's."

She turned it over and over, letting the sunlight catch it in a thousand scintillating prisms. Then she heaved a sigh. "Poor Marisa," she said. "I'll give it back to Ron. He can sell it. He's going to need the money with all those lawyers."

Mac nodded okay. It seemed appropriate.

They took a walk to the beach with the dogs, then Lev came to pick Allie up and drive her back to Bel Air.

She turned at the door, leaning against it, her hands behind her back. "I don't know what I would have done without you," she said softly.

Her eyes were that deep turquoise blue that searched the depths of a man's soul. Mac felt their pull, saw her beauty. Her gentleness.

"You'll manage," he said, kissing her on the lips.

He stepped back and they looked into each other's eyes one last time. Then, "Goodbye," she said, taking the dog's leash and walking outside to the car.

Neither she nor the dog looked back.

Sixty-Six

Allie went to see Ron at the downtown jail before she left for France. They met on either side of a glass partition and Ron was wearing the regulation orange jumpsuit. She thought he looked tired and sad.

"Why did you do it, Ron?" she asked.

He shook his head. "Because I could, I guess. It was just a game to me. Demarco was the one who took it seriously. Enough to kill for." He shook his head again. "Those poor girls."

Their eyes met through the glass partition that separated them.

"You look wonderful," he said. "Like my old Allie Ray."

"I'm going back even further than that," she said. "Back to Mary Allison Raycheck. No more movies. No more Hollywood. I'm putting the houses up for sale."

"Malibu as well?"

She nodded.

Looking relieved, Ron said, "Just save my trains, though."

"I'm going back to France."

He looked startled. "For how long?"

"I don't know. Maybe forever."

Their eyes met through the glass wall searching for the truth that somewhere along the line had gotten lost.

"Will you write to me?" he asked, and Allie promised she would.

The next day Allie and the new dog, Frankie, were on a flight to France.

Back at the Manoir, Petra welcomed her with kisses and cups of tea, and Robert Montfort welcomed her with open arms.

Later, Petra accompanied her to a *notaire*'s office in Bergerac and within a couple of weeks Allie found herself signing the documents that made her the new owner of five hectares of land with a two-bedroom, one-bath dwelling, a bunch of rickety farm buildings and a broken-down barn. The garden was still a riot of weeds, the rain bucket still stood under the drainpipe to catch the rainwater, and dragonflies still danced over the pond. Of all the splendid homes she had owned, Allie had never before felt this thrill of ownership.

Petra said she would be sad to see her leave the Manoir but glad that she was to be a permanent neighbor.

"I've gotten used to having you around, love," she said, dabbing her teary eyes with a pink silk scarf that just happened to be handy. "And don't you worry about the garden," she told her after inspecting it with critical blue eyes. "We'll have that knocked into shape in no time. To tell you the truth I think it looks just gorgeous as it is. Old Madame Duplantis lived here for as long as anyone can remember, until she went to stay with her only daughter in Bergerac a couple of years ago. It's been empty ever since.

"It'll need a bit of tarting up inside, though," she added, noticing the peeling flowered wallpaper and the rustic kitchen, which consisted of a small two-burner stove, a stone sink with a scrubbed wooden draining board, a table covered with red-flowered oilcloth and a couple of cupboards. It did have a nice stone-flagged walk-in larder though. Good, Petra told Allie, for keeping cheeses and eggs cool, as well as fresh veggies.

Robert came too, with an architect friend, who planned on knocking out a couple of the interior walls to open up the space, and who also redesigned the kitchen and the only bathroom. He mentioned that eventually Allie might want to think about renovating the barn. He had no doubt she was going to need more room. The work on the cottage would take a couple of months, they said, which made Petra laugh.

"Think more like six," she whispered to Allie. "You'll be stuck at my place for a while yet."

Meanwhile, there was a tired-looking old vineyard at the back of the property, a mere three hectares, but Robert said the land wasn't bad, and he could get it cleared and replanted for her.

Allie was thrilled. All of a sudden, she was a new homeowner and a future winemaker. And Robert Montfort's eyes were telling her things she half liked, half didn't.

A few weeks later Allie and Robert were having a picnic on the grass near her pond. The sound of hammering and the whine of tiles being cut had stopped for the day and they were finally alone. Robert uncorked the wine and poured her a glass.

"To us," he said, smiling.

"To us, Robert," she said, but she turned away from him as she said it.

"Mary," he said, making her smile this time because he still refused to call her Allie. "I never knew Allie Ray," he'd said. "Only *Mary.*"

"I want you to know how much I enjoy having you here," he said now.

She was watching the dog, Frankie, wading at the edge of the pool, searching like Dearie had, for frogs that jumped easily out of his way, sending him into a barking frenzy of delight.

"I feel like this is my true home," she said.

"But yet you go back to California all the time. It's as though you can't keep away."

"From Ron, you mean?"

"Ah, yes. The husband." He reached for her hand. "Promise me you'll let me know when there's any change in that."

"Yes," she said. "I promise." But in her heart, she already knew what her answer would be.

Sixty-Seven

Allie was in court every day of Ron's trial on tax evasion charges. She sat there, her blond head held high, immaculately dressed as always and alone except for her attorneys.

Mac and Sunny saw her briefly outside the courtroom. She came into Mac's arms, hugging him as though she never wanted to let go.

"Thank you for coming," she said. "Friends have not exactly been swarming. Not with Ron's disgrace and all the scandal, even though it was really Demarco who was the true criminal."

The trial resumed and they went back to watching. Mac was sorry he couldn't go every day, but his show was back on again and he was busy at the studios until late. Sunny and Sheila kept her company though.

In the end Perrin was given a hefty fine and sentenced to jail for a year. A nice white-collar open jail known as The Farm, the same place other famous wheeler-dealers had done time. Mac had no doubt that when they deleted the months Ron had already served, plus time off for good behavior, he would be out in much less than that.

A few months later he bumped into Allie again. Like him, she was a visitor at The Farm. She told him she flew in to visit Ron every two weeks. "Regular as clockwork," she added with a grin. She also told him that she'd had an offer from a well-known French director to be in his next film. "Just a small film," she said, "not one of your Hollywood productions. And I won't be starring, that'll be some young French girl. I'm looking forward to it," she said, surprising him. "After all, I'm a good actress," she added, and of course Mac agreed.

"Ron will be out in about six months," she said. "We're getting back together."

Mac's brows rose in surprise and Allie said, "Like all good criminals while in jail, Ron has repented his sins and promised to give up his 'bad ways.' Whatever that means," she added thoughtfully. "Anyhow, he's coming to live with me and Frankie at my little vineyard in France. I'm still helping Petra at the Bistro and Ron and I are planning on stomping our grapes together," she added with a happy laugh.

"Allie." Mac looked serious. "Why?"

"So, okay ... it's because I love him," Allie said simply. "I always have. And now I'm sure he loves me."

She gave him a happy smile, then twirled in front of him. "What do you think? Does it suit me?"

She had taken to wearing chambray shirts and Levi's and no makeup, and Mac thought she looked like the pretty small-town girl she'd always been at heart. And her large turquoise blue eyes could still melt a man's soul.

"I think you look great," he said.

Epilogue

The Colony homes are mostly empty in winter, when their owners flee all of ten miles inland to the more temperate climate of Beverly Hills. But Mac loved it then, even more than in summer. He loved it when it was gray and wild and lonely, when the waves surged at his little house demanding entrance and the wind rattled the shutters and blew smoke down the chimney.

It was kind of cozy here tonight, though, in the master bedroom, with a Bach CD playing and the fire lit and the curtains closed and the wind whipping the waves into storm force outside, and the candles flickering in the ever-present draft. Sunny was wearing his old green cashmere sweater and a pair of white sweat socks and nothing else. She was snuggled up beside him in bed, keeping a watchful eye on Tesoro, to whom Pirate and Mac had reluctantly granted visitation rights.

The Chihuahua had paced for the last hour, back and forth, back and forth. When she wasn't pacing, she was tugging at the curtains with her tiny paw and peering mournfully outside, tail drooping, ears back, the very picture of an unhappy exile. Meanwhile, Pirate sat on his haunch, his one eye following her every move.

Patient, Mac thought, that's what my dog is.

"Trust me," he said to Sunny, "I know Pirate. He's just biding his time. Like all men, he's waiting for that right moment to make a move."

Gazing at his Sunny, he wondered again why women always wanted to get married. Weren't the two of them perfectly good the way they were? Anyhow, he wasn't sure he was up to the job of being Tesoro's father. Plus Pirate wouldn't take too well to having a bossy female permanently around, infringing on his hard-come-by territory. Like him, Pirate had come up in life the hard way. Tesoro was like her mother, a lady— and you had better not forget it. Besides, two females in one small Malibu house? He sighed. It was simple math. Two into one just didn't go.

Tesoro finally settled at the very foot of the duvet, making it clear through the angle of her whiskers and her tipped-back ears that she was not about to move a single inch.

But then they spotted Pirate's black mutt nose sniffing over the end of the bed as he crawled sneakily closer. Pirate lay down next to Tesoro, nonchalantly making like he hadn't noticed her, though Mac could see a flinch waiting on his face in case he had to use it.

Sunny and he looked at each other, then back at their dogs lying side by side. Twenty ... thirty long seconds ticked by. They held their breaths.

Pirate glanced at Tesoro, then slowly, hesitantly, he lay his mutt head across the Chihuahua's tiny aristocratic paws. His eye watched her hopefully. Another ten seconds passed. Tesoro slid Pirate a sideways glance then burrowed her head

335

into the duvet, flicked her mini-tail over her nose, adjusted her ears back to normal and closed her eyes. Peace reigned supreme in Malibu.

"So that's it," Sunny said with a sigh of relief, cozying up under the duvet.

"That's what?" Mac asked, burying his face in her fragrant neck, ready to devour her.

"There's no excuse anymore. Tesoro and Pirate are best friends. They are sleeping together on our bed and nobody is killing anybody."

"So?"

"So there's no excuse for not marrying me." She turned her face to his.

"Maybe a wedding on the beach," Mac said, kissing her pouty mouth, clasping the soft cashmered length of her against him until he felt every heartbeat, every pulse, every throb of longing. "Yeah, a moonlit wedding with just a few good friends. And the dogs of course."

"What?" she said.

"Sunny," he whispered, in between kisses.

"Mmmmmmm?"

"Marry me," he said more firmly.

"I do," she said, and then they were tangled up in the sheets, laughing and crying together. Outside was a stormy moon and the slur of the ocean hitting the shore.

It was just one of those Malibu nights.

But this is where we came in.